MIDNIGHT
ON
STRANGE
STREET

MIDNIGHT
ON
STRANGE
STREET

K. E. ORMSBEE

DISNEY · HYPERION

Los Angeles   New York

First Edition, January 2020
1 3 5 7 9 10 8 6 4 2
FAC-020093-19340

Printed in the United States of America

This book is set in Adobe Caslon Pro, Unstable/Fontspring; Courier New/Monotype
Designed by Tyler Nevins

Library of Congress Cataloging-in-Publication Data
Names: Ormsbee, Katie, author.
Title: Midnight on Strange Street / by K. E. Ormsbee.
Description: First edition. • Los Angeles ; New York : Disney HYPERION,
2020. • Summary: After a tight-knit group of friends on a glowboarding team
discovers each has telepathic abilities, they catch the attention of Mr. Jensen, the
most powerful man in Callaway, Texas, and extraterrestrial forces, as well.
Identifiers: LCCN 2018057981 (print) • LCCN 2018061079 (ebook) •
ISBN 9781368052306 (e-book) • ISBN 9781368047685 (hardcover)
Subjects: • CYAC: Psychic ability—Fiction. • Friendship—Fiction. • Extraterrestrial
beings—Fiction. • Skateboarding—Fiction. • Racing—Fiction.
Classification: LCC PZ7.O637 (ebook) • LCC PZ7.O637 Mid 2020 (print) • DDC [Fic]—dc23
LC record available at https://lccn.loc.gov/2018057981

Reinforced binding

Visit www.DisneyBooks.com

SUSTAINABLE FORESTRY INITIATIVE — Certified Sourcing
www.sfiprogram.org
SFI-00993
Logo Applies to Text Stock Only

To Shelly Reed—
kindred spirit and friend through thick and thin

. . . a leaf of grass is no less than the
journey-work of the stars.
—Walt Whitman, *Leaves of Grass*

We are made of star-stuff.
—Carl Sagan, *The Cosmic Connection*

STRANGE STREET

I t was the last day of summer when the lights went out on Cedar Lane.

Life was utterly normal one moment, and *then*, at eight o'clock in the evening, on the twenty-first of September, the power left every house on the street. Ovens stopped cooking casseroles. Washing machines stopped cleaning muddied jeans. Televisions and computers zapped off. All of Cedar Lane went dark.

Then the blue light appeared.

As his fearful neighbors looked on, a man named Mr. Hernandez approached the light—which burned like a flame in the middle of the street, hovering above the asphalt without any visible source—and reached out to touch it. He let out a shout, running back to his wife and children to reveal the strange burns on his fingertips. They had a blue-silver sheen, and they bubbled long after Mr. Hernandez had made contact with the flame.

No one else dared approach the flame after that. Instead, all residents of Cedar Lane remained on their lawns, huddled together, watching the phenomenon in rapt horror. The flame did not expand. It did not diminish. It simply *burned*.

The local fire station was alerted. Firefighters arrived on Cedar Lane, their truck sirens shrieking, and quickly got to work. They aimed their hoses at the flame, releasing powerful blasts of water. But the blue light did not go out.

The neighborhood children were sent indoors, for what people kept saying was "safety's sake," though no one discussed what exactly "safety" entailed. The president of the homeowners' association proposed that the electric company be called, while Mr. Hernandez suggested a consult with the local university's physics department.

And while the neighbors were arguing, trying to figure out what to do next, an even stranger phenomenon occurred.

A little girl named Margot was the one who noticed it first. She'd been watching everything from her open bedroom window, when she shouted, "There it goes! It's *gone!*"

The adults stopped their squabbling and looked.

Margot was right: The blue flame, source of all their excitement in the last hour, was no more. It was simply, inexplicably *gone*.

Then, in a startling *whoosh*, the electricity came back to Cedar Lane. The streetlights flickered on, one after another, as corresponding bungalows filled with electric warmth.

The neighbors checked their clocks and digiwatches. It was nine o'clock, on the nose. An hour exactly had passed since the blue light had appeared. Now it had vanished.

And it never returned.

Hours passed. Then hours became days, and the days turned into months, and those months tumbled into years.

Even so, the memory of *the incident*, as it came to be called, forever hung over Cedar Lane. Some people called it a curse—the Curse of Strange Street. The account of what had happened that day turned to legend, only fueled further by the fact that, within the weeks that followed *the incident*, every one of Cedar Lane's residents moved away—some to retire to sunny beaches in Florida, others to accept jobs in another city or state.

And once they had left, their houses sat vacant for long stretches of time. Even when the houses were finally bought, their new owners rarely stuck around for long. People moved in, and people moved out, for over a decade of comings and goings. If you looked at the situation a certain way, you might say the houses were waiting—trying new owners, discarding them, waiting again—for the right inhabitants to show up.

For, though few people stuck around the neighborhood, two families had moved in and lived there for longer than anyone else, at numbers 23 and 27 Cedar Lane. If you asked either of these families, they would tell you that there was no silly curse on the street. People believed what they wanted to believe. As for the story about the blue light . . . *well*, that was closer to an urban legend. A tale from so very long ago.

Still, the houses on Strange Street waited.

ONE

THE NEW NEIGHBOR

"Cheap asking price for a charming bungalow like this," the real estate agent told the two visitors. "And in such a prime location! It should be selling for twice as much."

But Avery Miller and her mother, Ms. Rebecca Sills, weren't going to protest the house's price.

"It's perfect," said Avery's mother as she looked over the kitchen for a third time. "That backsplash and the new appliances—it must've been recently remodeled."

"Sure was," said Janice the agent, proudly patting her blond pouf of hair as though she'd done the remodeling herself. "Lots of work done. I simply *had* to track down the man who laid this tile. Isn't it exquisite? He ordered it all the way from St. Louis to . . ."

Avery had stopped listening to her mom's conversation with

Janice. There were better things to do with her time than learning about the origin of a certain kitchen tile.

"Mom," she said when Janice had taken a breath. "I'm going to check out the backyard."

"Oh, yes!" said Janice, with startling enthusiasm. "There's a swing set out there, too. Though it'll need new swings. Not in the best shape. Still! Bare bones, that's something. I've always thought—"

Avery donned her sunglasses and went outside.

The swing set Janice had been so excited about was only some poorly nailed planks of wood, splintered and rotted through. Nothing like the house, with its brand-new stainless steel faucets and its all-over smell of fresh paint. Avery wished it *were* a working swing set, because she wanted a place to sit and read the book tucked under her arm—*Hatchet*, by Gary Paulsen. Avery had been reading it in the car for an hour straight, and with only three chapters left, she was desperate to get to the end.

"Hey!" someone shouted.

Avery turned around.

"Hey! Over here!"

Avery turned again and this time saw a face peeking over the backyard fence.

"Hey," Avery said back. She approached a girl with brown hair and eyes, wearing a neon-green tee. A sucker stick poked from the girl's mouth. The candy clanked against her teeth as she spoke.

"You our new neighbor?" the girl asked.

"I probably am," said Avery, though she knew it was more than probable. There were fires and sirens back in California. Her mother loved that kitchen. And the price—as Janice said, you couldn't beat the price.

"Cool," said the girl. "My name's Dani Hirsch. I live at number twenty-three. You'll be twenty-five. And my friends the Gils, they live right there. Your other side, twenty-seven."

Dani pointed to a mint-colored bungalow with ocean-blue shutters. It looked like a gulp of freshwater against the blazing Texas sun.

"I'm Avery Miller," said Avery. "We're moving here from LA."

"Whoa, no joke?"

"My dad worked there. Well, *works* there. He makes documentaries."

"Oh wow," said the girl named Dani. "That's really cool."

"No, it's not. The bombings, you know."

Dani nodded solemnly at that. Everyone knew about the bombings, and the war.

"Mom wanted to leave," Avery went on, "but Dad didn't. Callaway is where my mom grew up. I was born here, actually, but we moved when I was one. Anyway, they fought so much about moving back, they ended up getting a divorce. Mom and I are sort of starting over here."

"Yikes," said Dani. "Sorry for your loss."

"It's fine," said Avery, though it wasn't. "We get a new house, and my mom said I can have a dog."

"Really?" Dani yanked the sucker from her mouth. "What kind?"

"Haven't decided yet."

"My parents won't let me get one," Dani said, adding a wistful sigh. "They don't believe in pets. It's the Hirsch Code."

"What's the Hirsch—?"

"So, did your mom come here for glow?"

Avery started at the girl's interruption. Then, understanding, she said, "Mom's in marketing, but not for Component G."

Dani smirked. "How official. Nobody calls it Component G around here, though. That's an insider tip: Call it 'glow.'"

Before the move, Avery had *known* about Component G, of course. There had been some kids at her school with glowboards. But she hadn't known all about its history until she'd read a book entitled *Callaway: An Origin Story.*

Decades ago, the government had sent out people to Callaway to investigate the appearance of a stark white substance, something between liquid and solid, and unlike any organic material the world had seen before. A rancher had first discovered the stuff in his well and, digging deeper, found a seemingly endless supply on his property.

The government had conducted tests and found that Component G was nontoxic and only a little practical. It wasn't powerful enough for weapons or heavy machinery, but it was innovative enough to be a commercial sensation. Its presence gave rise to a bustling new city over the course of those fifty years: Callaway. That lucky ranch owner became a prosperous man, the first member of the Jensen family dynasty. Soon, he established Gloworks, Inc., a factory that produced small household appliances and, most notably, a line of remarkably popular glowboards. Over the years, there were more glow discoveries across the globe, but Callaway remained the only American source of the stuff, as well as the most abundant deposit. And as a result, Callaway thrived, drawing people like Avery's mom to work and live there—even if it wasn't for Component G itself.

"Glow," Avery said, trying the word out. "Okay, sure."

"There you go," Dani said. "You'll be talking like a local in no time. In fact—"

"Danielle!" called a woman's voice.

"Crap. Gotta go." Dani pointed to the sucker. "You never saw me with this." Then she dropped the candy right there in the dirt and hopped out of sight.

"Bye," Avery said, a little too late.

Alone again, Avery shuffled around the yard, toeing sagebrush and dirt mounds. In the end, she decided this backyard wasn't a good place for reading—no trees that provided good shade, and no porch swing, like there had been in LA. Avery swallowed the scratch of homesickness in her throat. Maybe there wasn't a porch swing here, but there was no Hollywood either, and *that* was a good thing, wasn't it? Here, Avery wouldn't have to take second best to her dad's important job.

Avery's eyes started to water. She sniffed loudly and stomped up the porch stairs.

Janice had finished her riveting story about tile, and now

Avery's mom was at the kitchen counter, signing an important-looking document.

"A real steal," Janice was saying, looking on. "Lucky as two hawks with a carcass, that's what y'all are."

"Yes," Ms. Sills said when the paper was signed. "We're due some luck, aren't we, Vee?"

"Hm," said Avery, considering what the girl Dani had said: *Sorry for your loss.*

"I met a girl," she said. "The next-door neighbor. She seemed nice."

"Well, see! We're already settling in." Avery's mother looked like she very much needed to believe the words she was saying.

Janice smiled and leaned in confidentially toward Ms. Sills. "I'll be in touch, but between you and me, I foresee no trouble in closing the deal."

Together, the three of them walked outside, onto the front porch.

"There is one thing I'd like to know," said Janice as she locked the door. "How did you know the place was for sale? We haven't listed it online yet, and"—Janice pointed to the red *For Sale* sign planted in the front lawn—"I was right in the middle of putting that up when you two arrived."

Avery felt hot beneath her T-shirt. She shoved on her sunglasses to hide her eyes.

"Happy circumstance, I guess," said Ms. Sills, placing her hands on Avery's shoulders. "It was Vee's suggestion we drive through the neighborhood."

"Is that so?" Janice looked Avery up and down. "Well, happy circumstance, indeed."

With that, Janice left for her shiny white car, placing a call on her cell phone and chatting all the way. Ms. Sills and Avery got into their old station wagon.

"A new start," Ms. Sills told Avery, cranking the engine to life. "We're going to be happy here, Vee. I can feel it."

Avery looked through her pollen-caked window at the street sign marked *Cedar Lane*. She thought of the girl named Dani, who couldn't own a dog, but seemed nice enough. Yes, Avery thought. She could be happy here. She could feel it, too—a burning sensation inside her chest that flickered like a flame.

ONE YEAR LATER

The man in the navy suit looked out his window at the city—a tangled sprawl of marble and chrome, filled in equal parts by smog, businessmen, monuments, and elected officials. This place was nothing like his hometown of Callaway, a city filled with far more lawn chairs than lawyers. In moments like this, the man got homesick for Texas.

"Sir?"

A voice floated into the room, and the man in the navy suit turned away from the rosy, dawn-struck cityscape.

"Yes?" he said as a short, owlish man approached him.

"The report you requested," the man announced, handing over a folder he'd been holding close to his chest. "The readings are stronger than ever. It seems the DGE was right to focus its efforts in Callaway."

"Very good. That will be all, Smith."

The owlish man bent his head in acknowledgment. Then he shuffled out of the room.

The man in the navy suit opened the folder,

removing the most important of its reports: Callaway's glow activity reading, or GAR. A red-colored bar indicated all he'd been hoping for. With each passing month, the activity had been increasing. Now, according to the work of the government's top scientists, the GAR had at last reached a level deemed worthy of investigation.

"Yes," the man murmured. "I told them. I always knew." Looking up, he called out, "Smith!"

The owlish man reappeared at the doorway, adjusting his glasses with fumbling agitation. "Y-yes?"

Once more, the man in the navy suit looked out over the nation's capital. Soon, he would be leaving this sordid skyline behind. Soon, he would be going home.

"Get the department on the phone," he told the man called Smith. "It's time."

TWO

RACE DAY

ani adjusted her helmet and kissed her elbow pads. This was her good-luck ritual before every race, and this race—the May Day Draft Train Bonanza—was more important than all the ones that had come before. This time, her team was going to win.

"Hey, *ladies!*" called an unpleasantly familiar voice. "Hope you're not PMSing today!"

Mitchell Jensen, captain of the Grackles, was behind the spectator line with the rest of his team. He was also there with his dad, Carl Jensen, CEO of Gloworks, Inc., known around these parts as the King of Callaway.

So what, though? Dani thought. Mitchell's dad might run the city, but this was a speed race, and Mr. Jensen's money couldn't buy his son time. This was about the Sardines and what they could do.

"He's used that line before," said Avery, putting her hands on her hips and shouting back, "Super original, Jensen!"

Dani smacked her friend's shoulder. "Don't engage, remember? That only makes him do it more."

Avery shrugged, a little smile curling up her sunburned face. "He makes himself an easy target."

Dani rolled her eyes. In a lineup of nine registered race teams, theirs was one of only two with any girl members. Hazard Hill was a sea of guy skaters, all slapping each other's backs and calling each other "bro." If anyone made for easy targets, it was the Sardines, a team composed primarily of girls, and the only one in the league with a girl captain: Dani.

"Mitchell's a giant turd," said Bastian Gil, the Sardines' only boy member. "Just avoid the smell."

"*Bastian*," said Lola, tugging on her slider gloves. "Don't be mean."

Bastian tapped his twin sister's daisy-printed helmet. "How many times has he given you crap for this?"

Lola's mouth twisted.

"A *lot* of times," Bastian answered for her. "He's the enemy."

"Pfrsh!" Lola blew out a puff of air. "It's all in the way you look at things."

"Thank you, Lola," said Dani, "for those motivational words. Now, if you don't mind, I'd like to add some of my own."

The team huddled in a circle, placing their arms on each other's shoulders and ducking their heads until their helmets touched.

"Okay," said Dani, her heart beginning to pump with adrenaline. "We're ready for this. We've done the work, we've put in the practice, and we've beaten our best time. Most days, it's about the love of the sport. But today, it's about beating that jerk and his stupid team."

"*Dani*," protested Lola, but Dani continued. This was *her* motivational speech.

"They're the actual worst," she said. "We can't let them get first."

"Hey." Avery grinned. "You rhymed."

"No interruptions!" said Dani. "If we—"

"Yeah, Avery, stop interrupting," Bastian interrupted.

Dani gave all three of her teammates an irritated glare, but soon smiles cracked on every face, including her own. Dani guessed they wouldn't be the Sardines if she could ever get through a pep talk in one go.

"If we concentrate," she said, "and we listen to each other, and we focus on the goal, there's no way we can lose. Today is our day. We're gonna pulverize those Grackles. Are you with me?"

"Totally," said Avery, putting a hand in the middle of their huddle.

"Yep," said Bastian, adding his own.

"I guess," sighed Lola, gingerly placing hers atop the others.

Dani topped the right-hand pileup and shouted, "Today's our day!"

"Today's our day!" the others echoed, throwing their hands in the air.

Dani tried to ignore the snickering at her back. Mitchell and his teammates had started a chant of their own: "Smelly sardines! Smelly sardines! *Smellyyy sardines!*"

Super original.

"Hey," said Avery, leaning in close to Dani. "You cool?"

Dani shook the sound of the taunting Grackles out of her ears. Who cared what they said? What mattered was what Dani *did*. She gave Avery a thumbs-up.

Dani didn't have to ask Avery the same question. When it came to glowboarding, Avery Miller was always cool. She'd only been doing this for a year, but she was the second-strongest skater on the team. That's why Dani had placed her at the back of the draft train. Avery had the best control, as well as a knack for knowing the precise right time to whip up and cross the finish line.

Dani, the strongest skater, led the train. She took the brunt of the draft, set the pace, and forged their path. There was nothing Dani liked better than the few windswept moments between start and finish, when she was zipping into that wall of wind, her teammates at her back.

Dani loved skating the hill individually, too—just her and her board, leaving behind an aftershock of glow in the hot night air. That kind of skating required different skills, like better balance and navigation. But there was something special about draft train, and not just because it was the only Junior Glowboarding League event that the Sardines were old enough to qualify for. No, there was *magic* in a draft train. Together, linked hand in hand, the members of the Sardines became something beyond themselves, something bigger. When they were skating in perfect rhythm, Dani swore she could hear three other hearts beating in time with her own. Drafting made them a *team*.

Draft train was all about seconds and fractions of seconds. The teams skated one at a time, their only challenger the clock as they raced to see who could speed down the hill and whip up their crosser the quickest. Teams had to remain connected—hand in hand—until the last moment, when the crosser broke ahead of the pack and skated over the finish line, securing their official race time.

Today, the Sardines were last in the race lineup, which was both the best and worst position. Best, because the team knew the exact race time they had to beat: two minutes, eighteen seconds, set by the Grackles. Worst, because *everyone* knew the exact time the Sardines had to beat. And everyone was watching. The pressure was on.

We've done better than 2:18, Dani reminded herself. At last week's practice, the Sardines had managed *2:15.* They were ready.

Dani switched on her glowboard, which hovered inches off the ground, and concentrated on its familiar hum. There were a few stutters and coughs as it started up—to be expected, with a beat-up secondhand. But the board hadn't failed Dani yet, and it wouldn't in this race, either. It *couldn't.*

She crouched into position and tilted her chin up, focusing on the game official's laser flag. That flag was synchronized with the timekeeper's watch at the finish line.

Time. It was all about time.

"Mark!" the official shouted.

Dani's muscles tensed, all taut rubber bands ready to be flung free, over the starting line.

"Set!"

Today was their day.

"Go!"

The official brought down the flag.

And Dani was off, pushing her left sneaker against the asphalt track. From here on out, there could be no more contact with the ground; the team had to let their boards, the track's incline, and their formation do the rest of the work.

Dani's form atop her board was perfect, her timing just right. Every afternoon, on school days and weekends alike, she'd practiced until each muscle was in place.

Dani gained speed, the asphalt flashing beneath the board. *Time to link,* she thought, and in that instant she felt pressure on her hands, which she had clasped at her back like a duck tail. The pressure turned to a grip, as Lola curled her fingers into Dani's. Behind Lola, Bastian clasped his sister's hand, and behind him, Avery completed the chain. Dani felt the change and accommodated, tipping her head at exactly the right angle to press through the oncoming air.

Now came the very best part of the race. Dani shut her eyes as the growing speed thrilled up her bones. She felt *alive.* Deep inside, right above her stomach, a concentrated heat pulsed like a blue-hot star, urging Dani on, whispering, *Faster,* faster.

She opened her eyes to the rushing world—cedars, shrubs, and jagged stone walls—turned purple in the shadows of twilight. For this minute, the world was silent, save for the hum of four glowboards in alignment. Dani guided the train, leaning into the curves, shaving off milliseconds of race time with the precise bend of her knees. Then the Sardines swung around the final bend, and the finish line came into sight.

Spectators were shouting, some holding up phones, others signs. Dani blocked them out, keeping her head down and her thinking sharp. They neared the glowing red line, closer and closer. They had practiced this a hundred times before. Bastian would swing out Avery, and she'd cross the line ahead of the team, quick as could be. Closer and closer to the line until—

Now, Bastian! Dani thought.

But she didn't feel the change of weight in her hand.

Dani frowned. Bastian knew his cue. There was still time. Any moment now, he'd act. The moments passed, though, and only then did Dani feel the whip. Avery sped close by, but her balance was off, and she pinwheeled her arms as, together, she and Dani crossed the finish line. The Sardines broke away from each other and crouched, spinning to a stop with the aid of their slider gloves. For a moment, they were quiet, puffing out breath.

Around them, the crowd was cheering, but a cold surge of defeat filled Dani's body. They'd messed it up. *How* could they have messed it up? They'd practiced so much. Why had Bastian hesitated? Avery turned to Dani, like she was about to speak, but then Lola and Bastian were on their feet, locked in the arms of their parents, Mr. and Mrs. Gil.

"Way to go!" Mr. Gil cried. "We're so proud of you."

Dani stood, her arms tight against her chest. Mr. Gil was nice—much nicer than Dani's parents, who never showed up at races—but he was wrong. The Sardines had screwed up.

Mrs. Gil released Bastian from her hug and beamed at the rest of the team. "Well, you all are something," she said, pumping one fist in the air. "Go, Sardines!"

Dani smiled halfheartedly. Inside, though, a blue flame burned at her ribs.

"OFFICIAL TIME!"

A race official in a glowing green jacket was shouting into a bullhorn. Mitchell and the rest of his buddies had run down Hazard Hill to join the crowd at the finish line.

No, Dani thought. *I don't want to hear the time, not now.*

"Sardines!" the official called out, holding up his stopwatch. "Two minutes, twenty seconds!"

There was a giant whoop in the crowd. The Grackles were shouting and hugging, and Mitchell, who stood in the midst of it all, shot a big smirk right at Dani.

The Sardines had lost by two seconds.

Two whole seconds.

It wasn't their day after all.

THREE
CONSTELLATIONS

Bastian Gil sat in the dark, looking up at fake stars.

He'd created these constellations using a stepladder and sticky tack. There was Babe Ruth Major, a baseball bat in mid-swing, and Avast, the pirate hat. His favorite was *Martimus caninius*, a runaway dog mid-bound, leash flapping useless behind him.

Whenever Bastian got fed up with his current art project—a papier-mâché or a pastel self-portrait or a new glowboard design—he'd flip off the lights of his bedroom and crane his neck to trace the stars. But today, it wasn't a project that had Bastian frustrated. It was the May Day Draft Train Bonanza, and what had happened in the final seconds of the race.

As many times as Bastian had tried to reshape the memory, Dani's words were still there: *Now, Bastian!*

He had heard Dani speak—not in his ears, but *in his head*.

That wasn't right, though. Dani didn't belong there. No one belonged there but Lola. Bastian couldn't remember a time he hadn't shared thoughts with his sister. Twin telepathy—that's what they called it. That's what Bastian had always thought it was. He and Lola had never told another person about their secret.

But yesterday, on the racetrack, Dani had changed all that.

Bastian had been so shocked that his mind had gone blank. He'd missed the whip, throwing Avery out way too late. The Sardines had lost the race, and Mitchell Freaking Jensen had bragging rights again . . . and all because of Bastian.

He hadn't been able to face Dani or Avery after that. He'd stayed close to his parents, who, oblivious to the team's glum mood, had offered to take them all out for ice cream to celebrate their fourth-place "victory."

Of course Dani and Avery both had places to be, so in the end it was just the four Gils waiting in line at the Frozen Spoon. Bastian's double-scoop chocolate coconut fudge had tasted more like dirt than sugar.

At least Lola hadn't brought up their race time, or the fact that the Grackles' winning streak remained unbroken. For Lola, glowboarding was never about ranks or prizes, so at least *she* didn't hate Bastian. On the drive home, she'd reached across the backseat and squeezed his hand. *Don't worry,* she'd told him. *There's always next time.*

Bastian's skin had prickled at his sister's message. Maybe, if Bastian hadn't known what that connection felt like, he would have brushed off the incident at the race entirely. He would've explained it away, convincing himself that he'd made up Dani's voice. After all, whose first guess would be *telepathy*? But Bastian knew what telepathy was; he and Lola shared it every day. He knew, without a doubt, that Dani Hirsch had been inside his mind.

Had she felt it, too, on the racetrack? Did Dani know why Bastian had screwed up? A part of him wanted to walk down Cedar Lane, two yards over, knock on the Hirsches' front door, and explain everything. But what if Dani was still red-hot angry? She had a problem letting things go. Take Mitchell, for instance, or worse, Zander Poxleitner.

Then there was Avery. She would forgive him, Bastian knew, but he'd made *her* look like the bad skater.

How was he going to face the team again?

"Hi."

Bastian looked down from the stars, back to earth, where Lola was peeking through a crack at his bedroom door.

Time for Nando and dinner, she told him.

The thought was sudden, slicing through Bastian, and he winced.

"Bastian?" Lola said, concerned. "What's wrong?"

She pushed open the door and walked inside, flooding the bedroom with light. Bastian's constellations faded away to nothing but plastic adhesives.

"It's . . . nothing," Bastian said. "I'm okay."

"No, you're not." Lola knelt beside him, and Bastian felt a familiar soft prod at his brain. "You were like that in the car yesterday. What's going on? Are—" The prodding stopped, and Lola looked up, eyes big. "Are my thoughts *hurting* you?"

The twins had learned how to keep each other out of their heads when they were younger: They could build a wall, brick by brick, with thoughts that said *Private*, *Keep Away*, *None of Your Business*. Bastian built that wall now. Lola fell back, her butt smacking the floor. Then she readjusted her tilted flower crown, giving Bastian an injured look.

"You don't have to do *that*," she said. "Just tell me you don't want to talk."

Bastian looked away, to the framed photo sitting on his dresser. There was Nando in his college graduation gown and cap, one arm around each of the twins. What would Nando say if he were here now?

The door is always open, he'd told Bastian, the day he'd left for DC.

Bastian gritted his teeth. Before Nando had left Callaway, he and Bastian used to talk about things—*really* talk. About school, and about glowboarding, and especially about Bastian's art. His parents and Lola didn't understand. Mrs. Gil would say, *Oh, how beautiful!* And Mr. Gil would say, *That's impressive work.* And Lola would say, *I wish I could draw like that.* It was all nice stuff, but that was the problem: Bastian didn't want to hear nice things about his work. He wanted to hear *true* things. Like what he'd gotten wrong and what he could improve. For a long time, Nando was the only one who told him those real things. He told Bastian when his pastel landscape was oversaturated with green, and he told him when he thought Bastian needed to be more daring in his glowboard designs. Nando *got* art.

Then Bastian had met Zander—a new neighbor on Cedar Lane—and they'd become friends. After a while, Bastian had decided to share his designs. For the first time, someone other than Nando *got* Bastian's work, too. Zander had spent hours in Bastian's room, looking over his artwork. He'd told Bastian what he liked and didn't about his glowboard designs. Bastian had trusted his opinion; he'd trusted *Zander*.

Then Zander had moved away from Strange Street to another part of town and turned traitor, and once again, Nando was the only person left that Bastian could go to.

But now Nando was in a faraway city, where he'd grown a beard and changed his last name to Jones. Now he only called once a week, to talk to the whole family. He no longer looked at Bastian's art, and Bastian had no one else to ask about it. Now Bastian had no one to ask about *this*: Dani's unexpected thoughts in his head. He didn't want to tell Lola and freak her out. He definitely wasn't going to tell his parents.

The door is always open, Nando had told him. Bastian just wished Nando's door wasn't fifteen hundred miles away.

"Fine," Lola sighed, and Bastian realized that she had been waiting, all this time, for him to speak. "If you don't want to talk, that's fine."

Lola stood, her paper flowers bobbing on her head. She looked so serious, and Bastian felt a pang of guilt. On instinct, he made a funny face he knew would lighten things up and said, "It's a guy thing, that's all."

Sure enough, Lola broke into a smile. "Gross," she said, backing away. "Then I don't want to know. You are still coming out, right? After dinner?"

It was Sunday night—Sardines Night. And as much as Bastian didn't want to face Dani and Avery yet, not showing up would only make things worse. Sardines Night was a sacred tradition.

With a sigh of resignation, Bastian toppled the half-formed wall, opening his mind to Lola again. *Wouldn't miss it,* he thought, pushing the words to her.

"Good," Lola said, and then she set off down the stairs.

Bastian didn't follow right away. His blue flame welled and sparked, just behind his ribs, as he settled his gaze on his glowing desk lamp.

The lamp wobbled slightly, and then, in an instant, clicked off.

The lightbulb was still sizzling as Bastian headed downstairs.

The Gils ate family dinner together every night. No one had removed the fifth chair at the table, even though Nando had moved away ten months ago. He'd been hired to work a government job in Washington, DC, that was so secretive he couldn't say a word about it during his weekly video calls. Instead, Nando talked about the traffic and the cherry blossom trees, about his annoying coworker, Vincent Smith, and how the nation's capital was everything and nothing like it looked on TV.

Bastian figured that Nando's job had something to do with the war. Judging by the news reports and his parents' constant whispers about a "standoff," the Global War was getting bad. *Really* bad. Bastian had never felt too scared, living in Callaway. There were bomb sirens some days, but it wasn't constant, like Avery said it had been in LA, and like it was in all the big cities. Nando, though—he was in one of those big cities. He was in the most important city of all. Bastian worried about his brother. A lot.

At the end of every call on the digipad, Mrs. Gil asked Nando about his girlfriend, Ira. It was only a matter of time, said Mrs. Gil, before Nando married that girl; it was imperative that he give them fair warning so Mrs. Gil could book their tickets to Madrid, where she had grown up, and introduce Nando's fiancée to the family.

Luckily, Bastian's only obligation was to eat dinner, and so he took a seat at the table, placing a napkin in his lap. His mother was in the kitchen, pulling the casserole out of the oven and shouting something to her husband in Spanish. Most of these pre-dinner conversations ended as they did now, with Mr. Gil raising his hands and saying, "Vale, vale, tienes razón."

"You guys," sighed Bastian, "you know we don't like when you do that."

He looked to Lola, who nodded in agreement. In cases like these, Bastian was the designated twin spokesperson.

"So much attitude!" said Mrs. Gil, bringing the casserole to the table.

"It wouldn't make you so mad," added Mr. Gil, "if you and your sister had chosen to study the language."

Mr. Gil always called Spanish *the language.*

"French sounds nicer," Bastian said, still the twin spokesperson. "Plus, there are all those irregular verbs in Spanish."

Mr. Gil burst into laughter. "Do you hear that, Mar? *Irregular verbs.* Sebastian, where do you get these ideas?"

Bastian shrugged, placing a cherry tomato in the center of his salad.

"Your last day of seventh grade tomorrow," said Mrs. Gil, settling into her chair. "I can't believe it. Teenagers, already! Before you know it, you'll be leaving us for college."

"In *five years*," said Bastian. "That's not soon at all."

"It may not seem soon, but you'll see: Five years is a blink. You're simply growing up too quickly. And Nando gone off on his own...."

Though Mrs. Gil sounded perfectly upbeat, her eyes shimmered in the dining room light. Bastian wasn't the only one who worried about his brother.

Lola touched her mother's hand, smiling gently. "We're not *that* grown-up."

"One thing's for sure," said Mr. Gil. "You won't be doing any growing up without food."

With that, he slopped a big serving of casserole onto his plate. The family talked more about the end of school and the egg drop experiment the twins had recently conducted in science class. No one brought up yesterday's race, but the memory flashed in Bastian's head again: *Now, Bastian!*

Was it possible? Could Dani really speak in his head, the way Lola always had? And if *that* was possible, what else could Dani do? Could she also have . . . powers? Powers like his?

"Bastian."

"Huh!" Bastian started from his thoughts.

Everyone at the table was looking at him. His mother seemed both amused and a little concerned. "I was saying that the folks who moved into the Poxleitner house are selling the place *again*. And why don't I see Zander around these days? You two are still friends, aren't you?"

"Uh," said Bastian. "No. He hangs out with Mitchell now."

Mrs. Gil's face tightened. "Carl Jensen's son? That bully?"

"Yeah."

"Zander bullies you, too?"

"No," said Bastian, wishing this dinner were over. "I mean, he's not right-out mean, exactly. He just hangs with Mitchell's crowd and . . . well, he doesn't say anything when *Mitchell* is mean."

"I see," said Mrs. Gil, frowning. "So Mitchell's still bothering you?"

Bastian picked at his casserole. He *really* wished dinner would end.

Zander did more than stand back while Mitchell taunted Bastian. Zander was the *reason* Mitchell taunted. Sure, Zander had betrayed the other Sardines by leaving the team, but he'd betrayed Bastian the worst. He'd told Mitchell all about Bastian's art—secret, confidential things—and Mitchell hadn't let up about it since.

I hear you like to paint with pinks and purples, Mitchell had mocked more than once. *They your favorite colors, huh?* And just last week, Mitchell had slid a note into Bastian's locker, attached to a small tube of lip gloss. *If you're gonna act like a girl*, the note read, *why don't you look like one, too?*

As though being girly was an insult.

Bastian would never forgive Zander for what he'd done. Never.

"Lola," said Mrs. Gil. "What have those boys been saying?"

Bastian looked up, aghast. His mother was playing dirty.

"Um." Lola cast a wary look at Bastian. "They just...poke fun sometimes. Because Bastian hangs out with us, and we're all girls."

"Jealousy! That's all that is," said Mr. Gil, winking at Bastian.

But Bastian found it hard to believe that Mitchell Jensen could be jealous of anyone; he was the richest kid in town. He never had to worry about saving up for new glowboard equipment, and he bragged about how he'd been taking private skating lessons since he was four years old. What did Bastian have that Mitchell could possibly want?

Anyway, Bastian didn't like talking about Mitchell, and he didn't like it when his mother called what Mitchell did *bullying*, though Bastian guessed that was technically what it was. Repeating the stupid things Mitchell said only gave his words more power, and that made Bastian feel small and weak all over again. Like he hadn't done or been enough to stay out of Mitchell's way.

To his relief, the topic was forgotten when Mr. Gil brought up his work at the Callaway Wildlife Museum, which had recently acquired a tarantula. Lola covered her mouth in horror as Mr. Gil wriggled his hand toward the breadbasket, imitating the giant spider's scurrying legs. The table shook with laughter, and dinner carried on, but Bastian stayed quiet the rest of the meal.

"What're you thinking of, my brooding artist?" Mrs. Gil asked him as they were clearing the table.

Bastian was thinking of a lot of things. He was thinking of Dani's voice in his head, and of Zander's betrayal, and of losing to the Grackles, and of the blue flame that had been growing inside his chest, day by day.

Only, he couldn't tell his mother any of those things.

So Bastian said, "Nothing much."

And once the table was cleared, he followed Lola into the dark backyard for Sardines Night.

FOUR

HIDEOUT

Avery was late for Sardines Night, but she had a good reason. Sort of. She was reading an email. An email she'd read fifty times before.

Radar, the best Australian shepherd in all of Texas, sat by Avery's side, in front of the kitchen computer. He watched her intently, his head tilted, one ear floppy, the other pricked. Avery felt his stare and looked down.

"It's stupid to keep reading it, right?" she asked him.

Radar cocked his head.

"It's not like I'm *nervous*," Avery went on. "He's my dad, you know?"

Radar blinked at Avery.

"Fine," she sighed, turning her attention to the computer screen. "I guess I'm pathetic, or whatever."

There was a folder in Avery's in-box marked *Important*. She opened it now and clicked on the only item the folder contained: an email from her dad, Eric Miller, dated two months ago. For the umpteenth time, Avery read the letter's contents:

Hey, Veemeister!

Hope you're doing great. Mom says school is going well and you're really loving your sport competitions. She and I have talked this through, and I'd like to plan a trip to see you in Callaway this summer. The earlier the better, I say. Maybe June? Let me know what you think.

Love,

Dad

Avery clicked out of the email. She swallowed, trying to soothe her dry throat.

Her dad was coming to visit. It was only a matter of weeks now. And he hadn't canceled. He *always* canceled. Every day he didn't write her to say *sorry, plans have changed*, his promise felt a little more real.

"AVERY MILLER!"

Avery started, and Radar jumped to attention, directing a low *woof* toward the kitchen door. Through the glass pane, Avery saw Dani Hirsch standing with hands on her hips, her fair skin washed out by the porch light.

"Coming, coming!" Avery yelled, getting to her feet. She rubbed Radar's head—a quick goodbye—and hurried to the door.

When she stepped out into the hot, sticky night, she was met with Dani's glare.

"We've been waiting for you," she said.

Avery merely smiled and shrugged, then followed Dani, who was already forging a path through the grass toward the loose fence board that led to the Gils' backyard.

Avery's thoughts were still on the email.

Weeks.

Her dad was coming in *weeks*.

This time, it was really happening, and she'd be able to put her plan into action.

Avery crossed into the Gils' yard with a buoyant spring in her step.

Every Sardines Night began with the game.

That's the way things had been since the Sardines had formed two and a half years ago—way before Avery had moved to Cedar Lane. The Sardines gathered every Sunday night at eight o'clock sharp, after everyone's dinner but before anyone's curfew.

Sardines Night was a night for making plans and sharing stories inside Cedar House, the Sardines' official clubhouse in Lola and Bastian's backyard. It was a night to discuss glow-boarding techniques and upcoming competitions. It was also a night to talk about what was going on in the neighborhood and at school. Sometimes, it was a night to watch Radar perform the tricks that Avery had taught him that week.

Every Sardines Night was slightly different, but one thing was always the same: The night began with a game of sardines.

When Avery followed Dani into Cedar House, she found out that Dani wasn't the only Sardine in a bad mood. Bastian looked sullen, too, and Avery knew that was thanks to the way things had gone at the May Day Draft Train Bonanza. Dani and Bastian wouldn't so much as glance at each other, and Lola looked as uneasy as Avery felt. That's why Avery was extra grateful that it was her week to be It. She could escape from the simmering tension, while the other Sardines counted down her hiding time.

Sardines was the exact opposite of hide-and-seek, which was what made it twice as fun. Only one person hid, and everyone else sought. Once the first seeker found you, they squeezed in close, so the two of you were crammed like sardines in a tin. Then you kept on cramming until only one seeker was left. When that seeker found you, the whole group laughed and made a big deal about why it had taken the last Sardine *so long*.

Avery loved to be It. She liked the aloneness of hiding first. She liked how the waiting made her heart flutter and flip. It was almost as good as the feeling she got when she skated.

Now Avery stood outside the clubhouse, considering her hiding prospects. The official limits stretched from the Gil property straight across to the Hirsch lawn, and then the back fence up to Cedar Lane. Anything within those four lines was fair game—indoor or outdoor, upstairs or downstairs. Over the past year, the Sardines had used up most of the best hiding spots.

There was one excellent spot, though, where no one had hidden yet: the oak tree in the Hirsches' backyard. Avery had been eyeing it for a while now. The branches were sprawling and good for climbing, but they had been pruned so far up that those nearest the ground were a big reach away. The climb would require jumping, a good grip, and excellent sneaker treads. That, Avery guessed, was why no one had dared to hide there yet: It would take time, and it would be dangerous.

Tonight, Avery decided, she was brave enough to try.

She cut across the Gils' lawn and into her own, passing the broken-down swing set that she and her mom had never fixed up. She pushed open the loose fence board that led from her yard to the Hirsches' and, at last, approached the oak tree, which stood tall, shading a padlocked toolshed.

Even the lowest branch was high up, and Avery had to jump three times before she caught hold. She was strong, but most of that strength was in her legs—great for pushing a glowboard and keeping poised. There was much less power in her small, bony arms. Pain burned down Avery's shoulders, but she gritted her teeth and, step by step, inched her sneakers up the trunk until she was parallel to the branch, clinging for dear life.

"You're basically cheating!" shouted Dani.

"Stop following me!" Bastian cried.

Avery gulped. The sixty-second count was over, and the

others were coming to find her. In one big go, she heaved herself onto the branch so that she was facing the ground. She scrunched toward the trunk, panting. Once there, she contorted until she was on her feet, and then she really started to climb. She rose, up and up, until she finally settled on a branch that was sturdy and wide enough for sharing. There, she was hidden in a cloak of green leaves. For anyone to find her, they'd have to stand directly beneath the tree and look up.

Flush with triumph, Avery pulled a paperback from her back jeans pocket. She always had a book on hand for moments like this. Tonight, though, the moonlight was obscured by the leaves of the oak, and even with squinting, Avery couldn't make out the words of *Twenty Thousand Leagues Under the Sea*. Sighing, she tucked the book away. Without a story to distract her, her mind wandered where it almost always did these days: Glow in the Park.

Glow in the Park was, hands down, the biggest glowboarding event of the year. It began at dusk on the first day of summer, which this year fell on the twentieth of June. There would be a draft train—the only event the Sardines were old enough to compete in—as well as single speeds and duo racing, and for each race there were cash prizes. The first-place prize for the draft train competition was $500—a sum that Avery could hardly wrap her head around. The truth was that the Sardines really needed that money. Dani's parents had refused to buy her any glowboard equipment, which Dani claimed was their attempt to force her back into competitive swimming. Avery's mom was working overtime to pay the new mortgage, and she couldn't spare any extra change. Both Avery and Dani were skating with worn-out sliders and knee pads and out-of-date boards. Meanwhile, the Grackles got new equipment every single season, straight off the Gloworks factory belts, courtesy of Mitchell's dad, the so-called King of Callaway. Unless the Sardines won the money, there was no way they could keep up with *that*.

It all came down to Glow in the Park. If they didn't have the prize money to buy new equipment, they'd be through. You couldn't be a team after all, if only half that team had the right stuff to skate.

And Avery cared more than anything about keeping the Sardines together. After all the bad things that had happened in LA, she had made not just one friend, but three. Friends who didn't know about her problems in California. They hadn't known her dad or watched her parents divorce. They didn't know about a certain visit to the principal's office. They didn't know about Avery's ex-friend, Katelyn Sumner. Avery could lose a competition, but she couldn't lose any more friends.

The moon shone speckled light down through the oak leaves. Somewhere in the neighborhood, someone was barbecuing, filling the air with the scent of grilled steak and charcoal. Closer, a dog barked—Radar, in Avery's house. Closer still there came a sound: *thup, swish, thup, swish, thup.* Someone was walking through the grass, close to the tree.

Avery peered through the leaves, making out a pink-and-red flower crown. She sucked in her breath, like breath holding could make her invisible. Instead, it did just the opposite; Lola flinched at the sound, looking straight up and meeting Avery's eyes. Lola grinned, revealing the prominent gap between her front teeth. She waved at Avery, then looked around and whispered, "Coming up!"

"Careful!" Avery whispered back, but Lola was moving fast.

Lola was shorter than Avery, but she was strong, too. Avery watched, awed and a little envious, as Lola grabbed hold of the lowest branch and shimmied her way to a sit. She did so far quicker than Avery had, and seconds later, she was by Avery's side.

"That was impressive," Avery whispered to Lola. "Why haven't *you* ever hidden here?"

"I have, actually," said Lola, breathing hard. "But it was before you moved in, and it was in winter, when all the leaves were gone, so there wasn't a good cover like we've got now."

Lola offered a fist, which Avery happily bumped. Then the two girls watched and waited, swinging their legs in tandem, Lola's olive-toned knee knocking pleasantly against Avery's pale, freckled one. Lola had brought up with her the smell of jasmine and lavender—a soap she'd been using ever since Avery had met her. The scent made Avery smile contentedly. Secretly, she was glad that Lola had been the first one to find her. Over the past year, she'd grown closer to Lola than to the other Sardines. Avery loved talking—especially about the stuff she'd read in her latest book—and Lola was such a good listener and question asker. They had a joint cause, too: Lola, like Avery, didn't like it when the Sardines fought. Avery knew she could count on Lola to have her back when it came to group disagreements. In fact, Avery felt confident that Lola had her back when it came to *anything*. She hoped Lola felt the same way about her.

Now that Lola was here, Avery knew without a doubt who would find them next: Bastian. The twins were dependable that way.

Sure enough, one minute later, Bastian appeared beneath the tree, hands on his hips, looking left and right. Lola stifled a giggle into her knuckles. Again, Bastian swept his gaze across the yard. Then the winning thought occurred to him. He looked upward, and Avery and Lola waved down.

"Dani isn't going to like this," he said once he was settled beside them.

That was true. Dani always got miffed when the twins beat her, and she'd be especially insulted to find they'd hidden in her own backyard.

"Maybe I should climb down," whispered Lola, "and pretend to find you last."

"Don't you dare," said Bastian. "Dani has to learn not to be so competitive."

Avery suspected that Bastian was talking about more than just a game of sardines.

"There!" whispered Lola, pointing through the leaves. Dani stood on the Hirsches' back porch, arms crossed, surveying the yard.

Come on, thought Avery. *Please, come on and find us.*

It was almost as though Dani had heard Avery's request, because at that moment, she looked to the tree, and sudden realization spread over her face.

"Hey!" she called, jumping off the porch and hurrying toward the oak.

"Get ready," muttered Bastian, and seconds later, Dani was under their feet, shouting up through the leaves.

"You guys are the *worst*! If I'm not first, I'm always, *always* last."

"Twin advantage," Bastian shouted down. "We can't help it!"

"Twin advantage isn't a thing!"

"Sure seems like it is!"

Dani glared.

"Whatever," Bastian said. "We're coming down."

"No!" barked Dani. "The rules state that the last seeker has to *sardine*."

Avery looked over the branch where she and the twins sat. "I don't know, Dani. It's kind of a tough climb."

"What's that supposed to mean? You don't think I can make it?"

"No," Avery called back. "All I'm saying is that it doesn't make sense for you to climb up, only to climb back down."

But Dani wasn't listening anymore; she'd already jumped and grabbed hold of the lowest branch. She jammed her sneakers against the bark, hastily walking them up.

"Be careful!" called Lola.

"I *know*. What. I'm *doing*," Dani puffed back.

She did know what she was doing, but she was moving so *fast*.

"Hey!" called Avery. "Slow down, okay?"

Dani didn't slow down. She wrapped her legs around the branch, hoisting herself and, without pause, throwing her hands out to catch the next branch up.

One of her hands did not catch.

It slipped free, upsetting Dani's balance and sending her hurtling downward.

What happened next happened very quickly. Lola raised her hands to her mouth. Bastian shouted at Dani's descent. And Avery thought, *No, she can't hit the ground.*

The way Dani had thrown out her arms, the way she had twisted her back—Avery couldn't bear to watch the impact. Stubbornly she kept thinking it: *Dani can't hit the ground, she can't, she can't, she* won't.

That's when something inside Avery began to burn. It was a sensation she'd first felt at her old school in LA. It was the heat between her stomach and her heart that burned every time she skated downhill on a curve. She felt the blue light's energy, and suddenly she *saw* it, pulsing out of her. It washed around Avery, poured over the branches like water, rushed under Dani's back, and cradled her in its arms.

Then, in a *snap*, everything was fast and loud again.

"DANI!" Bastian screamed.

Dani lay motionless in the grass below.

"No," whispered Avery. "No, *no*."

She scrambled after Bastian and Lola, who were already halfway down the tree.

"Dani?" said Bastian, reaching her first. "Can you hear me?"

Dani blinked. Then she sat up.

"Uh," she said, touching her cheek. "I—I—"

"Where does it hurt?" asked Lola breathlessly.

"It doesn't. It . . . *doesn't*." A strange look crossed Dani's features. "It's like, I don't know. . . . It's like I landed on—on—"

Dani didn't finish the sentence, but Avery could: *You landed on light. Light that I* made.

Avery's hands shook as she and Bastian pulled Dani to her feet. There wasn't a scratch on Dani's body—no bumps or bruises that Avery could make out.

"Something caught me," Dani said, finally able to speak. She looked at the others, her brown eyes wide. "You saw it, too, didn't you? It was invisible, but it was *there*."

Now Avery's whole body was shaking. They *knew*. And everything was going to be different. No more glowboarding, no more friends. It was going to be exactly the way it had been in LA, with Katelyn Sumner, that awful principal, and her own dad.

But before Avery could run away, before she could watch her worst nightmare come true . . . something unexpected happened.

Dani said, "I thought I was the only one."

FIVE

BLUE LIGHT

"We gotta talk about it."

Dani's words broke the quiet.

The Sardines were gathered in a circle inside Cedar House, the clubhouse that Mrs. Gil, a contractor, had built for the twins in the third grade. There was a charge in the air— so strong, Dani could almost see it sparking in the dim light of the clubhouse. Something had happened in her backyard. Something *big*. If the others weren't going to speak first, then Dani would.

All eyes turned to Dani as she continued. "Well, don't we? We've been hiding stuff from each other. Keeping secrets. I think it's about time we talked about what's going on."

The Sardines didn't look at each other. The only sound was the angry buzz of cicadas outside.

"C'mon," Dani pressed, getting annoyed. "We all saw what

happened back there. I should be knocked out cold, but I'm not. So, which one of you did it?"

Still, no one spoke.

Dani wanted to shout in frustration, to get to her feet and storm out of Cedar House. She was about to do all of those things when Avery blurted, "It was me."

For a moment, Dani couldn't breathe.

Avery kept talking. "It was me," she repeated, softer than before. "I'm the one who broke your fall. It was like I was catching you, but not with my hands—with my *mind*'s hands. Like a fire came out from inside of me."

"A blue fire." Bastian spoke lowly, his face obscured in shadows.

Outside, there was a growl of thunder, and the clubhouse's twinkle lights swayed overhead.

Avery blinked. "Y-yeah. I mean, I've never seen it outside of myself. But, somehow . . . I've always known it's blue."

Dani coughed. It was all she could do with so little air in her lungs.

Blue fire. Wasn't that how she pictured the power inside of her? The power she'd discovered on her birthday, in September. The power she used to close doors and windows when she felt like it.

"Whatever it is," said Dani, "this flame—it's the reason we can move things without touching them. Right? That's what it is: We can move stuff with our minds."

"It's more than that," said Bastian, cautiously glancing at Dani, then Avery. "Can you all . . . *speak* with your mind, too?"

Dani blinked. "What?"

Bastian swallowed extra loud. "The race. Last night. I heard you in my head, Dani. All of a sudden, your voice was in my mind, telling me to whip Avery forward. It freaked me out, and ... I choked."

"You heard me in your *mind*?" Dani's eyes were as big as full moons.

"I thought it was something only Lola and I could do," Bastian said.

"Excuse me?" Dani's eyes got even bigger. She looked between Bastian and Lola, mouth agape. "You two can read each other's minds, and you *never told us*?"

Lola wrapped her arms around her knees. She looked uncomfortable, almost like she wanted to cry, when she said, "It's not that big a deal."

"Anyway," said Bastian, "if we had told you, you wouldn't have believed us."

Dani shook her head. "I don't get it," she said. "How could I have talked to your brain and not known I was doing it?"

"Who knows?" said Bastian. "Maybe you were thinking so hard at me, it just ... happened. Have you ever done it before?"

"What, *brain talking*?" Dani scoffed. "No way."

Bastian pointed to Avery. "Well, what about you?"

Avery licked her lips, looking nervous. "Not that I know of."
But I haven't ever tried before.

Dani gasped, pressing a hand to her forehead. Avery hadn't moved her lips; Dani was sure of that, she was looking straight at her. Even so, Avery's words had reached her mind.

"Wh-what's happening?" Dani demanded, looking wildly about. "How is this possible?"

"Twin telepathy," said Bastian. "That's normal for me and Lola. We've been connected since forever ago. But moving things, mind-talking with *you* . . . that's new. And I didn't start mind-moving until last year."

Softly, Lola said, "Me neither."

"When?" said Dani. She was formulating a theory now, as exciting as it was terrifying. "Can you remember exactly?"

Bastian and Lola looked to each other, as though having a silent conversation. Dani had seen that look countless times before. Only now, for the first time, she realized that the twins really *were* conversing.

"Maybe last February?" Bastian said when he and Lola were through. "Lola remembers her winter coat zipping itself up, right when she was thinking how cold it was outside. And I was making valentines. I remember: I almost knocked a jar of silver glitter off my desk. I caught it . . . but not with my hands."

"What about you, Avery?" Dani asked.

A funny expression crossed Avery's face. She looked down at the chipped nail polish on her right thumb. "Before I moved to Callaway. Right before summer."

Dani furrowed her brow as she put the pieces of her puzzle together. "And me," she said. "I shut a door without touching it on September third. I remember, because it was my birthday."

"Your birthday," Avery echoed. Now she also saw the puzzle, all its pieces aligning.

Dani pointed to the twins. "Last February." Then, to Avery. "Last May." Then, to herself. "September. Don't you see? When we turned twelve. We all started to move stuff *when we turned twelve.*"

"Telekinesis," Avery said. "That's the word for it. Moving things with your mind."

Dani and the twins stared at her.

"What?" Avery asked. "Didn't you guys look it up?"

Dani had. She'd searched the words "move stuff without trying" on the internet, back in the fall. But she hadn't heard a real-life person say the word "telekinesis" out loud.

Not until now.

Outside, the sky groaned irritably with more thunder.

"Telekinesis," Bastian repeated. "And telepathy—talking without speaking. That's what we have."

Dani made a face. "What we *have*? You make it sound like we're infected."

"How else should I say it?" Bastian asked. "If we can move stuff with our minds . . . if, maybe, we can all speak in each other's heads . . . that's not normal. Normal kids don't have tele-*anything*. So that makes us freaks, doesn't it?"

Dani flinched. *Freaks.* That was Mitchell Jensen's favorite word for the Sardines. Maybe the Sardines had powers—*blue flame powers*—but that didn't make them freaks.

"We shouldn't be labeling any of this," said Dani, "when we don't even know what this *is*. So let's get it straight: We can move things and say things with our minds. All of us?"

She looked around at the Sardines. No one was nodding, but no one was disagreeing, either.

"And what else?" Dani went on. "We've been doing this stuff since we turned twelve. Except the twin telepathy." She waved her hand at Lola and Bastian. "That's gone on longer."

In reply, Lola gave a timid nod.

Dani pressed her hands to her cheeks. "Okay," she said. "Okay, *okay*. We gotta come up with a game plan."

"What kind of plan?" Bastian asked, incredulous. "What can we do, tell our parents? Go to the doctor?"

"NO!" the three girls shouted together.

As though joining their protest, another bout of thunder rumbled outside.

"I don't want anyone to know," Lola said. "Why do they have to? It isn't like we're hurting anybody."

"Anyway," said Avery, "any grown-up is gonna think we're crazy. Wouldn't you? If you asked me right here and now if I believed in tele-whatevers, I think I'd *still* say no."

"So there's nothing we can do." Bastian turned to Dani. "Don't you think the rest of us have already thought this through? Haven't *you* thought about it?"

Dani slumped her shoulders, feeling defeated. "I guess I've been trying to ignore it, more than anything else."

"But what happened tonight..." Avery said quietly. "That's...harder to ignore. And hearing each other's thoughts is new, too. Like maybe the tele-stuff is getting stronger."

"We don't know that," said Bastian.

"But we do know that Avery saved me from falling out of a tree," Dani said, raising her voice. "She caught my whole body *with her mind*. That's not nothing. And it's not nothing that we all started noticing this stuff when we turned twelve. No one else gets a birthday present like that."

"We don't know that, either," said Bastian. "Maybe plenty of other kids have what we do."

"Oh, come on, Bastian," said Dani. "If everyone else was like us, don't you think you'd hear people talking about it? Don't you think you'd hear other voices in your head, or see stuff moving all on its own? You said it yourself: We're not normal."

"But why *us*?" Avery asked. "There's gotta be some sort of explanation."

"DANIELLE!"

Dani froze, hands clutched into the squishy sides of her beanbag.

She knew that sound. It was her mom, and it was her mom's *angry* voice. Panicked, Dani looked at her digiwatch. It was 9:43 p.m.—thirteen whole minutes past her curfew. Definitely not in accordance with the Hirsch Code.

"Crap," she said, leaping to her feet. "Crap, *crap*." Frantically, she looked at the others and said, "We're not done here. We'll talk about this tomorrow. After school, okay?"

Dani didn't wait for a response. She ran out of Cedar House, into the beginnings of a late-spring thunderstorm. The rumblings overhead were louder than ever, and rain *tip-tapp*ed on her head as she dashed across the Gils' lawn. A lightning bolt tore across the sky, illuminating the world in a ghastly hue.

In that moment, Dani got a strange feeling.

Even though she knew it didn't make sense, and it couldn't possibly be true, Dani felt sure that she was being watched by unseen eyes, hidden behind those storm clouds in the big Texan sky.

SIX

LAST DAY MAGIC

It was the last day of school, and it smelled like summer. The thunderstorm from the night before had cleared away, replaced by blue skies and a beaming sun, and the Gils' kitchen windows were open. A breeze blew in the scent of watered lawns and sunbaked roads.

Bastian didn't like for his parents to see his artwork, but Lola had no trouble sharing hers. Atop the refrigerator was a line of folded creations she'd made for her parents, composed of flowers and birds, all formed from pastel folding paper. The breeze blew the creations around, and Lola watched them shift and turn, a finch and a tulip dancing a waltz. She was so distracted by the dance that she didn't notice her mother until Mrs. Gil was standing directly over her and announcing, "Time for Last Day Magic!"

Last Day Magic was brown and white sugar, mixed together

with rainbow sprinkles, and it made Lola's breakfast oatmeal taste like hot ice cream. Since Lola's kindergarten graduation, her mother had shaken out Last Day Magic at the breakfast of every last day of school.

Today, Mrs. Gil shook the sprinkle jar with gusto, first over Lola's bowl, then Bastian's, who sat beside her at the table. Then she placed a kiss on both their heads and said, "Congratulations! Seventh grade is almost over."

Lola tried as best she could to smile. Normally, Lola gobbled up Last Day Magic, scraping her bowl clean of every bite. Today, though, the stuff tasted much too sweet. She could only manage a few swallows.

The kitchen television was on, playing a commercial for a used car lot. As the announcer shouted about bargain prices, another breeze blew into the house, this time picking up a yellow paper bird from the fridge. The canary swooped through the air, gliding out from the kitchen and onto the breakfast room table, landing a half inch from Lola's orange juice.

On a normal day, Lola would smile at this marvelous happenstance. On a normal day, she would be in a state of utter bliss, what with the nice weather and good food and the last day of seventh grade. Today wasn't normal, though.

Dani had said that the Sardines would talk more about the tele-whatevers after school, but Lola wasn't looking forward to that. She wanted things to go back to the way they were— before Dani fell from that tree, when no one was talking about "powers." She didn't want to talk about her and Bastian's twin telepathy, or admit that some days she folded her paper animals with her mind. It didn't seem right to talk about those things. It didn't seem safe.

Lola had felt the blue flame inside her growing stronger, flickering more insistently, day after day. It was as though there was too much flame for her body to contain, as though it were desperate to get out of her in any way it possibly could. Lola didn't like that feeling. There was a reason why Bastian was their twin spokesperson. There was a reason why Lola was content to be the one Sardine with no big job in the draft train competition. She liked to be quiet, and never so important that she'd stand out. And these tele-whatevers... they were the opposite of that.

On TV, the car lot commercial ended and the seven o'clock news came on. The newscaster spoke calmly, but all his words were ugly: "bomb" and "conflict" and "casualties." Mrs. Gil reached a sudsy hand from the sink, hitting the power button on the remote and turning off the TV in one succinct *snap.*

Lola didn't like to think about the Global War—not if she could help it. Especially not with Nando far away, in such a dangerous place. A "target city," the reporters called it. If the standoff ended, they said, and there was an "escalation," then DC would almost certainly be the first city attacked.

So Lola preferred not to think of the war at all.

"Seven o'clock," Mrs. Gil told the twins. "Off with you."

Lola and Bastian headed for the door, grabbing their backpacks and glowboards on the way out.

"Bye," Lola whispered back to the paper canary, still roosted on her place mat, staring at a bowl of uneaten magic.

At lunch, the Sardines sat together with a meal that befitted the last day of school: corn dogs, french fries, fruit cups, and double-fudge cake. Lola squirted an extra-large gloop of mustard on her corn dog, while Avery recounted what she'd been reading recently—in particular, a book about training Australian shepherds.

"Radar's going to be a pro," she told them. "The book said Aussies can jump as high as *four feet*. That's my goal. One day Radar will be able to jump over our *fence*."

"Sure," said Dani, who had been acting moody all through lunch. "But that kind of defeats the purpose of a fence, doesn't it?"

Avery frowned, and the Sardines grew quiet.

Lola smiled sympathetically at Avery. She found her hand beneath the table and squeezed it once—code for *You can tell me more when we're on our own*. But Lola didn't actually *think* the message at Avery. She didn't want to try.

Avery looked up at Lola's touch, and the softness in her hazel eyes sent Lola's heart into a funny rhythm—a *pit-pat* that was faster and lighter than usual.

Then the lunch table's silence was shattered by an unpleasant voice.

"Hey, losers! You cry yourselves to sleep all weekend?"

It was Mitchell Jensen. He was striding up to the table, simpering at the Sardines.

"Here we go," muttered Bastian.

"You know, Mitchell," said Avery, pointing her corn dog at him. "It's a good thing you're rich, or else no one would hang out with you."

"I'm not rich," Mitchell said, tipping his chin. "I'm *loaded*. And what about you all? Skating on garbage. I've seen your board, Hirsch; doesn't even stream right, it's so gunked up with bad glow."

"I could still beat you at single speeds, if I was old enough," Dani said with narrowed eyes. "My *garbage* board against your dad's nicest, newest invention."

"Cute," said Mitchell. The rest of the Grackles had now descended upon the Sardines' table—Ross Mondt, Kyle Bridges, and Zander Poxleitner. Mitchell gripped the edge of the table and leaned in even closer. "We're going to anni-hilate you at Glow in the Park. Get ready to eat the concrete." He pointed at Bastian. "Especially *you*, Gil."

Lola hoped Mitchell would say his piece and leave. All the while, heat was building inside her, a burning flame wicking up her spine.

Leave him alone, she pleaded silently. *Leave my brother alone.*

"You know Zander gave us the *whole* lowdown on you, right?" Mitchell said in Bastian's face. Lola could smell his breath—regurgitated cheese puffs. "You've got so many *feelings* about your paintings. And you joined the Sardines 'cause you knew no one else would take you but a bunch of *girls*."

Bastian glared at his tray of food as Kyle and Ross snickered, drawing closer to the table. Zander hung back, though, picking at his wristbands and staring at the floor.

"Hey, Zee," said Dani, glaring his way. "Your friends are super great."

Zander didn't reply, but Mitchell said, "At least he was smart enough to leave your dumb pack. How do you even spend your practice time? Giving each other makeovers?"

Leave us alone, Lola thought. *Leave us all alone.*

"Some crew you got yourself, Hirsch." Mitchell leaned in, punching Dani's shoulder. "The only way you could find some friends, huh? And the ones you found are total freaks who can't skate for crap."

LEAVE. MY FRIENDS. ALONE.

Suddenly, the world around Lola snapped in a bright blue light, and—

everything
slowed
down.

Mitchell's mouth moved languidly, each syllable emerging in a drawn-out groan. Dani took a full five seconds to blink. Lola looked at Avery's and Bastian's downcast expressions, at Dani's fists, clenched around her knife and fork. She looked to Mitchell's sneering, spiteful face. The heat inside became unbearable. Lola closed her eyes and felt the lurch of time speeding back into gear. And then—

Sound, startling and everywhere, and loud, loud, *loud*, like a thousand balloons popping, all at once. Lola opened her eyes to find the food from her plate suspended in midair—the half-eaten corn dog, the pieces of chopped-up pineapples and pears. It wasn't just her own food; the cafeteria was filled with floating school lunches, lifting higher and higher above the students' heads. Then, in a snap of a second, gravity did its work, and the hundreds of pieces of food all came crashing down.

The cafeteria erupted into screams. Lola placed one hand to her cheek, which had been smacked by a maraschino cherry. Dani wiped mustard off her nose. Avery's T-shirt was soaked through with cola. Their table was a mushy, messy disaster. Then Lola looked up and had to cover her mouth, quick, to keep from laughing.

Mitchell Jensen was covered in chocolate cake. It looked as though someone had smeared a giant piece of it, icing side up, all around his face, and topping it off was a dollop of whipped cream on the end of his nose.

Avery burst out in a cackle. "Oh my God," she said. "Oh my *God.*"

The screams in the cafeteria were turning to shouts and laughter. A boy from across the room yelled, "FOOD FIGHT!" And the food was flying again, this time catapulted from hands.

Something gloopy hit Lola's neck, but she didn't look to see what or wipe it off. She suddenly felt distant from the scene, and numb all over. She watched as adults hurried down the aisles, shouting for everyone to stop this instant and *put the food down.* Then she raised her eyes to Bastian's, whose mouth was slightly parted, his pupils wide.

Lola, his voice reached inside her head. *Lola, what did you do?*

SEVEN

SURPRISE

"**N**o food-related injuries. That's a relief, at least." Mr. Gil turned around at a stoplight to face the twins. "Bastian, are you sure your sister's all right?"

Bastian looked across the backseat at Lola, who had buried her face in her knees. There was mustard splattered on her torn pink tights and chocolate syrup crusted into her flower crown.

Lola, Bastian reached out for what felt like the hundredth time. *Lola, talk to me,* please.

But now, like before, Lola didn't respond. For once, she'd been the one to build a wall in her mind, made of solid brick.

Bleeeep!

The light had turned from red to green, and the car behind them honked again. *Ble-ble-bleeeep!*

Mr. Gil drove on, but his eyes stayed on Bastian in the rearview mirror.

"I think she's just scared," Bastian said, as twin spokesperson. But this time, he wasn't sure if he really was speaking for Lola. He wasn't sure of anything going on in his sister's head.

"Well, hey," said Mr. Gil. "There's nothing to be scared about now. You're all right. We're going home. And school is over, huh? All good things."

Bastian winced. It was clear that his dad was trying to be positive for the twins' sake, but his cheerful words fell flat. Bastian couldn't so easily forget.

Even now, blocks away from Taft Middle, he could hear distant sirens. The cafeteria had been a mess, kids chucking cake and handfuls of peas at each other, slipping on spilled chocolate milk, jumping from tables and chairs. Eventually, the adults had won out and brought order to the chaos, but not before getting covered in everyone's lunch. An army of fire trucks and police cars had arrived at the school, while teachers had ushered students out to the front lawn.

Bastian had eavesdropped on the teachers, who'd gathered in tight circles. A lot of them seemed to think that an explosive had been detonated; that was the only explanation for the sudden, violent burst of food. But there was contention over whether the explosive was planted by a student, or—far worse—an enemy sympathizer making a political statement. There had been plenty of those in other cities, bigger than Callaway. It wasn't unheard of.

But Bastian knew the truth: *Lola had been the bomb.*

"You two must be hungry," his father was saying now. "What do you say we make a pit stop at the Frozen Spoon?"

Any other day, Bastian would've jumped at the chance to order his favorite ice cream: a double scoop of chocolate coconut fudge. Now he shrugged and gave a halfhearted "Sure," while Lola kept her nose buried between her knees.

Bastian was also thinking of what Mitchell Jensen had said: *You know Zander gave us the* whole *lowdown on you, right?*

Bastian couldn't believe he'd been stupid enough to tell Zander about the emotions that certain paints brought out in him, how making a design was like composing a symphony, and every color was a different instrument's contribution. Back then, Zander had acted like he'd understood. He'd nodded along, probably making fun of Bastian in his head. Mitchell was bad, but Zander was the worst—because he'd been Bastian's friend. And now he hung back, quiet and smug, while Mitchell used all his insider information.

Bastian tugged on his seat belt, which felt suddenly too taut against his chest.

As Mr. Gil drove through the next intersection, the car digipad rang. He pressed the lit-up screen on the dashboard, and a moment later, their mother's frantic voice filled the car.

"Are they all right?" she asked. "Where are you now?"

"It's fine, Mar. They're okay. We're en route. I'm swinging by the Frozen Spoon first."

There was silence on Mrs. Gil's end. Then her voice burst from the car speakers: "*Ice cream?* Not a chance, Diego. What they need now is proper food, and no doubt a shower, and plenty of hugs. Bring them *home.*"

Bastian knew the tone his mother was using; there was no

crossing Maribel Gil when she spoke that way. His dad, it seemed, knew that as well. He took a sharp turn at the intersection, redirecting the car away from downtown Callaway and toward Cedar Lane.

Bastian wondered about the other Sardines. They hadn't had a chance to talk in all the confusion, before they were whisked away by their worried parents. What the Sardines needed, Bastian thought, was an emergency meeting. Lola had caused something *big* to happen at Taft Middle—something even bigger than what they'd seen the night before, in the Hirsches' backyard. The Sardines had to figure out what to do next, before their powers got even more out of control.

Bastian cast a furtive look at his sister. She had sat up, revealing a splotchy, teary-eyed face. Lola had always been the more sensitive of the twins, and Bastian didn't want her to hurt any more. But they had to get to the bottom of this, didn't they? If Lola could make an entire cafeteria explode . . . what else could she do? What else could *Bastian* do? The question made him nervous, but a little excited, too.

Mr. Gil pulled into the driveway of 27 Cedar Lane. He hadn't even turned off the engine, when Mrs. Gil appeared at the front door, waving and then running toward the car. The moment Bastian stepped out, she wrapped him in her arms. Then she was ushering him and Lola into the house, handing them fresh, fluffy towels and insisting they immediately wash off.

"When you're through," she said, directing the twins to the two upstairs bathrooms, "come to the kitchen. I'm making my couscous and fresh pink lemonade for the two of you."

Bastian knew better than to argue. Anyway, he loved his mom's pork and couscous recipe, handed down from her family in Madrid. And pink lemonade was both Lola and Bastian's favorite drink.

He scrubbed himself down in the shower, using globs of body wash to clean his skin of crusty foods and condiments. When he emerged from his bedroom, toweled dry and dressed in fresh clothes, he found Lola in the same state, standing across from him in the hallway.

Lola, he tried, for the hundred-and-first time. *Please talk.*

Lola sniffed. Droplets of water inched down her long black hair, falling to the carpet in silent *splat*s.

"I don't know ... what to say." Lola's voice wobbled. "I don't know what happened, Bastian. I didn't *mean* it."

"Of course you didn't," Bastian said. "You were mad at Mitchell, weren't you?"

That, at least, Bastian understood.

"Yes," Lola said, looking more frightened than ever. "I was mad, but I didn't mean to make everything *explode.*"

Then Lola began to cry. Silent tears slipped from her eyes, running down her cheeks.

"Don't worry," Bastian said. "It's going to be okay."

But the words sounded wrong once he'd spoken them.

The twins stood in the hallway, one crying and one confused, as the scent of saffron and cooked dates filled the air.

Bastian's stomach was growling louder than ever, but he found that he didn't have an appetite. Even the pink lemonade tasted too sour in his mouth. While he tried and failed to enjoy his food, his mother expressed her concern about the safety of Taft Middle School.

"...wholly unacceptable," she was saying to her husband, across the table. "I hardly think it's a coincidence that this explosion occurred on the last day of school. It seems deliberate, like a message. Whoever is responsible, it's clear they've been emboldened by all this violence broadcast around us. War should never be commonplace."

"Violence begets violence," Mr. Gil agreed.

It was no secret that the Gils were anti-war. They had taken the twins to several protests downtown and even farther off, at the state capitol in Austin. Bastian thought his parents were right about the war, but he wanted to tell them that they were completely wrong about Taft Middle. But he couldn't give away Lola's secret—*his* secret. Resigning himself to an uncomfortable meal, Bastian glanced out the dining room window.

Dani was there, standing in the backyard. She was waving a bright red flag over her head—the Sardines' code for an emergency meeting. Bastian sneaked a glance at Lola, who had also noticed the scene at their parents' backs.

"Um, Mom?" Bastian said, interrupting her point about international diplomacy.

"Yes, dear?"

"Do you think Lola and I could go outside? See, uh, the Sardines agreed to—"

"Bastian, you can't be *serious*."

He blinked, nonplussed. "I . . . can't?"

"*No.* Diego, tell them." Mrs. Gil looked to her husband for support.

"Sebastian," Mr. Gil said. "We still don't know the cause of that explosion at the school. There's been no official report. Tonight, at least, we don't think the two of you should be outside, unsupervised."

"But—" Bastian began.

"That's final," said Mrs. Gil. "You're not going out until we've learned more about what happened today. There's plenty to keep you and your sister occupied for the night."

And that was the end of the discussion.

Dani was still waving her flag forcefully, though she was obviously getting tired. Bastian watched his parents as they resumed their talk of the war. When he was sure they were both distracted, he met Dani's eyes and sent a thought her way:

Can't. Under house arrest.

Dani lowered the flag.

It's important. Bastian could hear the urgency in her thought.

Sorry, Bastian said back, shrugging helplessly.

Dani remained standing in the backyard, motionless, a moment longer. Then she slumped her shoulders and walked off. Bastian looked down to his plate, picking at his couscous.

That's when the Gils' doorbell rang.

Bastian gripped his fork. Was it Dani again? Or worse— was it the police? What if they had found a way to trace the explosion back to Lola? What if they were here to take her away? To take *all* of them away?

"I'll get it," said Mr. Gil, dabbing his mouth with a napkin and getting to his feet.

Bastian wanted to tell his father not to go, that whoever stood on the other side of that door might be dangerous—but all the warnings died in his parched mouth.

Mr. Gil disappeared into the foyer. Then the house fell silent.

"Diego!" Mrs. Gil called. "Who's there?"

"Dios mío," came Mr. Gil's voice from the other room. "I can't believe it."

No, Bastian thought. *It's really happening. They found out somehow, and they're here to take us away.*

He looked to Lola, fire in his eyes.

Then came the sound of the front door swinging open, and a shout from his dad—but not a shout of fear. A shout of *joy.*

"Surprise!" a second, familiar voice cried out, followed by boisterous laughter.

The sound of that laugh drew out a knowing, desperate feeling in Bastian's heart.

Could it be?

Was it possible?

"Nando!"

Lola's elated cry echoed off the dining room walls. Bastian turned, and there he was, standing in the foyer: Nando, taller and more muscled than ever, dressed in a smart suit. A grin stretched across his face as he dropped a green briefcase and opened his arms to Lola, who was running for him with incredible speed. She giggled as he picked her up and spun her around, like she was a little kid.

Just like that, Bastian's worries faded away. He felt young and silly and full of happiness. Nando was home. This was a hearty helping of Last Day Magic.

As it turned out, Nando's appearance was as much a surprise to his parents as it was to the twins. The five of them sat in the living room with tumblers in hand—pink lemonade for Bastian and Lola, red wine for the adults.

Mrs. Gil was shaking her head in disbelief. "Mijo, I simply cannot believe you!"

"It's technically a business trip," said Nando. "But good timing, huh?" He chucked Bastian's and Lola's shoulders. "Happy summer break, squirts."

"How long are you staying?" asked Lola, whose mood had transformed to bubbly since Nando's arrival. "A week at least, right?"

Nando smiled ruefully. "I can't really say, Lols. It's all up in the air at the moment."

A troubled look passed over Mrs. Gil's face. "What on earth do they have you doing here? Does it have to do with that new Citizen Force law they passed last week?"

Nando's work was classified, but their mother never missed a chance to try to trick out an answer from her son. Usually, Nando laughed the questions off, but tonight he stiffened, a hardness entering his brown eyes.

"I'm not at liberty to discuss," he said in a clipped tone.

Lola looked worriedly between Nando and her mother. "Well," she said, "that doesn't matter. What matters is you're *here*. I got new sliders, and Bastian and I have learned lots of skating tricks since last time. We'll have to show you tomorrow, okay?"

"I'd like that, Lols," said Nando, whose expression had turned kind again. "I might be tied up tomorrow, but I promise I'll watch before I go, okay?"

Lola nodded, still shiny-eyed. Bastian felt shiny-eyed, too. Maybe pink lemonade wouldn't make things right, but Nando? He could do anything.

A tinny beeping sound filled the room, and Nando looked at his digiwatch. Then he got to his feet, saying, "I've got a work call in half an hour. I should probably head upstairs and set up my things."

Bastian had been quiet this whole time, but now he saw his chance to really talk to Nando. He followed him upstairs, and when Nando reached the second-floor landing, he motioned for Bastian to sit. The brothers settled side by side on the top step, Nando resting his green briefcase against the banister.

"So," said Nando, "how're you holding up?"

Instantly, Bastian thought of the cafeteria, chaotic and covered in food. He thought of Dani falling from the oak tree, terror in her eyes. With effort, he shook the memories out.

"Great," he said. "I'm great."

"Still remember what I told you?"

Bastian nodded. "'The door is always open.'"

Only after he'd spoken the words did their meaning sink in. If the door really was open, was Bastian walking through it? He was worried. He was confused. He was *different*. But Nando didn't seem to see the guilt inside of him.

"That's my man," he said, clapping Bastian on the back.

So much for open doors.

There was, at least, one thing Bastian could still be honest about.

"I know you're busy," he said to Nando, "but maybe you could look at my art projects? I'm trying some new approaches, and... well, I don't know if they're any good."

Nando's digiwatch let out another round of insistent beeps. He looked down, reading a message that scrolled across the watch face, and then gave Bastian a distracted smile. "Sure thing, Bash. Not tonight, but sometime soon, okay?"

Nando got to his feet, picked up his briefcase, and was off, heading down the hallway.

The door is always open.

Bastian repeated the words to himself that night, as he lay awake in bed. The trouble, he thought, was that even though the door was open, he wasn't sure he *wanted* to walk through it. He wasn't sure he could be honest with Nando anymore.

These days, he had too many secrets to keep.

EIGHT

SILVER SUITS

A t Avery's. Back by dinner.

Dani left the note for her parents on the refrigerator digipad.

It was a lie, of course.

Dani had stood in Avery's backyard, same as she had the Gils', and waved the Sardines' emergency flag. Then, figuring that this situation was exactly what her newfound powers were good for, she added a telepathic shout for Avery's attention. But there had been no response. Maybe that was because the other Sardines had parents at home—parents who were keeping them locked away. Not Dr. and Mr. Hirsch, though.

It was funny, Dani thought. Her parents cared a whole lot about what she did, from the food she ate to the sports she played. But when it came to the mysterious cafeteria explosion, Dr. Hirsch had treated it like any other school event. She'd picked up Dani at Taft Middle and sped to Cedar Lane, talking all the while about how she simply had to make it back to her office for her two-thirty appointment. Then she'd dropped off Dani without so much as a "Stay safe," and screeched down the cul-de-sac, leaving her only daughter all alone in an empty house.

"It's fine, though," Dani said aloud as she washed her face free of a chocolate stain and then plucked a mysterious bit of meat from her hair. "It's better this way. Even if the others can't come, that doesn't mean I shouldn't go."

Because Dani Hirsch had a plan.

She left her house, glowboard in hand, by way of the back door. Then she paused on the porch and looked around, making sure no one was watching.

The first time Dani had done it, the day of her twelfth birthday, she hadn't even been thinking. She'd run outside, and the door had slammed after her. She'd explained it away as a gust of wind, but then it kept happening. Doors continued to shut behind Dani, without her so much as touching them.

It had taken Dani time to realize and believe. It had taken practice, too. But now she could do it on purpose. Now she could focus the bright blue flame inside toward the back door.

Shut, she commanded.

And *slam.*

The door closed and locked itself tight.

Dani crossed through the backyards of her other neighbors—the Arnolds, Lopezes, and Clarks. Only once she'd reached their end did she emerge onto Birch Street and click on her board. It sputtered, coughing out orange glow, then powered down. It had been doing a lot of that lately.

"Come on," Dani said coaxingly, running her hands down its sides. "You can't die on me now. Not until after the big race. Got it?"

She flipped the power switch again. The board rumbled, coughing out still more glow, but this time it maintained a gentle hum. Dani dropped it to the ground, where it hovered inches above the asphalt road.

"Thanks, pal," she said, mounting.

Then she was off, swishing around corners, hovering at intersections, and, above all, trying to stay inconspicuous— her beanie tugged low over her eyes, no showy glowstream behind her.

"It was me," Lola had whispered as they'd been shuffled out of the cafeteria by teacher aides. "I don't know how, I didn't *mean* it."

And then the adults had shouted for everyone to stop talking and file out silently.

Lola had caused the explosion; that's all Dani knew. Now she was determined to find out more.

Dani was going back to school.

The fire trucks were gone from Taft Middle, but some cop cars remained. Their silent lights whirled, flashing bright blue and red against the school's brick facade. Dani slowed and then cut off her board, hiding herself behind a thick-trunked tree across the road. There was yellow tape strung in front of the school's entrance, and two men in suits were talking by the front doors.

Then Dani noticed *them.*

There were a half-dozen figures on the school lawn, dressed in sleek silver jumpsuits that zipped up to the chin. Their faces were obscured by the dark visors of their metal helmets, and their hands were fitted with gloves. Not a single inch of skin was visible; in fact, the figures looked more like machines—heartless, faceless machines—than humans. They were gathered on the lawn in a precise formation of parallel rows, treading the ground with heavy boots and carrying long metal objects shaped like batons.

Dani recognized them; they looked like the figures she'd seen in textbook photographs of Callaway from fifty years ago, when Mitchell Jensen's grandfather had first discovered the glow and the government had sent inspectors to investigate.

The inspectors from those photographs—that's who these figures reminded Dani of now. They gave her the creeps. Their uniforms were slightly different, updated, but the metal instruments they were using, sweeping back and forth in slow arcs over the lawn—Dani knew what they were: glow detectors.

Is that what these suits were trying to detect? *Glow,* on Taft Middle property? Or were they searching for something else? Some*one* else?

Dani shoved her glowboard into her backpack. Then, noting one deserted corner of the school lawn, she emerged from behind the tree. She crossed the street as nonchalantly as she could and edged along the lawn. Then, in one go, she sprinted up the hill and hid herself in the juniper bushes by the school's front entrance, near the two men standing there, dressed in regular business suits. They were talking to each other. She crept closer, but then felt resistance. Her backpack strap had caught on a branch. Quietly, *quietly*, Dani freed the strap and crept closer.

"... reinforcements," said one of the men. "The local force isn't trained for this."

"They'll be here soon enough," said the other. "O'Brien says they're flying a team in tonight to handle the survey data. It'll be in federal hands from here on out. Well, and *his* hands, of course."

The first man put a cigarette to his mouth and lit it. Dani made a face and covered her nose.

"Think it's possible?" the man said around his smoke. "That we've got what *they've* got?"

"Wishful thinking, maybe. But if so, couldn't have come a moment too soon. No doubt they're already training theirs for combat. Wouldn't surprise me if—"

The school doors flew open. Dani ducked as a woman's voice boomed out, "Get in, both of you. He needs your signatures."

Dani sucked in a breath and heard a rapid series of sounds: the stamping out of a cigarette, footsteps into the school, and the slam of doors behind the government workers. Even after the sounds had faded, she remained where she was, crouched and unbreathing. At last, she exhaled and cautiously stood. There was no one left at the entrance guarding the taped-off doors. She could risk it, try to sneak in. But she had to be sure the area was completely clear. Dani turned to survey the yard...

...and found herself face-to-face with Mitchell Jensen.

"AAAH!" she shrieked, and ducked for cover once more.

Mitchell stood over her, venom in his blue eyes. There was someone by his side: Zander Poxleitner. Dani cast them both the dirtiest look she kept in her dirty look arsenal.

"What're you doing here, freak?"

Freak. It was Mitchell's usual put-down, but today it pained a tender spot inside Dani.

"Could ask you the same thing," she said, rising to Mitchell's eye level—though actually, *above* it. How had Dani not noticed before? She was taller than Mitchell Jensen. The revelation filled her with confidence, and she shoved her fists on her hips, staring him down.

"Don't play all innocent, Hirsch." Mitchell stepped so close that Dani could see the spittle on his lips. "I was there, in the caf. I know one of you freaks did it. I *know* it."

"Wow." Dani snorted. "That's some imagination you got. Didn't you hear? It was probably an enemy sympathizer."

"That's crap, and you know it." Then Mitchell's hands were on her shoulders, shoving Dani with force. She stumbled and fell, sprawling back into the juniper bushes.

"Hey, man, lay off!" a voice said. "Save it for the track."

Mitchell turned on Zander, red in the face. "Excuse me?"

"I said, save it for the track," Zander repeated. "This isn't the place to fight."

Dani struggled in the bushes, watching Mitchell elbow

past Zander and walk off toward the street. Then Zander was kneeling beside her, offering his hand.

Was he *crazy*? Dani glared, righting herself awkwardly on her own.

"You're not the good guy, you know," she spat when she was back on her feet, her blue flame burning stronger than ever.

Zander backed away. "I didn't say I was."

"And I don't need you to fight for me. I'm fine on my own."

"Yeah, I know that. I..." Zander's voice turned to little more than a whisper. "I know you, Dani. Even if you won't, like, look at me in school."

There was another sensation in Dani's gut, strange and unwanted, that had nothing to do with the usual flame.

"You're the one who's a traitor!" She folded her arms like she could hide behind them. "You moved away from Cedar Lane, and you never gave us an explanation. Why? Because you wanted to live in a cooler part of town? Probably Mitchell's neighborhood, right? We were a team, and then you left us for that...that *jerk*."

"Oh, like you weren't being a jerk before?"

"Excuse me?"

"C'mon, Dani. Things were great for a while. But then the races started up and you got so...competitive."

Dani bristled. "Are you saying girls can't be competitive?"

"Of course not!" Zander's dark eyes turned indignant. "You know, just because I skate with Mitchell doesn't mean I *am* Mitchell."

"But you *skate with him*. Even though he's awful to us. You stand there and let him say all those horrible things. You told him that private stuff about Bastian, too. Stuff he never even told the rest of the Sardines."

"I..." Why was Zander turning red? "Fine, you're right. I do stand there. And I did tell some secrets. That's not cool, I shouldn't...Look, I'm trying to figure things out. There's been a lot of stuff going on lately, and—"

"That's not an excuse!"

"Okay, okay, it's not." Zander scratched at his ear, looking down. "But you have to admit, back when you started getting so serious about racing? You made things really hard. You sucked all the fun out of glowboarding. And I wasn't the only one who thought that. I needed a break, to go back to having fun again. That's why I got into glowboarding in the first place. That's why I taught *you* to skate. I thought...it was a cool way to hang out."

The anger growing in Dani faltered, sent off-kilter by that weird *other* feeling. "So what?" she asked. "You teamed up with Mitchell to have *fun*? The Grackles are the most competitive team out there."

"Well, sure, but we still free skate a bunch, and there are parties, and we get new equipment—"

"Because Mitchell's dad *owns* glowboarding!" Dani shouted. Then she remembered where she was. Panicked, she looked around, sure someone had heard her. She had to get out of there, away from stupid traitor Zander. In a growling whisper, she said, "Just stay out of my way, you sellout."

With that, she freed her backpack, which had once again

caught in the bushes, and stomped past Zander, ignoring the sad look on his mole-marked face. She also ignored his stupid green jacket and floppy black hair, and the way he kind of smelled like a freshly opened can of Coca-Cola.

So what if she'd had a teeny tiny crush on Zander, back when they'd been friends? He'd joined Mitchell's pack. And he'd just called her a *jerk*.

Even now, his words blared in Dani's head: *I wasn't the only one who thought that.*

Who else had Zander meant? Who else thought that Dani sucked the fun out of glowboarding? Lola had never been as into races as the others, Dani knew. But Lola didn't think Dani was a *jerk*, did she? Did the others think that, too?

"Hey! You there!"

Shock zapped through Dani's bones.

They'd spotted her. One of the silver suits was running toward her, glow detector raised in a sinister hold.

Dani ran, flying across the grass, her sneakers pounding into the sidewalk, flinging her over the street until, back in the cover of her hiding tree, she pulled out her glowboard. This time, to her relief, it started up on the first go, and Dani skated off fast, into a bloodred sunset.

"A full-blown explosion. Who knew it would escalate this quickly?"

The man in the navy suit was sitting across a table from a young woman. As she spoke, she adjusted a bobby pin that held her high pony-tail in place.

"It's no surprise to me," the man said. "I was raised here. I remember the incident as though it were yesterday. I knew from that day on there was something special about Callaway." Here, the man smiled. "*More* special than glow."

The woman took a long sip of her Earl Grey tea. "You were right," she said. "Now the entire DGE knows it."

"And the contract?" The man in the navy suit tapped a stack of papers that lay between them. Most prominent on the page was the word "Gloworks."

After swallowing more tea, the woman said, "It would seem it's our best bet. The DGE has a history of making deals with private busi-nesses. Hopefully this deal, like all those that have come before, will be mutually beneficial."

The man in the navy suit nodded. "I feel confident of that. With the DGE's knowledge and Gloworks' resources combined? We'll track them down no matter what it takes."

The man in the navy suit meant every word.

NINE

THE MIDNIGHT MEETING

When Lola woke, it was not to the buzz of her alarm clock, but a faint brushing against her cheek. She swatted away the sensation, yawning, and held her pillow close. But the brushing returned, trailing along the curve of her ear. She sat up, blinking into the dark. The clock by her bedside read 12:00 a.m. exactly. Midnight. She still had plenty of sleep ahead of her. Lola rearranged her pillows and ducked back under her quilt. That's when she saw them: her paper birds.

They were gliding through the air—seven of them, in varying shades of violet and yellow and green. But no, not gliding, *flying*. They were *flapping their paper wings*. Lola sat up once more, wide-awake. She watched as the birds swooped in a circle, bathed in moonlight. How had they found their way here from the kitchen? How could they be *alive*?

A violet bird broke off from the circle and flapped up to Lola, skimming the edge of one wing across her forehead.

Come. She heard a voice in her head, twinkling and sharp, like a wind chime. *Follow us.*

Lola told herself to wake up. She rubbed her eyes and pinched her arms, but nothing roused her from sleep. So maybe she was awake after all. And why shouldn't she follow where her paper birds led?

She slipped out of bed, and the violet bird rejoined its mates. The birds' circle fanned out, then turned to a single straight line that shot out her bedroom door.

Lola followed.

Bastian woke to the sound of rustling paper. There was light streaming in beneath his door, from the hallway.

Weird, thought Bastian. The Gils always kept the hall light off.

He got out of bed and, thinking practically of intruders, grabbed a heavy brass paperweight from his desk. Holding it at the ready, he approached the door and listened. There was no sound of footsteps or whispers, just the faint, rustling sound that had woken him. Before he could lose his nerve, Bastian flung open the door, paperweight raised.

But there was no one there. He looked one way down the hall, then the other.

No robber, no stranger. Not even Nando, up to get a glass of water. No one.

Then a great *whoosh* passed over him, and Bastian saw

crumpled papers hanging in midair, surrounding him on all sides. They were half-finished, abandoned sketches of glowboard designs—all papers from the trash can beneath his desk. A folded sheet of neon green breezed forward and nudged his elbow.

Come, said a voice in his mind, light and clear, like a rushing stream. *Follow us.*

Bastian followed his artwork down the stairs.

Dani was dreaming of racing. In sleep, she felt the glowboard beneath her feet, her muscles finely tuned to it, swerving and hugging tight corners. In her best dreams, she beat Mitchell and his Grackles once and for all, sliding across the finish line and exulting in their defeat.

Dani heard the gentle hum of the board and the electronic *swoosh* as she kicked on the glowstream, which trailed behind her in a glowing ribbon of neon orange. She saw the stream shoot out sparks, cutting across the night and then fading from view, turned to vapor.

Only...

She wasn't dreaming the glowstream.

She was *seeing it.* She was suddenly awake, sitting up, and found that her glowboard was hovering above her bed, sputtering orange sparks into the dark. She yelped as more sparks blew out from the glow pipe. Then she lunged for the board.

But the glowboard did not want to be caught. It swooped out of reach, and Dani toppled off her bed, watching as the board flew to her bedroom door and hovered there.

Come. A voice clinked in her mind, like a butter knife tapping glass. *Follow us.*

Then the glowboard shot from Dani's room, and she had no choice but to chase it down.

"Radar? What is it, boy?"

Avery had woken to Radar's barking—shrill, nervous yips, as he danced close to her bed. She rubbed out the sleep from her eyes, and the shadowy forms in her room took shape.

Books. Books from her bookshelves were spinning around her bed in concentric circles. She ducked as the Merriam-Webster dictionary floated toward her face.

Radar kept barking, leaping to nip at the books nearest his jaws.

"It's all right, boy," Avery whispered, crawling from bed and patting him down.

But Avery wasn't sure if it *was* all right.

This didn't feel like a dream. The hardwood floor was cold and uneven beneath her feet. She could hear her breaths and feel the quick beat of her heart. Then a voice spoke inside her mind.

Come, it said, a woodwind melody. *Follow us.*

The books broke from their circles and swooshed in a flurry out the door.

With a whining Radar at her side, Avery followed.

The Sardines convened in the Gils' backyard, stopping outside Cedar House. For one instant, the midnight world was chaotic—the convergence of paper birds, crumpled artwork, books, and a rogue glowboard.

Then, in a burst, the objects dispersed, shooting back toward the houses whence they'd come.

All that remained were four friends and a dog.

Crickets sang around them, and the moon poured down its beams. A gust of wind shot through the backyard, and the door to Cedar House flew open. All together, the Sardines walked inside, where, silently, they formed a circle.

Then Cedar House filled with light.

A bright blue column shot down its center, as Radar barked wildly, straining against Avery's hold on his collar.

The column swelled, and so did the burning blue flames inside each of the Sardines. Then a voice spoke from the light:

Greetings.

We, the light beings, have taken note of your plight.

We planted the elixir here, in hopes that it would aid your civilization.

Instead, your own have turned against you because of your differences.

This world is not a hospitable place for gifted creatures like you.

So we have traveled from distant space to rescue the five of you.

We look . . . to meeting . . . the appointed date . . . when . . .

The voice was breaking up, garbled, like a broken transmission. The words turned indistinct, and then there were no words at all. The column gave a final swell, growing more and more unbearably bright until it forced Avery, Bastian, Dani, and Lola to shut their eyes.

Then there was silence.

Darkness.

The column was gone, and Radar began to bark once more.

TEN

THE MEANING OF
THE MESSAGE

A very was the first to speak.

"Whoa," she said.

There were stars in her eyes, specks of light left behind from the now-vanished column. Her knees felt more liquid than solid. She sank down into a beanbag, and soon so did all the Sardines. It was dark in Cedar House—too dark to see. Avery ran her hand against the wall until she found the clubhouse's single shelf. From it, she grabbed the emergency flashlight and switched it on. The Sardines blinked, taking in each other's stunned expressions.

Bastian was the first to actually speak.

He said, "Did . . . *aliens* just contact us?"

Avery laughed. She didn't know why. She laughed and found she couldn't stop. Dani and Bastian stared at her like she'd lost her mind.

"This is serious!" Bastian finally shouted over her giggles.

Avery wiped her wet eyes. "But it isn't really," she said. "It's hilarious. Aliens talking to *us*."

"We all heard the same thing, right?" asked Dani. "First things first. It's important we're on the same page."

Leave it to Dani to organize this, thought Avery. But the truth was, she was grateful. If anyone could help to make sense of the blue column and its message, it was Dani Hirsch.

"You mean how, apparently, we're in some sort of 'plight'?" Bastian folded his arms. "And how these light beings planted an elixir and are coming from distant space to rescue us? That's what I caught."

"What does that mean?" Lola asked in a threadbare voice. "Do they want to *abduct* us?"

The smile vanished from Avery's face. She didn't feel like laughing anymore.

"Yeah," she admitted. "That's kind of what it sounded like."

Lola sniffed, tugging at the lace of her nightgown collar.

"Sooo?" Dani drew out the word like an unanswerable question. "Who are these people? Why would they contact *us*? And rescue us from *what*?"

"Maybe," said Avery, "it's . . . a practical joke?"

She wasn't convinced by her own suggestion.

Dani wasn't, either. "A practical joke that woke up all of us with floating stuff and brought us out here and shot down blue light from the sky? Who could make a practical joke like *that*? Not even Mitchell's rich enough to do something that fancy."

Avery tried to swallow and found she couldn't. "It's too weird" was all she could say.

"Is it too weird?" asked Bastian. "Weren't we all in this clubhouse last night, talking about the stuff we can do? Is this any weirder?"

"The voice said there are five of us, though," said Avery. "In case you guys haven't noticed, we're only a four-person team."

The clubhouse was quiet. Then Avery noticed Dani and Bastian both looking her way. Though not her way, exactly. They were looking at...*Radar*. Avery's eyes got big. She turned to her dog.

"But...that's not possible! If you were one of us, you'd be able to talk. You'd..." Avery trailed off as she stared into Radar's eyes—one brown, one blue. She thought of all their games of Frisbee fetch, of dreaded baths and snuggle sessions over the past year.

"But he's only two," Avery said. "He's not our age."

"What's two in dog years?" asked Dani.

Avery scowled.

"Well," said Dani, "what other explanation is there? The voice said there are five of us, and there are *technically* five of us here."

"But...a dog!" Avery protested.

"That's the part you have trouble believing?" asked Bastian. "We're talking about *alien contact* here. And telekinesis. And telepathy. And—"

"Stop it!" cried Lola, shaking her head. "Everyone, stop! We're not focusing on what's most important here. *Whoever* contacted us, we didn't get their whole message. Don't you remember?"

Avery wrinkled her nose. How had the message ended? *Meeting . . . the appointed date . . . when . . .*

"It stopped," she whispered. "It cut out."

"That's right," said Dani, frowning. "They were talking about an appointed time, about—about—"

Dani was suddenly on her knees, searching the ground in the middle of their circle, where the column of blue light had once been. Somehow, Avery knew Dani wouldn't find any remnant of the message there. The light had simply *been*, and now it was gone.

"What are we supposed to do now?" asked Bastian when Dani slumped back from her unsuccessful search. "All we know is that *probably* aliens contacted us, and that, for some weird reason, they want to rescue us. The *five* of us. But why? And where? And *when*? We're kind of missing all the important details."

"Maybe they'll send us another message," Lola said.

"But maybe they won't," said Dani. "Maybe they'll show up in the middle of the night, like they just did, and abduct us on the spot."

A chill prickled up and down Avery's arms. Beside her, Radar whined.

"Don't . . . say things like that," whispered Lola.

Tiny tears were trickling down her face, and Avery's heart beat hard at the sight. Avery concentrated on the blue flame inside, and then she thought right at Lola, pushing words out to her: *It's okay, we'll figure it out. Together.*

Lola inhaled, sitting up straight and meeting Avery's gaze. Then Lola's thoughts came in, bright and somehow lavender-hued, the same way Lola's hair was so wonderfully lavender-scented: *Thank you.*

Avery inched a hand over to Lola's, took hold, and squeezed once—another way to say, *I'm here.* Lola smiled a little, even though fear was still in her eyes, and a flutter filled Avery's stomach—the kind of flutter she normally only got before a big glowboarding race.

Out loud, Avery said, "Maybe everything will make more sense in the morning."

Or maybe in the morning, this will turn out to be a dream, Avery thought, only to herself.

"Avery's got a point," said Dani. "It's after midnight, and we're tired. We'll be talking in circles if we stick around here. Let's get some sleep, and we'll discuss this tomorrow, at glowboard practice."

"Practice?" Bastian gawked at Dani. "You're thinking about *practice?*"

"Yes, I am," Dani said matter-of-factly. "Glow in the Park is still happening, isn't it? Nothing's going to stop us from winning that prize. Not the Grackles, and not even some weird alien message from outer space."

"Seriously, Dani, do you hear yourself right now?"

"Yeah, Bastian, I do," Dani said, raising her voice. "You

just don't get it because *your* parents buy you new boards every Christmas."

Cedar House fell silent, and Avery looked down, picking sand from her eyes. They really did need sleep.

The Sardines left Cedar House, trudging through the damp night, back to their homes. Radar trotted by Avery's side, glancing up at her every so often. When they reached Avery's room, he licked her hand and rested his chin on her lap, blinking his worried eyes up at her.

"Radar," Avery whispered, "are you one of us? Do *you* have tele-whatevers? Is that why the aliens want to rescue you, too?"

Radar kept looking at her. Avery tried again. "Can you understand what I'm saying?"

Radar stared up with his big, glistening eyes.

Avery decided to try something else.

Can you understand me? She thought the words and then pushed them from her mind toward Radar's furry head and floppy black ears.

Radar whined, pressing a paw into Avery's knee.

She gasped.

Did that mean yes?

Did that mean anything at all?

Avery looked around the room. All her books were back in their proper places, not a single one overturned or left open.

Maybe, Avery thought, she had simply imagined it all.

She would find out the truth soon enough when morning came.

ELEVEN

ERADICATE

I t was the first breakfast of summer break, and Dani was stuck slurping a power smoothie.

She had tried many times before to convince her parents that smoothies were the worst form of breakfast. They tasted like chalk mixed up with shoots and leaves, and Dani may or may not have secretly dumped out more than one smoothie in her bathroom sink.

Dani had made the mistake of actually *complaining* once, whining that Avery got to eat Eggos and Lucky Charms for breakfast and that the Gil twins regularly ate Spanish omelets with fancy Iberian ham. Dr. and Mr. Hirsch had curtly replied that Avery's mother was never around to monitor her breakfast, and the Gils were perfectly nice folks but incorporated far too much meat into their diets. As long as Dani was a Hirsch, said her parents, she would follow the Hirsch Code—and that code wasn't limited to food choices.

The Hirsch Code meant the hardest courses in school. The Hirsch Code meant no junk food, and absolutely no candy in the house. The Hirsch Code meant no pets, due to Mr. Hirsch's severe allergies. And the Hirsch Code meant an ongoing dedication to a legitimate sport. The trouble was that, in Dr. and Mr. Hirsch's estimation, glowboarding was *not* legitimate. Glowboarding was a fad that had arisen in the last couple decades and would fade away just as quickly. There were no college glowboarding scholarships, and there had been no glowboarding legacy passed down in the Hirsch family. Unlike . . . competitive swimming.

The fiercest fight of Dani's life had been convincing her parents to let her drop swim team that summer in favor of glowboarding. Dani could go to honors classes and even choke down nasty power smoothies, but she would *never* give up glowboarding. That spring, she'd spent many nights attempting to eavesdrop as her parents argued in loud whispers behind their bedroom door. In the end, they'd allowed Dani her glowboarding, but that didn't mean anything else changed. They didn't buy her equipment, like they had for swimming; it had cost Dani many years' worth of gift money just to get a mediocre board. The Hirsches hadn't attended a single one of her races, as they had her swim meets. There was always an excuse—a business trip or convention, a dinner date that simply couldn't be missed. Dani knew that the real reason was because her parents didn't approve. But she would take small victories as they came, and in the meantime, she'd drink her power smoothies without complaint.

This morning, all three Hirsches sat around the kitchen table. Dr. Hirsch's glasses sat perched on her nose as she read over the newspaper.

"Terrible," she said, tapping the headline that read *EXPLOSION AT TAFT MIDDLE CAUSED BY PRANK-ING TEENS*. "Glad they got to the bottom of it so quickly, though. Imagine, those eighth-graders rigging firecrackers in a public place. I'd like to know who their parents are. We've enough on our hands with this war without a scare like that."

Dani wanted to say, *If you'd thought it was so terrible, then you would've stuck around and not left me home alone.*

"How did they figure out who did it?" Dani asked instead.

"They say the kids confessed," Mr. Hirsch said between sips of goopy green liquid. "They're keeping their names private because they're underage."

Or because those eighth-grade kids don't actually exist, Dani thought. She was sure that the men in business suits she'd seen the day before had something to do with the fake story. Only the Sardines knew the truth. Only they knew it was *Lola*.

And we'll keep it that way, Dani thought resolutely. *Today, at practice, we'll figure out everything: the cafeteria, our tele-whatevers, and what happened last night in Cedar House.*

"I'm glad you're out of that school for the summer,"

Dr. Hirsch said. "They'd better put stricter safety regulations in place by August. Imagine if it *had* been a sympathizer."

Dani mashed her straw into a clump of unblended kale. Of course her parents believed the bogus story. Why wouldn't they? Her parents were always on the side of rational explanations.

These days, no one spoke about *the incident*, when a mysterious blue fire had burned in the middle of Cedar Lane. That day had been over thirteen years ago, before Dani's parents had bought their house for an excellent price. Before the Curse of Strange Street became legend.

There was no curse, Dr. and Mr. Hirsch maintained. The blue fire had been an anomaly, but the fact that there was no current scientific explanation for the phenomenon did not mean it was something to be afraid of. The trouble, said Dr. Hirsch, was that people were largely guided by superstition and emotion. Not every homeowner could be as perceptive as she, a licensed psychiatrist, was trained to be.

A slightly scary story—that's all the incident had been to Dani before. But now her mind was feverishly turning over a possibility. She'd never considered before that the blue light she felt inside had anything to do with *the incident*. Her blue flame had been personal, set apart. Now, though, she'd seen a bright blue column with her own eyes, right in the middle of Cedar House. Now she wondered if the incident that had earned Cedar Lane the name *Strange Street* had anything to do with her. And that wasn't something she wanted her parents to ever find out.

Dani slurped up more of her smoothie, and as she did, thick green bubbles appeared in the blended avocado and leafy greens. Dani stopped slurping.

But the bubbles kept appearing.

Dani frowned down at the glass. The smoothie wasn't just bubbling, it was ... transforming. Different hues of green, from the spinach, kale, cilantro, and apple skins, were separating and swirling outward. The lighter greens began to form a liquid pinwheel at the top of the drink, standing out starkly against a darker green background. Then the bubbling calmed, but the liquid continued to move. The pinwheel's arms extended, curling outward and detaching, morphing into shapes—into *images*, light green atop dark. Without knowing how it had begun, Dani found herself in the middle of a story.

A girl was mounting a glowboard, skating. Then she wobbled, her legs gave out, and she lost her balance entirely, falling forward onto the concrete.

There was a crackling sound in Dani's ears, and through it, a voice became clear. The voice spoke in Dani's mind, gentle, but insistent—a butter knife tapping glass.

Such pain in your world. Unnecessary pain.

The green liquid images transformed, this time rendering the figure of a group of boys, pointing fingers and laughing at a solitary girl.

At last, Dani understood: *That's me*, she thought. The girl who'd fallen from her glowboard, the girl enduring a bully's taunts—that was *her*. These were *memories*.

The voice spoke again, in her mind, though now it was

turning garbled, fuzzy with static. *We will rescue you... and eradicate... all that remain. We are... coming. At the appointed time... when...*

The static overtook the words, drowning out the rest of the message.

"WAIT," Dani shouted. "WHAT?"

She reached for the smoothie, but in her haste, she fumbled, knocking it over. The glass rolled along the table, then dropped to the floor, shattering.

"Danielle!" Dr. Hirsch cried, starting up from the table.

Dani gaped at the mess of broken glass and pulpy greens at her feet. The voice in her head was gone.

"I—I—" she stammered.

"What on earth is wrong with you?" Dr. Hirsch said, even as she hurried to the kitchen to fetch a dustpan for the glass shards.

"I didn't meant to," Dani finally got out. "I *swear.*"

"Help your mother clean it up," said Mr. Hirsch, sternly observing Dani from over his newspaper.

"Yes, sir," Dani said, getting to her feet and fetching paper towels from over the kitchen sink.

It was an unpleasant cleanup, and all the while Dani's mother lectured her about being more careful. Dani insisted again that it had been an accident, but even she had to admit, such an "accident" didn't look good after so many months of complaining about power smoothies. In the end, all she could do was sop up the remaining green gloop from the floor and follow her mother to the trash can.

"You're nearly a teenager, Danielle," Dr. Hirsch said. "You have to stop acting like a child."

Dani nodded morosely. "It *was* an accident. I just . . . haven't been feeling like myself lately."

Dani's parents exchanged a troubled glance, and then Dr. Hirsch sighed. "You know, dear," she said, in a gentler voice, "it's not too late to sign back up for swim team. Ms. Bettis has told me several times how much they miss you."

Dr. Hirsch had told *Dani* several times how much Ms. Bettis missed her. Dani was a natural talent, they said. Her mother had earned a college scholarship for swimming, and Dani could do the same.

Dani couldn't help that there were no college scholarships for glowboarding . . . yet. She liked swimming, but she *loved* glowboarding, and no amount of scholarship money was going to change that. The only money she cared about was the first-place prize at Glow in the Park that would buy her a new, dependable glowboard.

But Dani wasn't up for a fight, so she merely said, "Yeah, I'll think about it."

As she headed for the hall, Dr. Hirsch called out, "Danielle? Stay for a moment, please."

Dani froze. This wasn't good. *Danielle, stay for a moment* could never be good. Slowly, she turned to face her parents. Was she about to receive an infamous Hirsch Code lecture?

"Danielle," her mother said, "your father and I have been discussing this glowboarding business."

Dani's mind filled with a flurry of rebuttals: *It* is *legitimate, there's a cash prize, it's what I love, you have no right.* Before she could voice any of them, her mother continued.

"We know that, for whatever reason, you've fixated on this hobby."

Sport, Dani wanted to say.

"We certainly don't want to force you to do anything you don't want. But you're familiar with our concerns, and we think that, perhaps, you're not looking at this long-term. Swimming will be an asset to you in college and adulthood; glowboarding won't."

"You don't know that," Dani retorted. "More and more people glowboard. It's a real sport, with rules and regulations. Just because it's new doesn't mean it's not *legitimate.* Take Glow in the Park, for instance—they're giving away trophies. Cash prizes. What's not legit about that?"

"We're aware," Mr. Hirsch said, after he and her mother had shared another look. "In fact, Danielle, it's this new race of yours that got your mother and me thinking. We have a proposal for you."

Dani squinted skeptically. She wasn't sure if this was a trap, but "proposal" sounded a lot better than a lecture.

"What we propose is this," said Dr. Hirsch. "You clearly enjoy glowboarding, and you've told us that you and your teammates excel at it. We're giving you a chance to prove that to us, through hard work and dedication. You said there are trophies at this Glow in the Park—rankings, yes?"

Dani nodded cautiously. "And money. There's money, too."

"Right," said Dr. Hirsch. "We propose that if you and your teammates place first in your division, or category, whatever it might be—if you can distinguish yourself, can actually make *money* in this pursuit—then your father and I will be willing to fund glowboarding like we did your swimming. We're giving you a chance to prove that you can succeed in this field. That there are actual *benefits* to be reaped from competition."

Dani opened her mouth. Her veins thrilled with adrenaline. This was *way* better than a lecture. This was a gift. If her parents actually bought her equipment *and* the Sardines won Glow in the Park, they could buy so much more with the first-place prize: upgrades, extra glow cartridges, maybe even *uniforms*.

"However"—Dr. Hirsch cut into Dani's daydreaming—"if you do not place first, *you* will do something for *us*: You'll set aside this hobby and you'll rejoin the swim team."

Dani's mouth was dry from hanging open so long. She shut it, hit by hard reality. This wasn't a gift after all. This was a deal. A deal that would change *everything*. And Dani knew her parents would follow through; the Hirsch Code demanded strict adherence to all promises. For a moment, she considered the possibility of no more glowboarding. Of practice days no longer spent on Hazard Hill, but in chlorinated water.

It was worth the risk.

Because the Sardines *would* win. Dani had a plan.

"Deal," she said before she could second-guess herself. "It's a deal."

Dr. Hirsch raised her eyebrows.

"Very good," she said at last, reaching out a hand.

Dani shook on the agreement with all her might.

Dani headed to practice early. She was always first on Hazard Hill, and most days, she spent the free time working on her form, or thinking up new strategies for the team.

Today was different, though. Today, she was a girl with tele-whatevers who had received a message from aliens.

Eradicate all that remain. The words looped through Dani's brain, again and again, until they became a single word: *eradicate.*

Dani had barely gotten a wink of sleep the night before, thanks to that blue column, and now *this?* Memories in her power smoothie? A voice in her ear saying that aliens were going to wipe out the earth? And on top of all that, a glow-board agreement with her parents that could change the course of her life forever.

The strain of it all was beginning to take its toll. When Dani mounted her board on Cedar Lane, her hands shook, her balance uneasy. Her board sputtered pathetically, shuddering the whole way out to the hill. Dani wasn't much better; she wobbled at stop signs and nearly wiped out turning a familiar corner at Morris Avenue. By the time she arrived at the battered entrance gate of Hazard Hill, she was winded and flushed. She dismounted, pressing her hands to her knees, trying to breathe and right a spinning world.

Eradicate all that remain.

Set aside this hobby.

"Hey. You okay?" asked a familiar voice. A familiar, *stupid* voice. Skating up to her, a totally fake look of concern on his face, was none other than Zander Poxleitner.

"Leave me alone," Dani told him.

"You don't look so good." Zander hopped to the ground, grabbing his board from its hover and notching the power switch off. "Maybe you should sit down."

Dani glared at Zander but remained stooped, hands on her knees. If she stood up straight, she had a feeling she might pass out. She wasn't about to *sit*, though; she wouldn't give Zander the satisfaction.

"Fine," Zander sighed. "Have it your way."

"Where's your team?" asked Dani. The Sardines would be showing up soon, and the last thing they needed was a fight with the Grackles.

"Chill out, would you?" said Zander. "It's just me here."

Dani's fear instantly turned to suspicion. "Why?"

"Uh." Zander motioned around. "Some people like to skate on their own. You know, for *fun*?"

Dani risked standing so she could glare at Zander straight in the eye. "Oh right, and I don't know what *fun* is. Because I'm a total stick-in-the-mud."

"You said it, not me."

Now that she had a good look at him, Dani spied a cut beneath Zander's eye. It was thin but long, running from the crook of his nose to his ear.

"Where'd you get that?" she asked before she could stop herself.

Zander's hand flew to the cut. "It's nothing," he said. "There are these rosebushes in our backyard."

"Oh, at your fancy new house, huh?" sneered Dani. "And what, you shoved your face in them?"

"Yeah, sure." Zander spoke angrily, but his skin had turned a strange shade of purple, like he was ... embarrassed? That wasn't possible, though. Zander was a traitor and therefore incapable of shame.

The hum of approaching glowboards caught Dani's attention. She turned to see Bastian and Lola skating toward her.

"You should leave," she said to Zander. "The twins won't be any more excited to see you than I am."

"Yeah, got it," muttered Zander. "I was just finishing anyway."

He turned his board on, throwing it into a hover and jumping atop it. Then, smirking, he kicked on the glowstream—neon blue—and skated off, passing by Bastian and Lola with a flourish.

Jerk, thought Dani, even as she remembered his thorn-cut cheek.

TWELVE
TETHER

After reading the newspaper headline over breakfast and deeming that the outside world was safe, Mrs. Gil allowed Lola and Bastian outside to skate to Hazard Hill. Lola didn't feel like skating, and she was pretty sure the others didn't either, but once all the Sardines had arrived on the hill, Dani insisted they start practice immediately. She called out orders, timing draft train descents and giving Avery pointers on her finish line crossing. But for all Dani's efforts and all the team's attempts, their race time stayed awful, at two minutes and twenty-five seconds—the worst it had been in months. With every repeated attempt, Dani's commands grew shriller.

"You're not in sync!" she shouted. "Where is your racing *rhythm*? You have to be one with the board!"

The truth was, not even Dani was skating well. Lola

noticed her feet shifting awkwardly on her board, and after fifteen minutes of practice, she wiped out entirely, tumbling onto the asphalt and scraping up both knees.

Lola reached her first, kneeling down in concern, while Bastian and Avery came up behind.

"That's what you get," said Bastian. Immediately, his eyes got big with regret, but the damage was already done. Dani narrowed her eyes at him as Lola helped her to her feet.

"That's what I get for *what*? Trying to keep this team together?"

No, Lola thought to herself. *No, I don't want them to fight.*

Bastian, though, had committed to his side of the argument. "No one wants to practice right now," he said. "We're all too distracted."

"Oh really?" Dani shoved her hands on her hips, turning to Lola and Avery. "Is everyone *too distracted*? Do you all think I'm, like, sucking the fun out of everything?"

"Come on, you two," said Avery. "I'm sure Bastian didn't mean it that way, Dani. After last night, everybody's just . . . I mean, we're feeling . . . we're . . ."

Scared. I'm scared.

The Sardines turned to Lola, looking shocked. There was a strange, new sensation in Lola's mind. Her thoughts had reached out, first to Bastian, the same as they had for years. But this time, she felt the words duplicate and split, shooting out in two other prongs, toward Avery and Dani. There were new weights in her mind, like tethers held taut by three different hooks. The others must have felt it, too.

Lols, how are you doing that? Bastian asked.

Lola knew, even as her twin sent the words to her, that they were also reaching Dani and Avery. The energy pulsed from her, electrical threads that joined each mind to the others. Fear bloomed in Lola's chest. She shook her head and said, "I ... don't know. I just *am*."

Heaving a sigh, Lola sat down right there, in the middle of the track. The others followed suit, forming a circle.

Okay. Dani's thought shot along the connected threads, reaching each of their minds. *So our brains can all connect to each other at once.*

Lola *can connect us*, Avery corrected.

That's new. Bastian sounded excited, though Lola couldn't understand why. She shrugged uneasily.

I wanted Dani and Bastian to stop fighting, she told them. *I wanted us all to understand each other, so ... I joined us together.*

Good, thought Bastian. *Because we need to talk about what happened.*

It did *happen,* Avery asked, *didn't it? Last night wasn't a dream?*

As each of them nodded, Lola realized how strange they would look to an outsider: four kids gathered in a circle, none of them speaking a word, all of them nodding in unison. They'd look more than strange. They'd look ... frightening.

Like freaks. The words spilled from Lola's private thoughts for everyone to hear.

Don't think like that, Lols, said Avery. *We're still us. We're Sardines. That hasn't changed.*

Lola worried her lip with her teeth. *But the aliens said they're going to take us away. And we don't even know* why.

"THERE'S MORE!" Dani burst out, aloud.

"Whoa," Bastian said. "What're you talking about?"

"This morning," Dani said, not meeting anyone's eyes. "I was eating breakfast, and—I can't explain it exactly, but I know it was them. It was the same voice I heard last night. They showed me things. Things from my past. It's like they *know* my memories. And they told me . . . They said . . ."

"Hey," said Bastian, wide-eyed. "You gonna hurl?"

Dani did look close to puking, right there and then. She was paler than Lola had ever seen her, brow coated in sweat.

Dani shook her head, though, and carried on. "They said—I'm trying to remember it—something about there being pain, here on Earth. And then they said . . . they're going to rescue us, but they're going to . . . um, *eradicate* everyone else."

"WHAT?" the others shouted, in unison.

"Eradicate?" Avery repeated. "Like, blow up? *Destroy?"*

"Are you sure you heard right?" asked Bastian. Now he looked like the queasy one. "How did you hear them? Did the blue column come back?"

Dani shook her head. "No, they were in my head." She swallowed, then added, *Like we're in each other's heads. Like this. I know what I heard. Maybe I can't remember word for word, but that much was clear: They said* eradicate.

"No," whispered Lola, dropping her head in her hands. "No, that can't be right. It can't."

"Let's get one thing straight," Bastian said. "Why are they

trying to rescue *us*? You all remember what they said last night, right? About planting an 'elixir' here. About how people have turned against us because of our differences."

"Our differences," Avery repeated. "Like our tele-whatevers?"

"I mean, it fits," said Bastian. "It sounds a whole lot like these aliens have something to do with our powers. Almost like they *gave* them to us, with whatever this elixir stuff is."

"And other people have turned against us," Dani said slowly. "'So much *pain*.' When they told me that, they showed me a memory. It was of Mitchell being a jerk, like always."

Avery shook her head. "No way. Aliens wouldn't come here and rescue us because of *Mitchell*."

"I think it was a symbol," Dani said. "They used the memory to make a point, that's all."

"A point about how they're going to blow up the world?" Avery's voice was strained. "They can't do that. I mean, they *can't*, right?"

"If they can make stuff float and give us tele-whatevers," Dani said, "I bet they can do a lot of things. They're obviously way more advanced than us. Maybe *eradication* is as easy for them as smushing a bug with your shoe."

"What else did they say?" Bastian asked.

"That was it," said Dani. "One minute they were in my head, and then they were gone. It was like last night, the way the message faded in and out. But . . . there's something else, too."

The others waited expectantly for Dani to share, and at last, she did.

"I've been thinking," she said, "and it's only a thought—but do you think what's happening to us might have something to do with *the incident*?"

This wasn't at all what Lola had been expecting. She blinked at the thought, considering what she knew about *the incident*—what her parents had told her about the mysterious blue light that had supposedly burned on Cedar Lane years ago, before she was born.

"A *blue* light," she said aloud. "Like our blue flames."

"Exactly," Dani replied. "That fire was weird. Unexplainable, like our powers. And it happened on *our street*."

"Wait," said Avery. "What fire? What *incident*?"

"My parents always said it was more urban legend than anything else," said Bastian, looking thoughtful. "But... the legend *does* say there was a giant blue flame. It burned on Cedar Lane for an hour and then it disappeared. No one ever figured out why."

"I don't know if there's a connection," Dani admitted, "and it doesn't change anything for now. But... it's something to think about."

"Ugh," Avery said. She lay back in the dust, arms thrown over her face to shield it from the sun. "This is crazy. It's totally crazy. It can't be real life."

"See?" said Dani. "This is why I wanted us to practice. Because practicing is *doing* something. *Thinking* gets us all freaked out. So we figured out we can talk and move stuff with our minds. We're getting creepy messages from aliens. But there's nothing we can do about any of that. Don't you see? Right now, skating is the best thing. Skating is what we *know*, something we can *do*."

"But glowboarding isn't all there is!" Lola shouted.

Bastian raised his eyebrows. Dani and Avery stared at her, silent. Lola never shouted; that was new. But so was *eradication*.

"Did you forget?" said Lola. "I made a cafeteria *explode*. School got dismissed and firefighters showed up. Police, too. All because of me. I don't know about you, but I'm *scared*. I don't want something like that to happen again. I don't want to end up hurting somebody. Dani just found out that these aliens are dangerous. Well... what if *we* are, too?"

The circle was quiet, both inside their heads and out.

Then Bastian spoke. "Lola's right," he said. "We might be dangerous. We don't know how much we can do with our powers. And now, if these aliens really mean *eradication*, we have to find out more. We have to figure out how to stop it. We—"

"We have to stick together," Avery finished. She spoke the words quietly at first, then repeated them, louder. "Whatever happens, we stick together. We all moved to Strange Street. We're all *Sardines*. We ended up together for a reason—even if it was those aliens who did it, with their... *elixir*, or whatever. And sure, we're different, but we all have the blue light in common. So whatever happens next, we face it together."

"Okay," said Bastian, "but how?"

"I guess..." Avery took time to think, then spoke again, this time in their minds. *We carry on like normal. We all agreed, we don't want the adults to know. So we... what do they call it?*

Keep a low profile. If we don't, the grown-ups will take us to doctors or split us up. So we act like nothing has changed. We practice for Glow in the Park, like Dani said. But we can't deny there's creepy stuff happening, too. It's scary, like Lola said. So while we're acting normal we investigate.

I've already looked up tele-whatevers on the internet, said Dani. *It's all weird books and kooky blogs. Nothing that's gonna help us.*

No, said Avery. *I've read plenty of books about it, too. They're no good. I don't mean that kind of investigating. This kind we do for ourselves. We know we can say and move things with our minds, but do we know how* much?

The others shared uncertain glances.

I mean, Avery continued, *Lola just linked us together. We didn't know that was possible until now.*

Lola studied her crisscrossed legs, unsure if she liked all the new attention she'd brought on herself.

So, said Bastian, who sounded excited again, *you're saying we should figure this out by trial and error. Experimenting. Like in science class.*

Yes, Avery said. *The aliens—if they can speak in our heads, if they say they* gave *us our powers, then we need to understand what we can do. We need to figure out how to talk to them, to show them they're wrong, that they don't need to rescue or eradicate anyone.*

Bastian turned to Dani. *You said they spoke to you through . . . breakfast?*

My smoothie, Dani said. *They made stuff appear in it. Stuff from my past.*

114

So maybe food's the key, Bastian mused. *One thing's for sure: They're not getting their whole message through. If they contact us again, we have to pay close attention.*

The Sardines grew quiet. The sun beat down on their helmets, casting short shadows on the nearby boulders. Lola felt a sudden rustling sensation against her neck. She looked down to see the paper daisies from her homemade flower necklace slipping from their binding, one at a time, then wisping into the air in a soothing, sunlit dance.

Beside her, Avery sat very still, her hazel eyes crackling with energy as she focused on the dancing flowers. Then the daisies quivered for an instant and dropped from midair, piling one after the other in Lola's lap.

Lola gasped, then picked up a single daisy to study.

Avery released a long, rattling breath. She gave Lola a smile that Lola knew was meant only for her. Then she looked around at the others. "There," she said. "That's something new. Investigation number one."

"Maybe," said Dani, scrunching her nose in thought, "the more we practice, the more we can control it."

"And no one else can know about this," Bastian said. "Not our parents, *no one.*"

"Like a vow of secrecy?" asked Avery.

Dani nodded. "Yeah. A vow. Can we all agree on that?"

She looked around the circle, noting each member's nod, then nodding herself.

"Right," she said. "For now, we act like everything's normal. We focus on Glow in the Park. And behind the scenes, we investigate. See what our powers can do, and if we can make contact with the aliens again."

"And hopefully," said Avery, "we do all that before the earth gets destroyed."

"That's the spirit, Vee," Bastian muttered.

Once again, Lola wasn't paying strict attention to the conversation. This time, she'd seen a flash of movement to her right. She started toward it, but on closer observation, the only thing there was a small desert shrub.

"Lols?" asked Avery, looking at her with concern.

"I thought I saw . . ." Lola stopped short and shook her head. "It was nothing, though."

The other Sardines looked around, their brows bent and eyes alert, but further inspection showed that there really was nothing and no one around. Lola guessed she was only jumpy from all the secretive talk.

"Okay," said Avery as they got to their feet. "We've got a plan. But can I just say? It's really weird to think Radar's a telepath."

It was a big day for the man in the navy suit.

After years of waiting, months of monitoring, and days of investigation, they'd had their first breakthrough. They were one step closer to capturing *them*.

But now the situation was more complicated.

"You're sure this inside source of yours is reliable?" asked the woman with the high ponytail—his almost constant companion in the search.

"Believe me," said the man. "More than reliable. He's . . . very close to the situation."

"I didn't expect them to be so young." The woman tapped a glossy paper that lay on the desk before her. There were blown-up photographs, five in total, each neatly labeled with a name. She'd touched the one of a short-haired girl, labeled *Danielle Hirsch*. "They're *children*."

The man in the navy suit shook his head. "I can't believe it, either. It's not what we were expecting. It's . . ." The man trailed off, looking to a photograph labeled *Dolores Gil*. "It's almost incomprehensible. But you witnessed what they did at that school, and I have no doubt that incident was a mere fluke. Imagine what they'll be capable of when they use their powers intentionally. We must intervene before then. This secret can't get out to the public. In that, the interests of Gloworks and the DGE are aligned."

The woman continued to study the photographs with a furrowed brow. "What would you suggest as our next steps?"

"We monitor them," said the man. "For now, we gather information, and we keep quiet. We have to be absolutely sure, when we make our move, that it's the right one. We don't want anyone to get hurt in the process."

"No," the woman said, turning her darkened eyes to the photograph labeled *Avery Miller.* "We certainly wouldn't want that."

THIRTEEN

THE EMAIL

Ms. Sills wasn't around when Avery got home that afternoon, but that was no surprise; her mom often worked late, sometimes past Avery's bedtime. Days like these, Avery used the securipad to get in the house, entering the code—Radar's birthday—with practiced finesse. Radar greeted her, yipping happily, and Avery knelt to kiss his face, rubbing down his sides.

"Did you see squirrels today?" she asked him. "Did you show them who's boss?"

Radar wagged his tail.

Avery nodded her approval and let Radar out back. Then she turned on the oven and dug out a box of pizza bagels from the freezer. Her mother insisted that Avery eat fruits or vegetables with her meals, and every so often she *did* check the fruit basket. So begrudgingly, Avery took an apple up to her room while the mini pizzas cooked.

Since the move, Avery's bedroom had been painted a cheery green, though most of the paint was now obscured by stacks and stacks of books. That was all Avery had requested for Christmases and birthdays since she was eight years old: books and books, and more books. When she wasn't receiving books as gifts, she was visiting local yard sales, picking up paperbacks for quarters. Her collection had grown and was now composed of dozens of titles she'd yet to explore. In the end, when she and her mother had moved out to Callaway, books filled up two-thirds of Avery's moving boxes.

There were some novels she'd read over a dozen times—*A Wrinkle in Time*, by Madeleine L'Engle, and *Tuck Everlasting*, by Natalie Babbitt. Avery liked Meg Murry and Winnie Foster well enough, but her favorite characters were the Mrs. Ws and Mae Tuck. She liked to imagine what it'd be like to be a kindly supernatural entity, or to live forever and never age.

Lately, though, Avery hadn't been in the mood for immortal families. She had other topics on her mind, like *telepathy* and *telekinesis*.

When Avery's powers had first shown up, back in LA, she'd checked out lots of library books on telekinesis, but none of the descriptions sounded like *her*. And none of the books in Avery's current collection could give her answers to the questions she most wanted answered. Instead, Avery tugged out a yellow spiral notebook from under her bed. It was a journal, filled with half-finished entries that spanned over three years. Avery had never been able to turn herself into a committed journal writer. But when it came to this—the tele-whatevers— she figured she could make an exception. The Sardines had agreed to investigate after all.

Avery flipped open the book and wrote down a heading in pen:

A RECORD OF MY POWERS

She scowled at the page. No, not *powers*. That sounded terrible. She crossed out the word and thought some more.

A RECORD OF MY GIFTS

No. *Gifts* looked even worse. She crossed that out, too.

A RECORD OF MY TELE-WHATEVERS

Yes. That would do.

Beneath the messy title, Avery wrote down the following:

First Time: School Bathroom—Telekinesis

Second Time: Backyard—Telekinesis

Avery kept on this way until she reached

Twenty-Ninth Time: Sardines Night—Telekinesis

She remembered the horror she'd felt as she'd watched Dani fall from the oak tree. That night, the blue flame's power had poured out of Avery like waves. She hadn't done something as big as that since the first entry, marked *School Bathroom*.

Avery didn't want to remember that particular time. It was bad enough writing it down. Unbidden, the image of rushing water and yellow bathroom tile sprang into her mind. Avery felt as frightened as ever by the memory, but another emotion was building inside her: relief. At least she wasn't alone. What had happened in LA, what she'd done on Sardines Night—*she wasn't alone.*

With a sigh, Avery shut the journal and shoved it under her pillow. Then she looked at the apple she'd set aside, on her duvet. She looked harder, squinting.

Maybe food's the key.

Wasn't that what Bastian had said? Dani's breakfast smoothie had spoken to her. Maybe Avery's apple could, too.

"Hello?" she asked, tapping the apple's short, bent stem. "Aliens? Um, *light beings?*"

There was no reply. Avery sat up, grabbing the apple and holding it in both hands. She closed her eyes, and this time tried something new.

Speak to me, she thought, pushing the words upward. *I'm listening. Who are you? When are you coming to Earth? Could you not blow up our planet?*

She waited seconds, then more seconds.

Nothing happened. There was no voice in her mind, no visions like Dani had described. She just felt stupid.

Avery sighed and opened her eyes.

"Well," she said, "it was worth a try."

Then she took a chomp from the apple and headed downstairs to let Radar in.

The bright-eyed dog bounded inside and followed Avery to the kitchen computer. There, still gnawing away at her apple, Avery took a seat. She looked to Radar, who placed his chin on her knee, staring up with his brown and blue eyes. He always seemed to know when Avery needed some cuteness. She grinned and scratched him behind the ears.

Then she opened her email. There was one unread message in her in-box.

One unread message from *Eric Miller*.

Her dad.

The subject line read: *Callaway Visit*.

Avery swallowed, and swallowed again. Why did her throat dry up every single time she thought of her dad?

Maybe it was because she hadn't seen him for a whole year, since she'd moved from LA to Callaway. He'd said he was going to visit her last fall, and then again in December, for the holidays. But both of those times, he'd backed out of the trips. Both of those times, his work had won out. In September, he'd been invited to some big Hollywood party. And then, four months later, he'd been given the "chance of a lifetime" to film dolphins in New Zealand. *Dolphins. That* was a chance of a lifetime, but not Avery.

This time it's different, Avery thought as she opened the email. She was going to take him to Pizza Palace, the best restaurant in town. She was going to show him Taft Middle, where she went to school. They were going to take a drive downtown, and maybe even a day trip out to Austin. And best of all? The week was planned around Glow in the Park. Her dad was going to see her skate, see her compete, see her *win* first place.

Then he was going to figure it out. He was going to understand how wrong he'd been, back in that principal's office in

LA. He was going to realize how stupid he'd been to think all his projects were more exciting than his own daughter. He was going to *get* it.

But she was wrong. The email read:

Hey, Veemeister!

Hope all's well in sunny Texas. As much as I'd been looking forward to seeing you this month, I can't make it out this summer like I'd originally planned. Some work issues have arisen, and travel isn't an option at the moment. I'll plan another visit soon.

Love,

Dad

Avery swallowed. Her throat remained dry.

He was canceling. Only a few weeks out from the trip, and he was canceling *again*. Avery felt like crying. She felt like picking up the computer and smashing it on the ground. Radar whimpered, studying Avery with concern.

"Figures," she muttered, staring at the screen through brimming tears.

Work issues. Of course. It was always work. Avery could never be *that* notable; she wasn't documentary material, like watersheds in Iceland or dolphins in New Zealand.

Why had she thought this summer would be different?

Avery remembered with perfect clarity how her father hadn't defended her when the strange thing had happened, and when she'd needed him most. He'd sat in that principal's office and listened to the adults instead of her. He'd told Avery to grow up and stop inventing stories.

He had never been there for her. He had never believed her.

Avery looked back to the computer screen. Inside her, the blue light pulsed, strong and sure. And it was just then that the fire alarm started shrieking.

"The pizza bagels!" Avery moaned as the scent of smoke filled her nose.

FOURTEEN

FIGHT

"A crown? Mountain range. Shark teeth!"

Lola sat on the front porch by Nando's side, giggling as Nando tried to guess the shape Bastian was making with his glowstream. Bastian had run through this particular drawing five times now, with no success. There was sweat on his brow and frustration in his face.

Nando, Lola spoke into Bastian's head. *That's what it is. You're spelling his name, aren't you?*

Yeah, big help, Bastian thought back, kicking off the stream and returning to his starting point, in the middle of the Gils' driveway. *Don't give him any hints.*

"Lola," Nando whispered. "Give me a hint?"

Lola looked up at her older brother. Somehow he was larger than she remembered, taking up so much space and energy. When he'd left ten months ago, he had simply been Nando, her brother. Now he was a government worker with a job and secrets, a fake last name, and a small beard. The beard was definitely different.

In response to Nando's request, she clamped her mouth shut and shook her head.

"Come on," he pleaded. "I *know* you know. You two are always in sync."

Lola gave a giant shrug.

"You can't guess if you're not *watching*!" Bastian shouted at Nando.

"Okay, okay!" Nando said, waving. "I'll get it this time, for sure."

Bastian began again, carving over the concrete, a silver trail of glow shooting out in his wake. Lola could see it so clearly: the *N*, the *A* after it. How could Nando not?

An idea came to Lola. It was something she had never done before. An investigation.

Think ABCs. She formed the thought, her hint, and pushed it out to Nando.

Nando watched as Bastian formed the *D* and *O*. Suddenly, he pointed and cried, "Got it! A sailboat, right?"

Lola sighed. Nando couldn't hear her thoughts. Of course, she'd already suspected that. No one could hear her thoughts but the Sardines.

And the aliens.

But Lola didn't want to think about that right now.

Bastian hopped off his board, groaning. "*Nooo.* Not even close, man!"

"I'm out of practice." Nando laughed. "Give me a break, huh?"

The front door opened, and Mrs. Gil appeared.

"Okay, you goofballs." She swatted Nando's shoulder. "Everyone in, it's time to eat."

Bastian groaned again, but came running to the house, his board in hand.

"Tell me," Nando called after him.

Bastian shook his head—smug, but also a little annoyed, Lola thought.

"Nope," he said. "You still gotta figure it out."

For the first night in months, the fifth chair at the dinner table was filled. Nando's work hadn't let him come home for Thanksgiving or even Christmas, and Lola had started to fear that he might never get a break. But now here he was, and Lola was all smiles as she passed around a plate of asparagus, a platter of fish, and a pitcher full of pink lemonade.

"How was work, dear?" asked Mrs. Gil.

Nando looked up sharply at the question, and Lola was reminded of the almost angry way he'd answered a question like that on the night he'd arrived. Today, he had been gone all morning and most of the afternoon, and he hadn't said a thing about what he was doing in Callaway.

Lola held her breath, but Mrs. Gil spoke again.

"*Diego*," she said, turning to her husband. "How was work?"

"Hm?" Mr. Gil swallowed a bite of salmon and said, "Oh,

you know the museum. Office politics, kids tapping the glass. The usual."

"Mhm." Mrs. Gil nodded halfheartedly, still eyeing her eldest son. "Nando, dear, how is Ira? She must be missing you back in DC."

Nando gave his mother a look. "Really smooth," he said. "She's fine. Actually, she's in town."

Mrs. Gil's eyes got big. "What? And you didn't bother to tell us. She must come over for dinner. We want to meet her in person!"

Nando picked at his food. "She's not *just* my girlfriend, Mom. She's a colleague, and we're here on business. If there's time..."

"There has to be time!" Mrs. Gil insisted.

"Nando," Bastian cut in. "Will you still be here in two weeks?"

Nando, clearly relieved by Bastian's intervention, said, "I really don't know, Bash. This project of ours, it's a day-to-day thing."

"Well, if you are, we've got this race. It's called Glow in the Park."

"It's really something, Nando," said Mr. Gil. "Your mother and I attended last year. Oh...what's the tagline? It was catchy. Mar, what was it?"

"'The fastest night of the year,'" recited Mrs. Gil, who still looked peeved about the dropped topic of Nando's girlfriend.

"You know," piped Bastian, "because it's the shortest night of the year? But also a race."

"Now *that* I guessed," said Nando, winking.

"I hope there aren't any sirens this year," Bastian said. "Last time, they went off in the middle of single speeds, and everyone had to run home. The teams that won didn't even get their trophies until a week later. No awards ceremony or anything. And of course there wasn't *really* a bomb. Just another false alarm."

"That's the price of war," Nando said. "A small price, considering."

Lola frowned at her brother's tone. It seemed stiffer somehow, and brittle on its edges. Then her father spoke in a voice Lola *knew* wasn't good.

"No child should pay the price of war," Mr. Gil said. "No child should be afraid."

Nando cut aggressively into his salmon. "But they are, whether a war's going on or not. Kids will always be afraid, Dad. If it weren't a bomb, it'd be the bogeyman."

"So they've thoroughly converted you, then." Mr. Gil threw his napkin on the table, though he clearly wasn't through with his meal.

"Not over dinner," Mrs. Gil said, looking warningly between her husband and son.

Lola set down her knife and fork. Memories swept into her head of the weeks before Nando's departure, the nights she'd woken up to shouting from downstairs, the sullen dinner table glares, and the way her parents had cried so long and hard at the airport. How could she have forgotten all of that?

"Disagreement isn't disrespect," Nando said, his words

more brittle than ever. "We can have different thoughts on the war effort. I don't mind. You shouldn't, either."

"And I suppose they taught you all that at the academy," said Mr. Gil. "How to condescend to your parents. I suppose that's why you're ashamed to even use our name."

"I told you," Nando said, "the name change was for security purposes. It's standard."

"Standard," Mr. Gil scoffed. "Be honest, Fernando: You're embarrassed of where you come from."

"I'm not having this conversation."

"Because you're afraid of the facts."

"Because you're *cowards*!" Nando pushed away from the table, rising to his feet.

No, no, thought Lola, desperate. *It isn't supposed to go this way.*

"You live in your pretty suburban world," Nando continued in a raised voice, "where you have the luxury of preaching non-intervention. Where those sirens are only a precaution, not a threat of real danger. You don't live in the battlegrounds, the coastal cities. You're not affected. But I've seen it firsthand. I know what we're dealing with."

"You know nothing." Mr. Gil had not raised but lowered his voice. It came out like thunder. "And you presume to lecture your mother and father under their roof?"

Lola wished she could sink from her chair right into the floorboards. She didn't want to be here, to hear any of this.

"Right," Nando said. "I really thought we could move past this. But if that's how things are going to be ... My work provides free accommodation. I'll take advantage of that. It's what I should have done to begin with."

Nando walked off from the table, shoulders held high. Lola sat still, listening, as he ran up the stairs and into his room. She could picture him there, throwing open his green briefcase, packing away his things, *himself.*

For a moment, everything had been so perfect.

"You're just going to let him *leave?*" Bastian burst out at the quiet table.

Mrs. Gil shook her head, tears sliding down her cheeks. "Your brother is an adult, Sebastian. He's free to do what he wants."

"I knew you'd do this!" Bastian shouted, pushing out his chair.

Then he, too, ran from the room.

Lola looked at her plate, feeling suddenly tired.

"Can I be excused?" she asked. "I can't eat anymore."

Her parents exchanged a sad, helpless kind of glance.

"Okay," her mother sighed.

Lola got up, taking her plate to the sink, where she scraped the few remaining peas into the garbage disposal. At her back, she heard a slight, stirring sound—like a page being turned. She frowned, setting the dish down and looking toward the noise.

Lola gasped.

The windows were shut. There was no breeze in the kitchen, not even from an air-conditioning vent. And yet, clear as day, the folded creatures atop the refrigerator—Lola's folded creatures—were *moving.*

Lola stood still, skin prickling, mind alert, as she watched her paper flowers and birds rearrange themselves, unfolding and refolding, forming new creases and, eventually, new *shapes*. She opened her mouth, transfixed, as she began to recognize these forms. She knew, somehow, that a purple tulip—now turned to the figure of a girl—represented *her*, and a deep green canary had taken the triangular shape of a mountain—though not a mountain, exactly. Smaller. A *hill*.

Lola watched as the purple paper girl climbed to the hill's top and slid down, on a thin, rose-colored rectangle. A *glowboard*.

A fizzy sort of sound filled Lola's head. There was static, heavy at first, then fading as a voice became distinct. It spoke clear and melodically, like a wind chime.

We've seen where you gather. We will meet you there. At the appointed time, when . . . and . . . rescue . . .

The static returned, gobbling up the remaining words. Lola couldn't make them out, no matter how hard she pressed her hands to her ears.

"What appointed time?" she cried. *"When?"*

"Lola?"

Lola started, looking away from the refrigerator.

Mrs. Gil stood on the kitchen's threshold, a stack of dirty dishes in her hands. "Mija," she said. "What's the matter?"

Lola looked again to the top of the refrigerator, where the folded papers had been playing out their story. Nothing was amiss. The papers had resumed their former shapes—only pretty flowers and birds, arranged in a line, perfectly motionless.

"I—I—" Lola shook her head. "Um, nothing."

The concern hadn't left Mrs. Gil's face. "All right," she said slowly. "Just leave your dish there, dear. I'll take care of things tonight."

Lola nodded. "O-okay."

Then, without another word, she skirted around her mother and dashed from the kitchen. All the while, a growing conviction burned within her blue-flamed chest:

Hazard Hill.

The aliens planned to meet them on Hazard Hill.

When Lola reached the top of the stairs, she heard her brothers' voices. Tiptoeing, she made her way to end of the hall and pushed open Nando's cracked bedroom door. Nando and Bastian were sitting cross-legged on the floor. On the bed lay Nando's open briefcase, as though he had stopped mid-pack. Lola took a step back, wondering if she was intruding on something private. But when Nando saw her, he motioned for her to join them. Relieved, she stepped inside the room.

"Don't leave," she pleaded, taking a seat. "Things will be better in the morning. You can talk to Mom and Dad and work everything out."

"Lola," said Nando, shaking his head, "this isn't a work-outable thing."

"Sure it is," she insisted. "Everything can be worked out. If—"

"No, Lola. Not this. They don't approve of my work. They don't approve of *me*. I can see it all over their faces."

"But we approve!" Lola said, casting Bastian a frantic glance. "Stay for *us*."

Nando took Lola's hand and squeezed it at the knuckles. "Just because I won't be here doesn't mean I won't be around. We can meet up while I'm in town. The Frozen Spoon is still open, isn't it?"

Lola nodded and mumbled, "That's not the same."

"Did you really mean what you said?" Bastian asked Nando. "That stuff about the war. You think we should be fighting?"

Nando ran a hand through his messy black hair. "I think," he said, "we have to fight. It's awful, but it's an awful necessity. If we could find a way around it, any other solution . . . I would take that in a second. I would."

There was a faraway look on Nando's face. If only, thought Lola, he could share the connection that she and Bastian had. Lola looked away, trying to ward off tears. That was when she spotted the folder resting on Nando's bed. It was open, a single sheet of paper visible. She squinted, making out the letters *DGE*, written in a large, bold font.

"Nando," she whispered. "What are you doing here?"

Nando caught her gaze. In an instant, he was on his feet, grabbing the folder and slamming it shut. "It's— That's—" There was a wild look in his eyes.

"It's confidential, Lols," Bastian muttered. "How many times does he have to tell you?"

"But," said Lola, "we're your *family*. I get not telling Mom and Dad, but who would Bastian and I tell about your work? We don't know any enemy spies."

Nando dropped the folder into the open briefcase on the bed. "It's protocol," he said, gruffly. "These secrets aren't like other secrets. They're the government's."

He turned to face them, and Lola could see that wild glimmer still in his eyes. "You wouldn't want to make a traitor of me, would you?"

On instinct, Lola thought of Zander Poxleitner, and of Mitchell and his Grackles. She grimaced. "No, of course not."

At that moment, the briefcase, which must have been sitting too close to the bed's edge, toppled over, sending papers and clothes tumbling out. Nando shouted, and Bastian hurried to his side, beginning to gather the scattered items.

"No, no!" cried Nando, waving him off. "Don't look. It's got to be— Both of you, stay away!"

"I'm just trying to—" Bastian began, but Nando cut him off with a bellowing *"NO."*

Bastian shrank away, and Lola got to her feet, joining Bastian where he stood. Together, they watched their brother collect the fallen papers.

DGE, Lola thought. What did those three letters mean?

Nando threw papers into folders, tossing them into the briefcase, along with socks and shirts. When he'd recovered everything, he clasped the case up tight.

"I'm . . . sorry," he said, turning to face them. "I'm sorry, Bash, Lols. This is why I shouldn't be here. I shouldn't have come in the first place. That was a mistake."

Lola knew Nando didn't mean to hurt her, but his words stung all the same. She was still smarting from the pain as she hugged him goodbye, and as she and Bastian watched him descend the stairs, then slip quietly out the front door and into the night, without a word to their parents.

Only after the door had slammed shut did Bastian unclench a fist, revealing to Lola the crumpled paper hidden there.

FIFTEEN

THE MEMO

Dani was awake when the *plink*s began.

Plink against her window. Then, moments later, another *plink*. Finally Dani threw off her duvet and crawled out of bed.

Lola stood beneath her window, a pile of mulch flakes in hand. Dani opened the window just as Lola tossed up a piece, which pelted Dani soundly on the cheek.

"Oops!" Lola whispered, dropping the flakes and covering her mouth. Her daisy crown seemed to droop in embarrassment.

Really, Lola. Dani formed the thought and pushed it down. *We share thoughts now, remember?*

I know, Lola replied. *But I wasn't sure if my thoughts could wake you up.*

Dani began to protest, but stopped herself when she saw the urgent expression on Lola's moon-drenched face. "Coming,"

Dani whispered instead, climbing out the window and carefully making her way down the back-porch trellis.

She followed Lola through the sliding fence board, crossing through Avery's backyard and into the Gils'.

Bastian and Avery were already in Cedar House, Radar curled up between their beanbags, his eyelids drooping. As Dani and Lola stepped inside, he raised his head and let out a welcoming *woof.*

"Hey, boy," Dani said, absently rubbing his head. She took a seat. "What's this about?"

The twins shared a look. Then Bastian cleared his throat and held out a single sheet of paper. It was wrinkled and bent, as though it had been through a good wadding-up and smoothing-out. Dani took the paper and held it between herself and Avery so they could both read its contents in the beam of the clubhouse flashlight.

DGE Departmental Memo

Concerning the contract with Gloworks, Inc.,
for use of facilities and delivery of new resource.

Negotiations proceeding as planned.
Deadline for contractual agreement June 20.

Dani frowned over the words. She read them again, even after Avery had crossed her arms and said, "Uh-*huh.*" Something about this memo made Dani feel uncomfortable. Alarmed.

"What's DGE?" she finally asked, handing the paper back to Bastian.

"No clue," he said. "But whatever it is, I think they're the people Nando is working for. And it looks like they're making some kind of deal with Gloworks."

"With *Mr. Jensen*," said Avery, looking ill. "Gross."

"It does explain why they're in Callaway, though," Bastian said.

"But why?" asked Dani. "Why would the government want to make a deal with a *glowboard factory*?"

Bastian shrugged. "Probably not so the head of the FBI gets a new pair of sliders."

"Maybe," Avery said slowly, "they've come up with a new use for glow."

"How?" said Dani. "Glow is *glow*. They did all those experiments when it was discovered, for weapons and big machines, and those didn't work, no matter how much of it they used."

"But maybe it's different now," said Avery. "You read that about a 'new resource.' Maybe the government's got some top secret ingredient that will change everything. They've got something Gloworks needs, and Gloworks has something *they* need."

"Yeah, but what?" Bastian recrumpled the paper, tossing it to the ground. "What's Nando doing here? Why is he here *now*?"

"The silver suits," Dani whispered.

"What?" asked Bastian.

She looked up. "I didn't tell you all. So much weird stuff

has happened, I forgot. But yesterday, after the cafeteria . . . you know . . . I skated out to the school to see what was going on. When I got there, there were these people in silver suits with glow detectors. And these other guys—I think they were with the government. It wasn't just firefighters and police. They were *other* people. And they were looking for something."

Lola picked up the memo, smoothed it out, and began to fold it into neat creases. After a few moments, she held up a newly formed creation—a graceful swan—and looked at the others with widened eyes. "Aren't you all thinking it? What if this has to do with . . . *us*? Those silver suits didn't show up until *I*—"

"This isn't your fault, Lols," Avery said, gently placing a hand on Lola's knee.

"But," said Lola, "it could still be about us. And the aliens." Then a new, frightened look crossed her face. "They . . . spoke to me. Tonight."

"*What?*" On instinct, Dani scooted closer. "How? What did they say?"

Lola looked uncertainly at Dani, then the others. "It wasn't food this time. It was my artwork, in the kitchen. But it was like you said, Dani: The paper turned to memories—*my* memories. They were showing me glowboarding on Hazard Hill. And they said that's where they're going to meet us. They started to say when, but the message broke up. It got all fuzzy, and I couldn't get them to come back."

"Oh man," said Avery, putting a hand to her head. "Oh *man*."

"The *when* is kind of important," Bastian said. "It'd be nice to know what day they plan to wipe out humanity."

"Don't say that." Lola shook her head fiercely. "That's not going to happen."

"It will," Dani said, "if we don't figure out the rest of the message. Lols, were you trying to talk to them?"

"No." Lola sniffed. "No, it just *happened*."

Dani nodded, thoughtful. "It was the same with me. But it doesn't mean reaching out won't work. We should still try."

"I did," Avery said. "Turns out talking to an apple doesn't work."

"Lola," Bastian said. "The aliens showed you memories. And they showed you memories, too, right, Dani? Of Mitchell being a jerk."

"Yeah," Dani said, not sure where Bastian was going with this.

"Well," he said, "maybe that's important. They're sending us messages telepathically, but for some weird reason, their words keep breaking up. Maybe it's an alien translation thing. Or maybe their spaceship, or whatever, is too far away from Earth. But it sure seems like they put a lot of stock in memories. And if they communicate using our memories, maybe we can communicate back the same way. Not through words, but pictures. If we can *show* them all the good things about Earth—our families and glowboarding and stuff we like—maybe they'll see it doesn't deserve to be eradicated after all."

"But how do we do that?" Dani asked. "We can share thoughts, but I've never shared a *memory* with any of you."

"Try now," Bastian said. "Send me something."

Dani, still uncertain, scrunched up her face. Bastian readied himself, placing his palms flat on the clubhouse floor, trying—Dani guessed—to open his mind.

Then Dani shut her eyes and conjured one of her favorite memories. It was a warm April day, and she was inside the Gloworks store on Main Street, trying out a glowboard for the very first time. Sure, Zander was in the memory—*that* wasn't pleasant—and sure, the board was way too expensive. But this was the day everything had changed. This was the day the thrill, the possibility of skating had first entered Dani's heart.

She remembered the dappled sunlight in the store, the glossy green of the board, the way her foot first wobbled, then steadied. She remembered Zander's stupid smile and the scent of fresh, new plastic in the air. Then she took all those memories, bundled them together, and tried to send them to Bastian.

Moments passed. Then Dani opened one eye. *Well?* she asked Bastian. *Did you get it?*

Bastian's face fell. "Nope," he said, for everyone to hear. "I heard your thoughts just now, but...I didn't see anything."

Dani shrugged.

Bastian, however, wasn't giving up that quick. "Maybe," he said, "it takes practice. Maybe we should work on taking memories from our heads and pushing them out."

Dani scoffed. "You make it sound easy."

"Well, why not?" Bastian was growing more enthusiastic. "Maybe it's like glowboarding: We practice, and we get better.

We put together a whole collection of our best memories. Then, once the aliens get here—whenever that is—we can show them all the reasons why Earth isn't a bad place."

Lola was nodding. "I agree with Bastian. We should practice. We should try."

Bastian turned to Dani. "If they've reached out to you and Lola, there's a good chance they'll reach out again, maybe to me and Avery. And if they do, we've got to be ready for it."

Bastian pointed to the paper swan in Lola's hands.

"Now, what about this?" he said. "And the silver suits you saw. They could have something to do with us, too."

"Or not," said Dani. "We don't know that for sure. Maybe Nando and all this DGE stuff has nothing to do with us. A weird coincidence, that's all."

"I don't know," said Avery. "The timing is kind of suspicious, isn't it? I mean, Nando got here right when the weird stuff started happening."

"What're you saying?" Lola asked. "You think Nando is doing something bad?"

"*No,*" Avery said quickly, looking almost apologetic. "I mean, I bet he doesn't think it's bad. But he *does* have a top secret government job. And why is he in Callaway when there are plenty more important things to do in DC? It's just... weird."

Radar barked—in agreement, it seemed, with Avery's assessment.

Lola, however, was shaking her head. "I know Nando. He's a good person. The *best*. He wouldn't do anything bad, and he definitely wouldn't do anything that would put us in danger. Like Dani said, it's a coincidence."

With that, she set the swan in the center of their circle. All eyes turned to the paper animal. Dani was thinking hard. She knew as well as the rest of the Sardines that something was happening here. Something scary, maybe wrong. All they had right now, though, was a bunch of maybes.

"Man," she mumbled. "I miss when we just came here to play sardines."

SIXTEEN

FREE SKATE

Hazard Hill was, hands down, the best place to downhill glowboard in the city—maybe even in the whole wide state of Texas. According to Lola's mother, when Callaway's new Component G industry had boomed fifty years ago, people had moved from all over, and apartments and houses couldn't get built fast enough. Hazard Hill had been planned as an exclusive, upscale community, complete with fancy gates and a giant swimming pool. The developers had even planned to change the name to *Heartland* Hill, to make the place more appealing. Then things went bad. The investors bailed, and the project was never finished. All that remained of Hazard Hill was the paved road that wound from its base to the very top: the perfect downhill track.

The hill was a good distance from Cedar Lane, a half-hour skate through neighborhood streets, and then out of the city, on through craggy desert terrain. Today, Lola pushed and carved along the desert road, allowing the rhythm of the board to guide her through the air alongside Bastian and Avery. Dani was already out at the hill, as she always was before practices. Lola had once asked Dani what she did out there, and Dani had replied, simply, "I *envision*."

When Lola and the others reached the hill's base, there was no sign of Dani, so they skated on, adjusting to the incline of the track. They sped up and up, as the city grew smaller, sprawling out beneath them. There were no guardrails on the track, just brush and boulders to hide the steep drop-off. The highest a glowboard could hover was one foot, tops. If you skated off those cliffs, you'd fall right to your death.

So Lola skated with feeling, but with caution, too, hugging the corners of the track, bending her knees and grazing her sliders when needed. At last, they reached the hill's flat crest, and there was Dani, carving slow circles on her board. Dani had stopped wearing her old orange-rimmed glasses after her bat mitzvah last September; Lola thought the contacts made Dani look older. Or maybe, really, Dani was getting older. Maybe they all were.

"Good!" Dani shouted when she spotted them. "You're here. We can start."

"Hello to you, too," said Avery.

"We can be polite again once we're back to two fifteen," Dani said. "Let's get to the game plan, huh? I got a new practice angle. I call it . . . *tethering*."

Lola's heart took a dive, landing in her stomach. "You

mean," she said unsteadily, "what we did yesterday? Sharing our thoughts?"

"What *you* did yesterday," Dani corrected.

Lola cleared her throat. "Just because I did it first doesn't mean I'm the only one who can. I'm sure we can all...um, *tether.*"

But Dani was shaking her head. "Nope. I've been trying to connect our thoughts since you guys showed up. Feel anything?"

"N-no." Lola faltered, then turned to Bastian. "You try. Imagine little lines connecting us all. Focus your blue flame. It's easy."

Bastian frowned but closed his eyes, concentrating. After a long moment, Lola heard his voice in her mind, asking, *Like this?*

She turned eagerly to the others. "Did you hear him, too?"

Dani and Avery looked blankly back.

"Well, try again!" Lola said, more desperate. "I'm sure we can all do it."

"We can't, Lola," Avery said softly. "I've been trying, too. You're the one who has the power. *Just* you."

Tears were forming in Lola's eyes. "But I—" *I don't want the power,* she thought, only to herself.

"Lola." Avery touched her elbow. "I know you're scared. It's a super-scary thing. But, for whatever reason, you can do something awesome. Something none of us can."

"Look," said Dani, beginning to sound impatient. "If I

could connect us, I would. It'd make sense, me being captain and all. But you've got the power, Lols. And you can really help us out."

Lola asked, "Help us out how?"

"Can you connect us right now?" said Dani.

Part of Lola didn't want to, but another part...that part was curious. Yes, she was scared, but she was with her friends. They had tele-whatevers of their own. They wouldn't let her powers get out of control, not if they could help it.

So Lola focused on the blue light inside. She pushed the light out, quickly finding a link in Avery's mind. Then Bastian's—a worn and familiar thread. Last of all, she reached out to Dani. And just like that, the Sardines were connected.

Tethering, Dani began, without missing a beat, *is what's going to win us this race. Think about it: What team wouldn't kill for the chance to link minds? We'll all be in each other's heads. Never out of sync. If we focus, we can be in perfect harmonization.*

Is that a real word?

Dani responded to Avery's interruption with a pointed look. *Yeah. It is.*

Because it sounds like a disease, said Avery, who seemed unbothered by looks, pointed or otherwise.

"This is what I'm talking about!" Dani threw her hands in the air. "We have to *focus.* Eyes on the prize. Stop with the stupid jokes!"

"Um, Dani?" Lola said, in what was barely more than a whisper.

"Yeah?" said Dani irritably.

"Are you saying you want me to tether us when we're racing?"

"Yeah."

"I just..." Lola's cheeks grew hot. "I don't know if I can do that. I've never tried."

"Well, that's what practice is for," Dani said. "We'll work on it. Anyway, Lola, it's not like you do a ton when we draft train. You're not leading or whipping or crossing. You're just *skating*. Now you've got something extra to do, like the rest of us."

Lola bit her lip, feeling a flash of anger. Dani didn't understand. Lola *liked* the fact that all she did was skate. She didn't want more responsibility. She'd never asked for it.

"Hey," said Avery. "Dani, give her a break, okay? This is new to Lols. It's new to all of us. We need some time to let it sink in."

"But we don't have time," Dani retorted. "Glow in the Park is in—"

"We *know* when it is," Bastian cut in. "In less than three weeks. You won't let us forget."

Dani's face turned purplish red. "What's that supposed to mean?"

"It means," Bastian replied, "that sometimes you make glowboarding...not so fun."

The color in Dani's face intensified, then drained away entirely.

"Hey, I get it, Dani," said Avery, glancing between her and

Bastian. "We all think it's worth training so hard for draft train. Right, Bastian?"

Bastian stared at the ground, making a noncommittal grunt.

"But," Avery continued, glancing at Lola, "you know, we stopped going to all the events around here that don't give trophies. And, well . . . sometimes those were more fun? Because there was less pressure."

Dani shook her head. "But the Grackles don't compete at those, either. If we want to stay competitive, we have to *compete*. In real races. With prizes. Like Glow in the Park."

"Sure," said Avery, "but some of us aren't as competitive."

Avery was talking about her, Lola knew. And Avery was right: Over their many months of practices, as the other Sardines had focused on form and efficiency, Lola had felt an itch, a deep-down desire to simply *coast*, her mind free of the microseconds she had to beat. That itch had been building inside her, hot and blue.

Lola wasn't sure what gave her the confidence—the fact that Bastian and Avery had spoken first, maybe, or the new discovery that she could tether when nobody else could. Or maybe it was the softness in Avery's eyes when she looked Lola's way. Whatever the reason, Lola found her voice.

"Maybe," she said, "we could do something different today. Maybe we could free skate?"

Dani blinked at her, uncomprehending. "But this isn't free skating. This is practice."

"I know," Lola said, nervous, but now determined to say

what she had in mind. "It's pretty clear, though: We're all stressed out after what happened at the race. And then the message. And our powers. Well, and whatever 'DGE' means. We can't exactly get *harmonization* if we're stressed."

"But that's not the point of—"

"*Please?*" Lola didn't like interrupting. She hardly ever did. But if Dani was going to ask her to tether, then Lola was going to ask something in return. "You always say we'll free skate if we have time, but then we practice so long, we never do. I think it'd be nice to, you know, have some fun. Like before. *And* I think we'd all tether a lot better afterward. It's easier for me to connect us when our brains are calmer."

Lola wasn't sure if this last part was true, but she decided it was worth saying.

Dani was quiet. Scarily quiet.

"I'm with Lols," Avery piped up. She shot Lola a wink that filled her heart with relief. "Maybe we'd all skate better if we loosened up. And then we can really focus on . . . um, *tethering*."

Dani faced them all, her arms crossed tight. "You think so, too, Bastian?"

"Sure," said Bastian. "Free skate would be nice."

A few more seconds passed, and then Dani heaved a beleaguered sigh. "*Okay.* This is a democracy, or whatever. I'm not going to, like, *force* everybody to practice."

"So," said Lola, a little uncertain she'd heard Dani right, "we can free skate right now?"

By way of reply, Dani jumped on her board and took off down the hill.

"Eat my dust!" she shouted back at the others.

"Hey!" Avery laughed. "This isn't a race!"

Dani called back, "Then how come I'm winning?"

The others hurriedly dropped their backpacks and rummaged out their gear. Lola tugged on her slider gloves, checked the strap of her helmet, and mounted her board. Then, with a big starting kick off the ground, she zoomed down the track. Lola gulped down the onrushing wind and let it flow inside her. She bent her knees and tilted her body in time with the rhythm of the road. She breathed in the hot June air as dust and rock flew past.

The downhill ride was always too short. Too soon, the track flattened, ending at the half-built residential gate. Lola slid to a stop across the finish line, breathing deep and hard. She shaded her eyes and looked up to see Bastian and Avery neck and neck, both skating with their glowstreams on. Bastian's stream was silver, a liquid wave fluttering out behind the board. Avery's was green, a faint lime shine in the sunlight.

As they reached the hill base, Avery cut a sharp turn, sliding in front of Bastian and whooping in victory. Bastian tried to pull back and avoid her glowstream, but it was too late. At the last minute, he sprang off his board, jumping over the solid green stream as his glowboard shot beneath it. Then, *smack*—his sneakers connected with the board. He wobbled once, then regained his balance, and carved into a stop. Avery was already off her board, her stream vaporizing behind her.

"Dude!" she shouted, running to Bastian. "That was *awesome*. Did you see him, Lols? Dani, did you *see* that?"

Bastian looked flushed but gratified. "It was instinct," he said.

"See?" Avery said to Dani. "Lola was right: Free skate's great for practice."

Avery shot Lola another wink, and Lola felt flushed with happiness.

"See you all at the top!" she shouted, mounting her board and pushing uphill in a new burst of energy.

The Sardines kept it up, straining uphill and coasting down, weaving in each other's paths in effortless crisscross patterns, occasionally kicking on their streams, sometimes falling down. Lola fell once after knocking into Bastian's stream—a hit that shredded up a layer of skin on her forearm. She didn't mind the asphalt's burn or the prickling blood on her skin, though. This was what glowboarding was about: mistakes and tumbles and finding things out for yourself.

On her seventh time up the hill, Lola swung to a stop, dismounting for a moment to catch her breath. She walked to the edge of the hill crest, looking out. There was Callaway, a shiny new city made of metal and glass, winking in the lowering Texan sun. In the distance, large factories rose, manufacturing the many forms of Component G that would be sent across the country and the world.

Avery joined Lola, crunching through loose red rocks until they were standing side by side.

Hey. The word entered Lola's mind, sounding tentative.

She turned and found Avery's face radiant in the orange light. Lola felt a fluttery burst of nerves.

She'd been upset with Avery the night before, when she'd suggested that Nando might have something to do with the silver suits. The truth was, Lola herself had been bothered by the way Nando had left home. He'd been so secretive, so on edge...as though he had something to hide.

But that's what it's like to work for the government, Lola told herself. *It's nothing to be suspicious of.*

She'd known Nando her entire life. Maybe he was moodier than usual, but he was still her brother, and she trusted him. And now, as she met Avery's hazel eyes, the remainder of her bad feeling faded away.

Lola smiled, and when she did, Avery's thoughts poured out with more confidence: *You know, you don't have to tether us if you don't want. Dani's got big ideas, but that doesn't mean you have to go along with them. You do what's right for you.*

Lola studied the sunlit cityscape, squinting in thought. *I know,* she said after a while. *I've thought it through, though. I want to help. I'm still scared, I guess, but...I'm a little excited, too?*

Avery nodded. *Yeah, I get that.*

That's when Lola got the idea to try something new. An investigation. Pressing her tongue against her teeth, she envisioned a memory of herself throwing a Frisbee for Radar in Avery's backyard. Then, carefully, she attempted to send the memory Avery's way.

"Huh," said Avery, pressing a hand to her forehead.

Lola's breath hitched. "What?" she asked hopefully.

Avery shook her head, looking dazed. "Was that you?"

Lola grinned. "It worked," she said. "You saw it?"

"It was blurry," Avery said. "But I knew it was from you. A memory, right? You and Radar together."

Lola nodded, a thrill racing down her arms.

Bastian and Dani came over to where the girls were standing, but Lola didn't want to tell them about the success of her investigation just yet. She wanted to keep the memory between her and Avery—something special, shared by the two of them. And Avery, it seemed, felt the same way.

In silence, the Sardines looked out over their city.

"Sometimes," whispered Lola, "I feel like I could fly. Like there are wings inside me, even when I'm not on my board."

She wasn't sure what she was saying. She was probably too pepped with adrenaline, speaking nonsense the others would laugh at her for. Nobody laughed, though. They kept staring down on Callaway, and Avery replied, "Sometimes I feel that way, too."

Lola didn't respond; she only smiled. Under her ribs, in the blue-flame place, sparks showered down. Maybe the Sardines were different, with their tele-whatevers. Maybe they were on a mission to stop aliens from destroying the planet. But for now? They could free skate. For now, they could be regular kids.

SEVENTEEN

CHANGING CHANNELS

A very was about to punch in the code to the securipad when she realized the back door was cracked open.

"Mom?" she called, walking into the kitchen.

From upstairs, Radar barked excitedly. He scampered down the stairs and ran for Avery, wagging his tail in a frenzy. Avery knelt, petting him and planting kisses on his head. Then she pulled back and gave Radar a somber once-over.

If you could understand me, you would *think back, wouldn't you?*

Radar barked twice. But did two barks mean yes or no?

Or nothing at all?

"Hey, sweetie." Ms. Sills walked into the kitchen, phone in hand.

"You got off work early," Avery said, giving Radar one final, cautious pat.

"More like *on time*, for once." Her mother laughed ruefully.

"This overtime is killing me. But it's our busiest season. Shouldn't last much longer." She reached Avery, drawing her into a big, swaying hug.

Radar jumped beside them.

"I promise, hon," she said, planting a kiss on Avery's head, "July will be better. We'll do all sorts of summery things. The pool, Putt-Putt, maybe even a weekend getaway? Just you and me, girl."

Avery nodded. "I'd like that a lot. I feel like..."

Like you're never here, Avery wanted to say, but she stopped short. Saying that would only make her mom feel worse, and Avery knew she couldn't help the overtime at her marketing agency. Avery had learned to make the most of nights like this, which were fewer and farther between since they'd moved to Callaway.

"Can we order a pizza?" Avery asked.

Ms. Sills grinned so wide that dimples formed in her cheeks. She held up the phone. "It's like you're reading my mind."

Avery grinned back, but inside she felt like someone had punched her right in the kidneys.

Like you're reading my mind.

Avery sat at the kitchen counter as her mom called Pizza Palace.

"Yes, extra cheese *and* extra sauce," Ms. Sills said, shooting Avery a conspiratorial wink. "A two-liter comes with that? Then of course we'll take it! What kind? Uh, we'll have..." Ms. Sills motioned to Avery for a suggestion.

In a split second, Avery decided to try. If her mom could hear her thoughts, that would mean they were connected somehow. It would mean that Avery wasn't a freak, that she and the Sardines weren't the only ones.

Dr Pepper, Avery thought, desperately pushing the thought out toward her mother.

Ms. Sills blinked. She raised her brows expectantly. "Hon?" she whispered loudly. "What do we want to drink?"

She hadn't heard. Of course not.

Avery mumbled, "Dr Pepper, I guess."

Ms. Sills shot a thumbs-up. "Dr Pepper. Yes, and could we order an extra cup of garlic sauce? Oh, and what the heck, some more marinara sauce, too. Do you have that spicy kind? Arrabbiata? Yes! Perfect."

It's not exactly perfect, Avery thought. *You don't know who I am. I don't know who I am. Extra garlic sauce won't fix that.*

The garlic sauce didn't fix anything, that was true, but it did make Avery and her mom pretty happy, at least for the moment. They licked grease off their fingertips as an old movie played on television. And because Ms. Sills insisted that Avery eat a vegetable, even on pizza night, they finished off their meal by chomping on celery sticks.

"A palate cleanser!" Ms. Sills declared, dipping her celery into a big cup of ranch dip.

Avery liked when her mother joked around and wasn't talking on the phone about credit card bills, or locked in her home office, typing away at a work project. For now, she and Avery could stuff themselves silly and laugh at the goofiest parts of the movie. When the next round of commercials began, though, Ms. Sills muted the television. She had a suddenly serious look on her face.

"Vee," she said, "your father called this morning."

Avery's throat went dry. "Huh," she said, picking at a stringy bit of celery.

"He says he emailed you."

"Yeah."

"And you didn't write back."

Avery sniffed. "I've been busy."

"Vee."

"What?"

"We've talked about this before, sweetie. Just because your father and I don't get along anymore, that doesn't mean—"

"Well, what am I supposed to write? 'Okay, wow, you can't visit *again*. Big surprise.'"

"*Vee*."

"What?!"

"Your father still—"

"He'll never visit," Avery interrupted angrily. "He doesn't care. He's got all these exciting *projects*, so why does he need me? He didn't even fight to get, like, one *iota* of custody, and—and—"

Avery suddenly felt much too full.

"Vee." Her mom squeezed Avery's shoulder. "I'm so sorry. You know I didn't ever want you to take sides in this divorce, and I told myself I'd never speak ill of your father. But...

canceling again, it isn't right. I told him that. I told him everything he was going to miss. You're an amazing kid. He should appreciate that. And . . . I hope you know, just because I can't always make it to your events, that doesn't mean I'm not rooting for you. I am. I brag about you to my coworkers, just ask."

Avery smiled a little, but the blue flame still burned.

"He offered to reschedule," her mom said very softly. "He says he can come in August."

Avery thought about it. Then she said, "I don't want him to come."

"Sweetie, I—"

"You can tell him that: I don't want him to come *ever*. He'd only make everything terrible again."

"Vee," her mom said gently. "What do you mean?"

Avery slumped into the couch and glanced up to find that none other than Mr. Carl Jensen, the King of Callaway, was on the television screen, advertising a popular Gloworks, Inc. gadget: the hoverstand. The commercial cut to a white screen, bright with the bold yellow words *GLOWORKS: THE FUEL OF THE FUTURE*. Avery scowled, trying to form an answer to her mother's question.

"He doesn't *get* me," she finally said. "At school, he didn't stand up for me. He took Principal Grisham's side. And he didn't even ask me what happened first. He assumed it was my fault. And it wasn't. And that—that wasn't right." Avery wiped hot tears from her eyes. She didn't want to cry about her father. She didn't want to think about him at all.

Her mom wrapped an arm around Avery's back. "I know that hurt, sweetie. I'm so sorry."

Avery didn't want to think about Katelyn Sumner, either, but every bad thing that had happened in LA, before the move, bubbled to the surface of her mind: the rumor Katelyn had spread all around the sixth grade; their confrontation in the girls' bathroom; Katelyn's big, unbelieving eyes as the faucets shook and then flew from their sinks, water bursting out all around them, the broken mirrors and chipped yellow tile.

Katelyn had blamed it on Avery. She'd claimed that she'd overheard Avery planning to vandalize the bathroom, and that she'd seen her do it with her own eyes. The adults had believed Katelyn, and her dad had believed the adults. Avery had been suspended and scheduled for therapist visits, to work on controlling her anger.

Then Avery had moved away with the one person who didn't think she was guilty of anything.

The trouble was, Avery *was* guilty—just not in the way that anyone else thought. She had vandalized the bathroom, but not on purpose, and not with her hands. It had happened in a burst, all the anger welling inside, fueling that hot blue flame. She'd been as shocked as Katelyn. But what Katelyn didn't understand was that Avery couldn't control it, and that she was just as scared. No one understood. Especially not her dad.

"Dad doesn't get me," Avery said again, with more resolve. "And I'm fine without him. I don't want to see him again."

"That's your decision to make," Ms. Sills said after a moment of quiet. "But why don't you sleep on it, okay? If you

162

feel the same way in the morning, I'll call and tell him whatever you want me to."

Avery curled into her mother's side, breathing in the scent of garlic and cinnamon. "Okay."

"Vee."

"Yeah?"

"Are you happy here? In Callaway?"

Avery peered up at her mom. "Yeah. I am."

"I loved growing up here; this town holds a lot of memories for me. Coming back felt right. It felt almost—well, you'll think this is weird, but it felt like I was being drawn by magnetic force. Sometimes I forget, though, that you don't share my nostalgia. I know this has been tough. These past few years haven't been easy, Vee, but . . . we're going to make it through."

"Yeah, Mom." Avery gave a small smile. "I know."

The television image flickered, breaking up.

Then a sharp pain sliced across Avery's eye.

"Ow." Avery pressed a hand to her forehead.

"Sweetie?" Her mother looked at her in concern.

The television flickered more strongly, cutting the movie into strips of fuzzy black and white. Then the sound came back on, and the channel switched entirely. Pictures of tanks and fast-flying planes filled the screen. A reporter appeared, shouting over an engine's roar about the deployment of troops, enlisted through the newly instated draft.

"What on earth?" Ms. Sills grabbed the remote and pressed at its buttons.

Avery sank into the couch cushions, her eyes transfixed

on the screen. The image there was changing again, taking on a familiar form. Avery saw *herself* on the television with Dani, Bastian, and Lola, all of them huddled together in Cedar House, around a blazing blue column. This memory was recent. *Very* recent.

Static filled Avery's ears. She winced, shaking her head, trying to free her mind of the sound, but then she began to make out a voice. A woodwind melody.

We will come for you at the time we came before. On the day when ... sun ... the end ...

The static grew louder, drowning out the voice.

"No!" Avery cried, jumping to her feet. She ran to the television, placing her hands on the screen, but the image there— her memory—was fading away, too. *Wait!* Avery tried with all her might to reach out with her thoughts. *Don't stop yet. I know what time you mean, but what day?* When?

Avery covered her ears. She shut her eyes. She tried to concentrate. Everything was suddenly too loud.

Then the sound cut out, and the pain in Avery's head vanished.

She opened her eyes to find that the television screen had gone dark. Across the room, her mother held the remote close to her chest, breathing hard.

"What in God's name was that?" she whispered.

Avery realized that her hands were trembling. She dropped them from the TV. "I—I don't know. Did you ... see it?"

"I saw a news broadcast that I absolutely did not tune in

to," Ms. Sills said, tapping the remote. "This cable company is the worst. I'll give them a call."

"A news broadcast," Avery said slowly. "That's it?"

Ms. Sills met Avery's eyes. "Hon? Are you all right?"

"Y-yeah," Avery said. "Sorry. It's just annoying. I really liked that movie."

Her mom smiled sympathetically. "It looks like the cable's out for now. Why don't you pick a DVD? I'll call and find out what the problem is tomorrow, I promise."

"Sure," Avery said. "Sounds good."

But guilt was pooling inside her, the same as it had been in the principal's office, all those months ago. This wasn't a cable problem. This was *her* problem.

The aliens had given her a message: They would come for the Sardines at the time they had come before, in Cedar House.

Midnight.

EIGHTEEN

A NEW KIND OF PRACTICE

"**M**idnight? Midnight *when*?"

"That's what I'm trying to tell you: The message broke up before I could figure it out. All I heard was something about 'sun' and 'the end.'" Avery shivered, even though the sun was beating down on Hazard Hill.

Bastian felt like shivering, too. He wasn't sure he wanted an answer to his question. What if the *when* was a week from now? What if it was tomorrow? Or *today*? He may have had a plan to talk to the aliens, but he didn't exactly feel like meeting them yet. Not for a while. Actually, *not ever* would've been great.

"Okay, let's think," said Dani. She looked around the circle of Sardines, who'd gathered at the top of the racetrack for practice. "We know three things for sure: midnight, Hazard Hill, and . . . eradication."

Avery shivered again.

Lola whimpered, "I don't want to think about any of this."

"Too bad," Dani said. "Because whether we want to think about it or not, aliens *are* contacting us, and obviously, they think we're smart enough to put this message of theirs together."

Bastian picked at the shoelace of his left sneaker. Aliens were contacting the Sardines—that is, every Sardine but *him*. He was the only one left who hadn't received a weird memory message. But maybe that was a *good* thing. If he'd worked on his memories enough by the time the aliens contacted him, maybe he could convince them single-handedly to not blow up Earth.

"So," Dani said, "how do we feel?"

Bastian looked up, at a loss. "How do we feel about *what*?"

"Your plan, obviously," Dani said through a huff. "Do we really think this memory communication stuff is going to work?"

Bastian sighed. Why did Dani have to make everything an almost fight?

Maybe you're jealous, he wanted to say, *because I came up with a plan before you did.*

Rather than talk, though, Bastian thought. And rather than think in words, he thought in pictures. He conjured the memory he'd been working on in his spare time: his tenth birthday, on the Gil family's vacation to the Grand Canyon. He pictured the vast expanse of giant red ravines, envisioned the open blue sky and shimmering sun, recalled the fresh cantaloupe his father had cut into for their picnic. Then he took each of those images and pushed it, resolutely, toward Dani's mind.

Dani opened her mouth. She stared at Bastian, panicked at first, then comprehending.

"Whoa," she said, touching her forehead.

"You see it?" Bastian asked, excited. He hadn't attempted to share a memory until now; he hadn't even tried it out with Lola.

"So it *can* work," Dani said.

Now it was Bastian's turn to be huffy. "I told you it would."

"Lola and I have been practicing, too," Avery piped up. She looked to Lola, smiling. "Things are still kind of fuzzy right now, but we can definitely share pictures. It's a start."

At that moment, an image appeared in Bastian's mind: a brand-new glowboard under a pair of yellow sneakers—*Dani's* sneakers. Then the image flickered and disappeared.

Bastian smirked at Dani. "See? Even you can do it."

"Ha, *ha,*" Dani said humorlessly. "Of course I can; I've been practicing. But just because we can send memories doesn't mean it'll work on the aliens. Do you really think we can convince them that way?"

"Well," Lola said, "what else can we do?"

Dani didn't have an answer for that. "Whatever," she mumbled. "We're wasting time now. The only thing left to do is wait for the aliens' next message."

"And work on our memories," Bastian added. "I think we should make a point to do it every day, before practice.

Memory tests. We each share one memory. That'll keep them fresh."

"Yeah." Dani nodded, businesslike. "Then that takes care of that. Now, let's do what we came here to do, and *skate*."

"Tethering," said Dani once they'd gotten their boards and their gear and lined up. "It's how we're going to win."

Lola had been dreading practice for this exact reason.

Free skating the day before had been so relaxing, so freeing, so *good*. For a couple hours, she'd remembered how fun skating could be, with no rules or limitations, and no trophies to win.

Now that was over.

Glow in the Park was on the horizon. There was a flock of Grackles to beat.

And Dani seemed to think that winning depended on *tethering*.

"I don't see how it's going to make a difference," Lola said, toeing her hot-pink glowboard. "We already skate in a good formation."

"You're not looking at the big picture," Dani said as she strapped on her helmet. "If we can share thoughts, that changes *everything*. We'll skate better, faster. We can *talk* to each other. We could never do that before."

That much was true, Lola had to admit. The draft train involved skating against a wall of hard, loud air. Even if someone shouted from behind or ahead of you, their words would be almost impossible to catch.

"It's a glowboard team's dream," Dani went on. "Imagine if

the Grackles could do this. They'd jump at the chance. And we should, too."

"I don't see why everything has to be about the Grackles," Lola mumbled, but when Dani fixed her with a stink eye, she sighed. "*Fine.* How exactly do you want to practice?"

"I think we should start small," Dani said. "Form our train two at a time. Me up front, you behind, like normal. But just the two of us to start out. We'll head down the hill, staying in each other's thoughts at all times. When we're comfy with that, we add Bastian, and then Avery."

Lola nodded, though out of obligation, not enthusiasm. What if she got out of control, the way she did in the cafeteria? What if, instead of sending food into the air, she sent Dani flying over the edge of Hazard Hill?

Lola. It's going to be okay.

She turned to Avery, who was smiling encouragingly at her. *And remember, you don't have to do it if you don't want.*

The look in Avery's hazel eyes filled Lola with confidence. She nodded, then turned back to Dani.

"It's worth trying, at least," she said.

Dani kicked on her glowboard and hopped on. "That's the spirit," she said, motioning for Lola to join her on the track.

Lola kicked on her own board, hovering a few inches above the ground. Pushing off, she skated up and grabbed Dani's hands, which she held behind her back—their usual racing configuration. What wasn't usual was how Lola reached from her mind to Dani's. She didn't merely send thoughts her way, like she would if they were having a conversation. No, if they were going to stay connected all the way down Hazard Hill, while skating, they needed an actual *connection*. So Lola took a hook from her mind—the kind she used to tether the Sardines together—and cast it out for Dani to catch.

Got it? Lola asked.

The tether took hold as Dani replied, *Got it. Now, on the count of three. One, two . . .* three.

Dani pushed off the track—one strong kick from her left sneaker. Then they were off, gathering speed. The sensation was familiar to Lola, but odd, too—she was used to Bastian's hands in hers, to the weight of both him and Avery behind her, forming their complete draft train.

Bend to your right, Dani instructed.

Lola, noting the curve in the track, adjusted the bend in her knees. In that moment, she felt a snipping sensation, behind her eyes. Her tether to Dani—it was pulling apart.

Dani, wait, Lola said. *I'm losing the tether.*

Make it stronger! Dani thought back.

But there was no strengthening this thread. *Snip, snip*—the sensation came on again, harsher than before, until, suddenly, there was a final *snap*.

Lola cried out, tumbling back and falling off her board, hitting the track with a hard *thump*. Dani, meanwhile, was falling forward, waving her arms in a wild attempt to regain her balance.

"AAAH!" she shouted, before toppling off her board and landing on her hands and knees, skidding to a stop.

"Lola! Dani!"

Lola looked back to see Avery and Bastian running to catch up with them. Grimacing at the pain in her backside, Lola grabbed her board—hovering stationary beside her, right at the spot where she'd fallen off. She was grateful, at least, for the board's security feature. Dani, however, was not so lucky. Her board—a way older model—was still hovering its way down the track, coughing out gunky orange glow in its wake.

"NO!" Dani shouted, scrambling to her feet and chasing after it.

"*Ouuuch*," Avery said, groaning sympathetically as they watched Dani hurl herself onto the board, face-planting once more on the track. Then, kneeling beside Lola, Avery asked, "You okay?"

Lola nodded weakly, rubbing her head. Her tether to Dani was completely gone, and judging by the look on Dani's face as she came storming up the track, Lola decided that was a good thing.

"What was that, Lols?" Dani demanded once she'd reached them. "We were doing really well. You have to focus."

"I *was* focusing," Lola retorted. "I told you to wait, I felt the tether snapping. I've never done this before, not when we're skating. If you'd *listened* to me—"

"Lols is right," Bastian said. "Cut her some slack, okay?"

Dani looked as angry as ever at first. Then a moment passed, and her glare lost its force. She looked to the ground.

"I'm . . . sorry," she said. "I guess I've been a little . . . overexcited about this."

"A *little*?" Bastian snorted.

"Okay," said Dani, "*a lot*. It's just, I don't know if you guys understand the potential of tethering like I do. If we master this? We can be the best skaters on this track. Better even than all those high schoolers doing single speeds. We could make a name for ourselves. If we race fast enough, we wouldn't just beat the Grackles, we'd set a record no one else could beat. We'd show that we're *legitimate*."

Lola watched in wonder as Dani spoke. Dani *could* take the fun out of practice, and right now, Lola was more than a little annoyed with her. But she still admired how passionate Dani got about glowboarding. When it wasn't annoying, it was kind of... inspiring.

You sure you're okay?

This time it was Avery, back in Lola's head. Her words were gentle, careful—the way they always were.

Lola brightened. She had an idea.

"Dani," she said. "I'll try it again. But, um, this time... can I skate with Avery instead?"

"I don't see how it's going to be different," Dani said from the sidelines, arms crossed.

Avery smiled. She and Lola, they understood each other. That had been clear from the first thought they'd shared, and it was even clearer now as Lola placed her hands in Avery's and lined up behind her on the racing track. Lola's thoughts appeared in her mind, lavender-hued and full of warmth.

Feeling okay? Lola asked.

I should be asking you that question, Miss Scraped Knees, Avery replied. Then she nodded. *I'm ready whenever you are.*

Ready, Lola said.

Then she pushed off the ground, and they were off, skating downhill.

Avery wasn't used to the position of lead, but she knew the basics. She bent her knees and tilted her head forward, using her helmet to take the brunt of the wind as they gained speed.

Still okay? she asked Lola.

Yep. You? the lavender thoughts replied.

Oh, watch it! Avery shot back as she noted a large chunk of rock ahead—too large for their hovering glowboards to crest. *Bend to the left.*

It happened in an instant: She and Lola both leaned, changing the course of their glowboards, perfectly aligned.

Now back on track, Avery said, and again, in tandem, they returned to their path.

Avery's smile had turned to a full-blown grin. It was *working.*

But at that very moment, she felt a pinch behind her eyes.

The tether, Lola said, frantic. *It's breaking again.*

That's okay, Avery replied. *I'm letting go. We'll spin out.*

With that, Avery released Lola and, crouching, lowered her hands to the track. Her sliders screeched against the asphalt, and Avery caught a whiff of burning rubber—*not* what you wanted from a stop, but with worn-out sliders like hers, it was the best she could expect. And even though she stopped several yards farther down the track from Lola, she did *stop*.

When she did, the pinching sensation in her head let up.

Avery rubbed at her eye and looked to where Lola was getting up from her crouch.

Still there?

Lola smiled. *Yeah, I am. That was a way better ending than last time.*

Avery jumped to her feet at that. "We did it," she said aloud. Then, calling up to the distant figures of Bastian and Dani, *"We did it!"*

Lola shook her head as the girls walked in step, back up the hill. "Don't be *too* happy," she said, "for Dani's sake."

Avery laughed. "Sure," she said. "The tether *did* still break. But we *did* do it, Lols. Do you think it's something you really can practice? Something you could do with all of us, as a team?"

Lola pressed her tongue to her bottom lip in thought. "Honestly? I didn't think so before, but... maybe it's possible. If I can keep practicing with you and *then* add the others, I think I'll be able to do it."

"Well," said Bastian as the two reached the top of the track, "that looked a little better?"

"How did it feel?" asked Dani.

"I mean, so-so," Avery said, shrugging. "But it definitely helped."

"See?" Dani said, grinning. Then, looking a little more

abashed, she turned to Lola. "Um, I *am* sorry for being pushy before. If you don't feel like you can—"

"No," Lola interrupted. She cast a shy smile at Avery before going on. "I think I can do this, actually. It'll take work, like you say, but . . . I do think this will help us skate better. And I'd like to do my part to help out the team."

Dani grinned again. "Cool. So, how about you two try that again?"

Dani left Hazard Hill with energy buzzing in her veins.

Usually, practice left her sore and a little grumpy, but today, she'd skated way less than normal, using most of her time to coach Lola and Avery as they formed their tether and traveled, little by little, farther down the track. Then, in the last hour of practice, Bastian had joined the formation, and the markers were set back again. At first, the three of them had tumbled to the ground within a second. But over time, they added yards, the team using their shared thoughts to skate as one.

Dani called her shouted orders coaching, but she knew, really, she wasn't doing much. This power—this *tethering*—was Lola's. And even though Dani felt a little jealous that she wasn't the one who could tether, she'd been satisfied watching her teammates figure out what she'd known from the start: These new powers of theirs? They were good for something. With these powers, the Sardines were going to win.

Anyway, Dani thought, once she'd arrived home from practice and made her way to her room, *I can't do* everything *on this team. If I were tethering, who'd be left to tell everyone what to do?*

Dani also had to admit that free skating the other day had been... nice. She'd forgotten what it was like to skate for *skating*'s sake—no worries about time, formations, or the next competition. Maybe, she decided, once Glow in the Park was over, she'd reinstate free skates as a regular Sardines tradition. It seemed good for morale.

That, and Zander's words were still stuck in her head: *You made things really hard. And I wasn't the only who thought that.*

Dani sat on the edge of her bed, glaring at her sneakers, concentrating on the blue flame inside. With laser focus, she untied the laces of her right sneaker, then the left—all with her mind. Still filled with adrenaline, Dani did more: She concentrated harder than ever and used invisible hands to tug the shoes from her feet, carrying them across the room toward her open closet.

She'd never done *this* before. Today, because of all that buzzing energy, she'd felt she could. And she *had*.

"Danielle!"

Dani jumped at her mother's shout from downstairs. The shoes fell from midair, landing inside the closet with a *thud*.

"Danielle, time to set the table! Right now!"

"Coming!" Dani shouted, but she didn't move.

Even if Zander was right, and the others did think she sucked the fun out of everything, *they* didn't have unreasonable parents like she did. The Gils loved watching Lola and Bastian race. They supported everything the twins did. And even though Ms. Sills was busy with work, at least she didn't call what Avery did a "hobby."

Dani, meanwhile, had the Hirsch Code to contend with, and an agreement with her parents that she couldn't bring herself to tell the Sardines about. The others couldn't possibly understand what winning meant to her. Glow in the Park wasn't just about beating stupid Mitchell, traitor Zander, and their horrible Grackles. It was about proving herself.

And tethering? That was the key to proving, once and for all, that the Sardines were a team to be reckoned with, and that Dani Hirsch really was the best in her sport.

"Danielle!" her mother called, harsher than before. "I won't ask again!"

With effort, Dani got to her feet and headed for the door. She'd show her parents that glowboarding was as legitimate as any other sport. She'd show them with a first-place trophy.

NINETEEN

GLOW EXPO

Days passed, each June afternoon hotter than the one before, and the Callaway sun burned bright, anticipating its longest day. There had been no more night visions, no columns of light, no messages. All of Bastian's questions about the aliens remained unanswered. Somehow, life began to feel almost normal again.

Tethering while skating had been a mess at first. Dani had finally joined the draft train formation, and though Lola could technically tether all four Sardines, the connection started out shaky, cutting in and out with every curve in the road. The Sardines' stray thoughts wandered in—Bastian's new ideas for a sketch, Avery's craving for Pizza Palace cheese sticks. But just like with normal skating, the more the Sardines practiced, the better they became, until all that remained inside their tethers were pertinent thoughts about balance and speed. As the tethering improved, so did the Sardines' draft train time. It returned to 2:15 and then, with more practice, went all the way down to 2:13.

Bastian was secretly proud that, during the "memory tests" at the start of each practice, his memories were the strongest of all the Sardines. By now, he was so used to thinking of his favorite memory—the Grand Canyon one—that he was having *dreams* about it. If the aliens saw that, they'd know how beautiful Earth was. If they saw how happy Bastian had been on that vacation, they wouldn't have a reason to abduct him, or any of the Sardines.

Bastian remained the one Sardine the aliens hadn't contacted on his own. It wasn't from a lack of trying, either. Every night at his work desk, while stooped over his most recent glowboard design, Bastian reached out, using his thoughts and, more recently, his memories, searching for a recipient above—past the fake constellations on his bedroom ceiling, up in the true vastness of space. He knew one thing for sure: Whenever the aliens did reach out to him, he'd be ready.

The waiting was difficult, though. And lately, Bastian had begun to wonder if waiting was even the right thing to do.

"I've been thinking," he said at the end of practice one day, "things have been quiet lately. It's been days since we've heard anything from the aliens."

"We have to be patient," Lola said gently. "We have a time and a place. All we need is a date. They'll tell us soon."

Bastian shook his head. "But what if they don't? Why do we assume they'll reach out again? Every time they've contacted us, their message has cut out. How do *they* know what we've received and what we haven't? I know we said the only thing left to do is wait. But...well, what if it's not?"

Dani was studying Bastian, her brow creased. "What do you mean?"

"I mean, we've been waiting around for the aliens to tell us a date when *they* come for *us*. Well, what if we're thinking about it wrong? What if, instead of waiting, *we* reach out to *them*?"

"But we've tried that," Avery said. "You told us you reach out every night. And talking to that apple didn't get me anywhere. I bet Lola and Dani have tried, too, right?"

Avery motioned to the girls, who nodded.

"Yeah, I know," said Bastian. "But maybe we've been going about that the wrong way, too. I've been thinking about it a lot—their message that night, from the blue column. They said they planted an *elixir* here. They made it sound like that elixir is why we have our tele-whatevers. Well, haven't you all been wondering what that elixir is?"

"Sure," said Dani, patting her chest. "It's the blue flame we've got inside."

"I think it's more than that," Bastian said. "Listen, it's only a hypothesis, but I've been thinking...what if the elixir is... glow?"

"What?" Dani looked incredulous.

"Think about it," said Bastian. "Component G only showed up fifty years ago."

"Technically," said Dani, "it was *discovered*."

"Okay, sure," Bastian conceded. "But it's new, and it's

different. The government did all that testing on it, and glow isn't like anything else on Earth. Well, what if that's because it's not *from* Earth?"

"So," Dani spoke slowly, "you're saying that glow and our tele-whatevers are connected?"

"I get it," Lola said, nodding. "Maybe glow affects us in a way it doesn't affect other people."

"So, what if it does?" asked Dani. "What difference does that make?"

"Okay, listen," said Bastian. "I know this probably sounds too weird, but I've been thinking of a plan. A way we can stop waiting around and *do* something. Say the elixir *is* glow. And say the aliens planted glow here in Callaway fifty years ago. Well, it sort of makes sense that they'd be drawn to it, right? It's their own substance after all. Maybe it's how they found *us* in the first place—because of the glow *in* us—like Dani said, our blue flames. But they keep breaking up, right? It's like the connection isn't strong enough. Well, what if all the aliens need is more *glow*? Like, glow is an antenna that can reach out to them? And if we surrounded ourselves with a *ton* of glow, their transmission might come through. Then they could find us, and we could share our memories, like we've planned."

The circle of Sardines was quiet.

"You're right," said Avery. "It *does* sound too weird."

"I don't know if it would work," Bastian admitted. "But to me at least, it's better than sitting around, waiting, worried about missing the aliens' message and getting the world *eradicated*."

"I agree with Bastian," Lola said. "At least it's something to do."

"Okay," said Dani, folding her arms. "Say we try this plan. Where do we surround ourselves with a *ton* of glow?"

Bastian looked at his sneakers, more nervous than he'd been before.

Dani caught on. "Nuh-uh," she said. "No way."

"What?" asked Avery. *"Where?"*

Bastian summoned the strength to look up again and say, "Glow Expo."

Avery blinked. "But...that's at Carl Jensen's place."

"Yeah," Dani cut in hotly. "That's why we *never* go."

Never was dramatic, Bastian thought. This was only the second year they'd done Glow in the Park and the second year they'd decided not to go to Glow in the Park's pre-race party, Glow Expo. The event was literally in Mitchell Jensen's backyard. It took place five days before the race—in this case, *tonight*. There was a cookout, fireworks, and even swimming at the huge lake on Carl Jensen's ranch. There were also exhibits from glow companies all over the US, featuring their latest products. And of course, Gloworks, Inc. was the biggest exhibitor of them all. The Sardines stayed away to avoid the Grackles; Dani called it "protecting team morale." And Bastian was the last Sardine who wanted to run into Mitchell, Zander, or any of the Grackles. But if his plan could work... well, wasn't it worth the risk?

"C'mon," he said. "Team morale is fine, Dani. And I think we can all admit, Glow Expo looks pretty cool. Carl Jensen's ranch is huge—plenty of space to keep away from the Grackles. *And* plenty of space to try our plan. There's going to be so much glow there, from Gloworks and all the other vendors."

Dani shook her head. "This is stupid. We don't know that your plan is going to work. We don't even know if glow *is* the elixir."

"I'm not saying we do," Bastian replied. "But we might as well try. I'm tired of waiting."

"I guess," said Avery, "the worst that can happen is that it doesn't work."

"And if it does," said Lola, sounding hopeful, "we can share our memories with the aliens, like Bastian said. We can convince them to leave Earth in peace."

"And *then*," Avery added, nodding toward Dani, "our concentration will be even better for Glow in the Park. You know, because we won't be worried about the world blowing up. That'd be a good thing, right, Dani?"

Dani twisted her mouth, as though she were trying hard not to smile. Bastian could tell, she'd been worn down. The Sardines were going to Glow Expo. They were going to try his plan.

Now Bastian just hoped the plan would work.

"I didn't think it'd be so . . . pretty," said Lola.

Jensen Ranch was aglow with lights. Bulbs were strung from cedar trees to oaks, and a giant patio stretched before Bastian and Lola, looking out over Jensen Lake. The sun was setting, casting umber hues on the water. Cicadas buzzed loudly. Festive guitar music piped from the speakers. All around, guests were laughing and talking, and the scent of grilled corn and fresh watermelon wafted down from the barbecue tent. Lola looked enraptured by the sight, and Bastian couldn't blame her. Glow Expo *was* way prettier than Bastian had imagined.

Still, the thought of Mitchell Jensen growing up here, with a giant lake and patio, made Bastian want to puke. Mitchell had everything a guy could want, so why did he see the need to ruin other people's lives? Bastian would never understand.

"Avery!" Lola cried, waving.

Bastian watched as Avery emerged from the dim tree line, where a makeshift dirt parking lot had been set up, complete with glowboard racks. Radar was trotting happily ahead of her on a leash. When Avery spotted the twins, her face lit up, and she ran to meet them, Radar bounding by her side.

"This place is out of control," she puffed out. "Who knew there were so many glowboard stores? There are, like, *a hundred* tents over there."

"Thirty," Bastian corrected. "And most of them are Gloworks-sponsored. That's what it said on the Glow Expo website."

Avery waved him off. "Whatever, it's a lot. You were right, Bastian: There's a *ton* of glow here. Do you see that display?" Avery pointed farther afield, toward the lake. "I heard some kids by the glowboard racks talking about it. It's this new thing called glow boosters. They make your boards go, like, turbo speed. But the Junior Glowboarding League hasn't approved them yet."

"Good," said a new voice—Dani's. The Sardines turned to where she was approaching them from behind. "Because we sure couldn't afford them."

"I mean, yeah," said Avery. "But they're *cool*."

"Whatever," Bastian said, shrugging toward the vendor tents. "We're not here for that stuff, anyway." He looked to the lake and pointed toward a distant spot, where a copse of trees bordered the water's edge. "I've been scoping it out, and I think that'd be a good place. We'll be close enough to all the glow, but far enough away to do this privately."

Dani nodded at the proposal, but Avery and Lola were distracted, looking toward the barbecue tent. Radar, too, had pricked his ears and pointed his nose toward the scent of food.

"Hey," said Dani, snapping her fingers in front of their faces. "Focus. We came here to talk to aliens, remember?"

A group of older teenagers passed by just then, and two girls glanced at Dani, whispered, and burst into laughter before heading on.

Dani's cheeks pinked, and she whispered, "The sooner we try this out, the sooner we can *leave*."

Bastian didn't like how dismissive Dani sounded—like she thought his plan wasn't going to work. But he did at least appreciate that their interests were aligned. Lola and Avery, on the other hand, were still distracted.

"The food's free," Lola offered, a little sheepishly.

"And it smells amazing," Avery moaned. Beside her, Radar whined in agreement. "C'mon, we'd be stupid not to . . . you know, take advantage."

"Seriously," said Dani. "You want food catered by Mitchell's dad?"

"Well, *yeah*," Avery said. "He's, like, a billionaire. It's about time he shared the wealth."

"Don't you remember why we're here?" Bastian protested. "*Light beings*, not roasted corn."

But Lola and Avery were whispering conspiratorially, and Avery piped up to say, "We'll be *five minutes*, tops. We'll meet you right where you said, at those trees by the lake!"

Before either Bastian or Dani could protest, Avery was off, along with Radar, tugging Lola behind her. Lola glanced back once to give Bastian an apologetic grin. Bastian sighed and rolled his eyes at Dani.

"*We* can head down there at least," he said.

But now even Dani was glancing toward the tents. "I mean," she said, "if they're going over there anyway . . ."

Bastian gaped. "Seriously? You, Dani Hirsch, are going to eat Jensen food, too?"

"Well, I'm hungry," Dani admitted. "All we had for dinner tonight was this weird quinoa bake. I'll be down there in five, too, okay? We'll do a better job if we're not starving."

Bastian watched as the last of the Sardines abandoned him. Then, shaking his head, he stomped down a slight embankment, steering clear of the tents and heading toward the lake. He was so focused that he didn't notice anyone approaching him until there was a hand on his shoulder.

"WHOA," Bastian yelped, jumping away from the touch. Then he saw who it was: Zander Poxleitner.

Bastian scowled. "What the heck do you want?"

Zander blinked at Bastian. There was a weird look in his dark eyes, like . . . regret? Only, that couldn't be right.

"I didn't think you'd come to this," Zander said. "Are the others here, too?"

"Yeah," said Bastian, resuming his stomp toward the lake. "Yeah, we are. Now go report that to Mitchell. You tell him everything, don't you?"

To Bastian's irritation, Zander followed him. "Hey. *Dude.* Can't we even talk?"

"No."

"Why not?"

Bastian turned on Zander, planting his feet in the grass. "Seriously? *Why not?* Let's just forget the fact that you left the Sardines to become a Grackle; you're the one who told Mitchell about my art. Private stuff. Stuff I didn't even tell *Lola.* And all that stuff you fed him? That's his ammo. You get that, right? You betrayed us. You betrayed *me.*"

That look was back in Zander's eyes. In fact, it was all over his mole-marked face. But Bastian didn't buy it.

"I didn't betray you on purpose," Zander said very quietly. "Any of you. I still thought of you as my friends. I thought the Grackles were my friends, too. *That's* why I told them those things about your art. It wasn't because I wanted to hurt you. If I'd known what Mitchell was going to do—"

"But you *did* know!" Bastian shouted. "You knew he was a jerk when you left us. And that's what makes you as bad as him. That's what makes you *worse*. Because you knew how terrible the Grackles were, and you joined them anyway. For what? Fancier equipment? Better friends? Well, I really hope that's working out for you."

The words were out before Bastian could consider their importance. He saw hurt flash across Zander's face, and then . . . resignation.

"Fine," Zander said. "I don't know why I even tried to talk to you."

"Yeah, me neither," said Bastian, still red-hot with anger.

With that, Zander turned around and left, heading up the embankment, back toward the tents, the music, and the crowd. Bastian watched him go with clenched fists, warding off stinging tears that threatened to spill.

Forget Zander. Bastian was here for one purpose, and one purpose only.

He set out once more toward the lake.

TWENTY

CONTACT

Dani bit into a steaming piece of corn on the cob, which she'd slathered in hot sauce and sprinkled with cotija cheese. She watched from the food tent as partygoers gathered and mingled around her. Some of these people were her age—fellow skaters or kids interested in the sport. Most of them, though, were older teens and adults—members of the adult Glowboarding League, or businesspeople, or curious locals. Glow Expo brought out a lot of Callaway residents simply because they didn't have anything better to do until the Fourth of July.

Dani would be lying if she said she hadn't wondered about Glow Expo the year before, when she'd made the other Sardines promise to boycott it. Back then, Zander had just left the team, and Dani had been raw over his betrayal. Now, a year later, she still felt on edge. This was Grackle territory, and she sure hoped Bastian's plan was worth it.

The corn, Dani had to admit, was decent. She finished off the rest of it, dumping the cob into a nearby trash can. Then she sidled up to Lola and Avery, who were sitting side by side at a picnic bench, sharing a plate of barbecue and coleslaw. Radar sat at their feet, happily nibbling bits of brisket that Avery occasionally lowered to his mouth.

"Do you think it will work?" Dani asked, taking a seat at the table. "Bastian's plan?"

"Yeah," Avery said. "I mean, I hope it does."

"I'm nervous about it," Lola offered, in her quiet way. "I guess . . . well, I guess I've been scared to try."

Dani pointed to their plate of food. "Hence the procrastinating."

"Speak for yourself," said Avery, taking another bite of slaw. "I really wanted the food. You know when it's Carl Jensen, there's no expense spared."

Dani glanced down the embankment, toward the trees by the lake. She couldn't see Bastian, which must have meant he was well and truly hidden away.

"It's pretty cool here, actually," Avery went on. "I don't think our team morale is suffering."

"Yeah, well, it might be soon," Dani said. "We'd better head down there, or Bastian is gonna get mad. He already kind of is. We *did* come here for his plan."

Avery pointed her fork as Dani. "Then how come you're up here procrastinating, too?"

It was a good question, but Dani shrugged it off. The truth was, she was afraid that Bastian's plan to reach the light beings wouldn't work; but she was more afraid that it *would*. And then what if they couldn't share their memories, like they'd planned? What if they couldn't convince the light beings to spare their planet? What *then*? All this to worry about before Glow in the Park. These aliens had thrown a real wrench into Dani's plans.

Lola wiped her hands on a paper napkin and stood, taking away her and Avery's plate and dumping it into the trash.

"You're right," she said. "We shouldn't upset him. Let's be brave and go."

Together, the three girls headed down to the water's edge, Radar trotting ahead, leading the way to the dense copse of cedar trees until Lola spotted Bastian ahead. They hurried their steps to join him where he stood.

Bastian's arms were folded tightly across his chest. As Dani suspected, he wasn't happy.

"Whoa," said Avery. "If I wanted something chilly, I would've gone to the Popsicle tent."

Lola giggled, Dani smirked, and even Bastian cracked, the lines in his face relaxing.

"Whatever," he said, shaking his curly mop of hair. "Can we all focus now?"

Avery stood up straight and saluted, causing Radar to let out a low *woof*. Lola nodded. Dani said, "What's the precise plan?"

Bastian's eyes lit up; this, it seemed, was the question he'd been waiting for.

"Before," he said, "when the light beings contacted us together, we gathered in a circle. So I'm thinking we do that, and we join hands. You all brought your glow cartridges, right?"

The girls nodded, and Dani pulled out a clear plastic cartridge from her back pocket. Its contents were nearly drained, but what remained was an orange-colored substance: glow. Avery, Bastian, and Lola produced theirs, too—far fuller cartridges, their contents colored green, silver, and blue.

"Okay," said Bastian. "Let's place them right there." He pointed to a patch of grass. "All together. And we'll form a circle around them. Combined with all the glow up the hill, they'll form a beacon."

Dani gave Bastian a skeptical look. "Says who?"

Bastian shrugged. "It's a *hypothesis*. We're testing it out."

"Okay, *okay*," said Dani, setting down her cartridge as Bastian had directed. Then, stepping back, she joined hands with Avery and Lola. Avery kept Radar's leash looped around her wrist, and the Aussie took a seat between her and Dani, looking up at the group.

"Now," said Bastian, "we summon the light beings here. We close our eyes, and we think up the memories we've been practicing."

Dani watched as the others shut their eyes and grew quiet, concentrating. Sighing, she finally closed her own eyes and conjured up the memory she'd been reliving lately: the first time she'd set foot on a glowboard. She focused on the thrill she'd felt, on the wobbling of her legs as she found her balance. She focused on the bright green body of the board, trying to draw out as vivid an image as possible. Then she envisioned sending that memory up—past the cedar treetops, past the clouds and the stratosphere, into distant space, wherever the aliens might be.

Seconds stretched out, turning to a full minute. The circle remained quiet, and the only sounds came from the distant Glow Expo crowd—strains of music, laughter, and conversation.

Soon, Dani couldn't take it anymore. She chanced a peek at the rest of the Sardines. Their eyes were still closed. The sun was lowering, casting warm rays through the cedar branches. Trickles of sweat had begun to run down Dani's forehead and the back of her neck. She coughed, causing Bastian to open an eye.

"Stop looking," he hissed. "Concentrate."

"*You're* looking," Dani countered. "And let's face it, nothing is happening." She motioned to their collection of glow cartridges. "This is stupid."

Now Avery and Lola also opened their eyes. A flush was spreading over Bastian's face. "We haven't tried long enough," he insisted. "Take it seriously, Dani. You have to *want* it."

"Says who?" she said. "C'mon, we're taking a stab in the dark. You think the aliens are really going to see our memories?"

"*We* can see each other's memories," Lola offered. "Dani, just try it. Bastian's right: We haven't given it enough time."

Dani grimaced, but said, "Fine. Let's try it some more."

She shut her eyes and, once again, focused on her memory: the musty, old sweat scent of the glowboard shop, the tremble in her knees as she'd mounted the board. Moments passed, Dani focusing solely on the images from her past.

Then Bastian's voice broke the silence. "Hang on."

Dani's eyes fluttered open. "What now?"

Bastian shook his head. "We're all trying to reach the light beings on our own. But why do that when we can reach out *together*—the four of us as one?"

He turned to Lola, who was nervously biting her lip. "Lols," he said, "do you think you can tether us?"

"Um . . ." Lola cleared her throat. "I can try."

Dani watched as light sprang to Avery's eyes, then to Bastian's. Then she herself felt a familiar sensation in her head: a rope thrown out for her to catch. Dani took hold, and instantly, new images rushed into her mind: Radar catching a Frisbee, rainbow sprinkles atop oatmeal, the vast sprawl of the Grand Canyon.

All right. Bastian's voice shot along the tether. *Let's try this again. All together. Everyone focus, hard.*

The sensation that Dani felt then was new: Her memories began to merge with the others, swirling together in a bright blur of color. She heard Lola's thoughts: *Please, reach us, light beings.* She heard Avery's: *Hey! Can you hear us?* She heard Bastian's: *See our memories. Understand.* Then she added her own plea, directing it upward: *It'd be nice if you could make contact right about now.*

Inside Dani's chest, the blue flame waxed larger. Her ribs began to feel hot and fragile—as though they might break. She could feel heat on her face, could sense the blue flames in all the others, expanding, sizzling along their tethers, merging into one raging fire.

Then, in an instant, there was a loud *POP!* Dani's tether snapped, sending her sailing backward. She landed on her back with a hard *thud.*

Blinking in bewilderment, Dani looked around. The other Sardines had been thrown back, too, and like her, they lay sprawled on the ground in a state of shock. Radar stood over Avery, whimpering and pawing at her shoulder.

"What was that?" Avery asked. Slowly, she sat up, rubbing down Radar's fur in a daze.

"I—I'm sorry," Lola said, collecting herself into a sit. "The tethers broke. It was . . . *too much.* I couldn't hold them all at once."

Bastian said nothing. He had risen to his feet and was staring up at the sky.

"Bas—" Dani began, but he waved violently, a plea to be quiet.

Dani said nothing else, only got to her feet and then helped up Lola. The girls gathered close to Bastian as he stared upward.

Then, at last, he dropped his gaze and let out a long, defeated sigh.

"Nothing," he muttered. He motioned limply to their collection of glow cartridges. "Guess it was a stupid idea after all."

"We did feel *something*," Dani offered. "That big popping sound. You all heard it, too, didn't you?"

"Yeah," Avery said. "We all got thrown on our backs. That's not nothing."

"It was our blue flames," said Lola, looking contemplative. "All of ours, they joined together. For one moment, it was all *one* flame."

"Yeah," said Dani. "That's what I felt, too."

"We didn't reach the aliens, though," said Bastian, stooping to pick up his cartridge. "I'm . . . sorry. I really thought it might work."

"You don't have to apologize," said Lola, kneeling to place a hand on his. "I'm glad we tried. It seemed like a good idea."

So they'd combined their blue flames into one. Maybe that was cool, but from what Dani could see, it didn't make a difference. It wouldn't help their race time, and it certainly hadn't put them in touch with the light beings. It seemed they were stuck waiting like before, back at square one.

Dani felt weary. She rubbed at her eyes and shrugged. "Well, that's that," she said. "Guess we can head ba—"

She didn't finish, though. She'd turned toward the trees and come face-to-face with someone.

Not a Sardine.

A Grackle.

Mitchell Jensen.

Dani sucked in a breath.

A smirk stretched out on Mitchell's face as other figures emerged from the trees: Kyle Bridges, Ross Mondt, and none other than Zander Poxleitner.

"What I want to know," said Mitchell, throwing out his chest, "is what you Sardines are doing on *my* property."

"Talking to aliens," Avery said. She grinned, even after Bastian had punched her in the shoulder.

Dani could see Avery's point: Why bother lying? The truth was so ridiculous, no one would believe it.

Mitchell gave Avery a dirty look. "Freak," he said. "No one invited you here."

"No one needed to invite us," Bastian shot back. "It's a public event."

Mitchell fixed his eyes on Bastian. "Is that so, Gil?" he asked, sauntering up to him. At his back, Ross and Kyle snickered. "I don't think it's so public if you're banned. And I ban you. All four of you freaks. But especially *you*." Mitchell reached out a finger, poking Bastian hard in the chest. "I don't like girly boys on my property. So *leave*."

Bastian's lip was trembling. There was heat in his eyes, and Dani could swear his glare was tinged with blue.

"Hey, *hey*," said Avery, waving her arms between Bastian and Mitchell. Beside her, Lola's small hands had balled into fists. "It's whatever. We were leaving anyway."

Bastian was still glaring—no longer at Mitchell, but beyond him, at Zander.

"Nice, Zander," he spat out. "You really are a snitch, aren't you?"

Zander had gone horribly pale, and Dani was close enough to hear him mutter, "I didn't tell him you were here."

"Yeah, right," Dani scoffed. "Like we'd ever trust the word of a traitor."

Mitchell let out a high-pitched, unkind laugh. "Poxleitner, a traitor? At least he had some sense." Mitchell returned his glare to Bastian. "Unlike you."

Dani watched then as, in a horrible instant, Mitchell puckered his lips and spat right into Bastian's face. The glob of bubbly saliva landed on his left cheek.

Bastian said nothing. He only lifted his arm and wiped the spit from his face while Ross and Kyle howled with laughter. Rage swelled inside Dani, stoking the hot blue flame. She felt nearly ready to burst with it, and across from her, she saw Lola's arms trembling with anger.

But before they could do anything, Radar let out an angry howl and lunged forward, snapping at Mitchell with bared fangs.

"Yaaah!" Mitchell shrieked, stumbling back. "What the heck, Miller?"

Avery had pulled back Radar by the leash, but she didn't seem perturbed by her dog's snarls. "He never acts this way. I don't know, seems like he smells something he doesn't like."

Mitchell, having regrouped with the Grackles, had regained his composure. "You just keep him away from me," he ordered. "I mean it. Keep that stupid dog away, or I'll have him *taken* away. Don't think that I don't know the people who can make that happen."

Avery's eyes narrowed. "You leave Radar alone!" she shouted.

"Come on," Dani said to the Sardines. "Come on, let's go. Let's just go. Don't engage, remember?"

She didn't look at any of the Grackles—Zander included—as she marched away from their pack. She heard the others following suit, walking behind her, and she didn't look back again until they had cleared the cedar trees and reached a slope of grass that led up to the glowboard racks.

She noticed first that Lola was crying, her head on Avery's shoulder. Bastian looked angry enough to burst into flames.

"Don't let them get to you," she ordered. "Sardines are stronger than that."

Even as she spoke the words, a great *boom* resounded in the sky. Dani looked up, startled, to see the first of the Glow Expo fireworks exploding, showering silver sparks across the dusky sky.

It was a beautiful sight, she had to admit. A beautiful sight to end an ugly night.

So much for team morale.

"It's here."

The man in the navy suit looked up from the papers on his desk—ledgers, figures, and memos, all important to his job, but none so important as what the woman with the high ponytail held in her hands.

"The report," the woman said, laying a stiff sheet of paper before him.

On the paper was a graph, and on that graph was a severe spike, dated the night before.

"This event produced more concentrated activity than we've ever seen before," said the woman. "An all-time high in GAR. They're getting stronger. Much stronger."

"Yes," mused the man in the navy suit. "They are. And at a far quicker rate than we anticipated. Than *you* predicted. We can no longer sit back and observe. We need to act."

"What do you propose we do?"

The man swiveled his chair toward the office window. He looked out on the city of Callaway—*his* city. His home. Soon, he would be this city's hero.

"The key," he said at length, "is stealth. I want the subjects trailed and observed. Eyes on each one of them, at all times. This incident has proved what I've suspected: The subjects possess an inextricable connection to glow. So glow is what we'll use to bring them to us."

The woman lingered, her brow creased.

Slowly, the man in the navy suit swiveled to face her. "What is it?"

"It's only . . . they *are* children."

"Don't you think I know that?" the man replied, heat in his voice. "But it's what's best for them, as well as for this country. They don't know their own strength."

"And we do?" the woman asked. "Do you think turning them into weapons is what's *best* for them?"

The man rose from his chair. "Believe me, I understand the gravity of the situation. My work is, and has always been, a matter of gray areas. So please, I ask that you trust my decision. That's what this relationship is based on, isn't it? Trust."

The woman with the high ponytail was silent for a moment. Then, nodding stiffly, she answered, "Yes. *Trust.*"

TWENTY-ONE

THE UNWELCOME VISITOR

"Up you go. You'll be the turret."

Avery was in her bedroom, training her eyes on a small, square book entitled *Pacific Volcanoes*. The blue flame flowed through her, picking up *Pacific Volcanoes* and carrying it through the air, resting it gently atop a three-foot-high stack of books.

Building book towers was a much better use of energy than worrying about the big race in a few days' time, or about an alien threat to abduct her and destroy the earth, or about the fact that the Sardines' plan to contact the light beings had failed tremendously.

The night before, the team had trudged, defeated, away from Jensen Ranch. In silence, they'd unlocked their glow-boards from the rack.

Then Bastian had said, in a small voice, "It was only an idea."

"We tried," Lola had added.

"Yeah," Dani had said. "Looks like all we can do is wait."

"It doesn't mean my memory plan is wrong," Bastian had said almost pleadingly. "I still think we can convince the aliens that way. We should keep on practicing sharing our memories. We should be prepared for when they *do* reach out."

No one had responded to that. Avery, for one, had felt exhausted. Whatever sensation the Sardines had created together in that copse, with their hands joined tight—whatever had made that loud *POP!* and knocked them off their feet—had drained the energy from Avery's body. And so, with no other plans or conclusions, the Sardines had skated back to Cedar Lane.

Now, in the morning light, a small but sturdy fear sat in Avery's gut, near the place where the blue flame burned. As she felt it stir, she shook her head and concentrated, raising *Tuck Everlasting* high in the air. Radar happily barked at the soaring book.

Avery focused extra hard, fanning out the book's pages and carefully positioning it over the tower to form a hardcover roof.

The kitchen digipad rang, breaking her concentration. *Tuck Everlasting* quivered, then dropped to the ground, and Avery jumped to her feet.

Avery ran downstairs, skidded into the kitchen, and punched the answer button on the digipad.

"Hello?" she said breathlessly.

"Vee, is that you?"

Avery froze. She knew that voice. Deep, smooth, and clear. Her father.

"Uh. Yeah?" She turned to Radar, who had followed her downstairs.

Help me out, she thought to him, but of course, Radar didn't speak.

"I'm glad you're home," Mr. Miller was saying. "Your mom said to call first but, well... I've called. And here I am."

Avery frowned at the digipad's call screen. "Wait. What?"

"I'm right outside, Veemeister!"

There was a knock at the front door, and Avery's heart gave a massive *thud.*

Her father. Her dad was *here, at the house.*

No. That wasn't right. Avery wasn't expecting this.

Forcefully, she punched the end call button and turned, staring at the door.

The knocking continued.

Help me, she thought again to Radar, but he was too busy barking at the commotion. With dread, Avery walked to the door. She undid the locks and opened it to find that, sure enough, her father, Eric Miller, was standing on the front porch.

"Veemeister!" He flashed a radiant grin. "How's it going?"

Avery stared. What did he want her to do? Give him a hug? Say *It's so nice to see you?*

Yeah, right.

Avery crossed her arms. "What are you doing here?"

Radar was barking wildly and leaping around. Avery shooed him back and stepped out on the porch, closing the door behind her.

Mr. Miller's smile fell only a little. "Well, when your mom told me how disappointed you were that I had to cancel my trip—"

"A third time," Avery interrupted, glaring hard.

Her father's smile faltered again. "Yes, well, when she told me that, I reconsidered. She said this Glow in the Park thing was a big deal for you. A kind of once-in-a-lifetime event. I didn't want to miss that."

Avery kept on glaring. "What about your important work stuff?"

Mr. Miller shrugged casually. "I decided I could put that on hold."

"Huh," Avery said. "Well, too late. Mom told you I don't want to see you, and I don't. So you can go back to California, or whatever."

This time, her father's face fell all the way. "Veemeister," he said—now less of a shout and more like a plea. "I thought, once you saw me, we could . . . talk. Maybe set some things straight?" When Avery didn't reply, he said, "I guess I should've listened to your mom."

"Guess you should've."

Avery knew she was being mean. Maybe too mean. Guilt

tapped on her heart, making her suddenly uncertain. Her dad looked so downcast. Like maybe he really had come to patch things up. Maybe he'd even come to apologize for not taking her side in the principal's office all those months ago.

"I don't think you should come inside," Avery said, lessening the venom in her voice. "Not without Mom's permission."

"Yeah, I see that now. I guess I just got . . . I wanted to see you, kid. I didn't think."

The guilt tapped harder on Avery's heart. That's why her dad had come here, unannounced? Simply because he wanted to see her? *Her.* His Veemeister.

Maybe, she thought, she shouldn't turn him away so fast.

"I dunno." She swung her arms, not meeting his gaze. "The race is coming up, so I'm kind of busy. But we could maybe get breakfast together, if you want. If Mom's cool with it. There's this place called Pizza Palace? They have a brunch buffet."

"Pizza for breakfast?" Mr. Miller said, laughing. "I'm in. And don't you worry, I'll be at that race. It's why I'm here, remember?"

Avery looked into her father's eyes. She knew them very well—they were her own after all. That's what her family and friends always said: Avery got everything from her mom, except the bright hazel eyes.

"So . . . you're coming?" she asked him. "You're gonna watch me race?"

Mr. Miller knelt before his daughter. Normally, Avery would find this annoying, him treating her like a little kid.

But now, for some reason, she didn't mind. Maybe it was the smile on her dad's face, or the warm way he said, "Wouldn't miss it for the world."

Inside the house, Radar continued to bark, pressing his nose against the storm door and glaring at Avery's dad.

Mr. Miller laughed again. "Your mom told me you got a dog. Aussie, right? Seems like a good one."

"He is," said Avery, smirking back at Radar.

It's okay, she tried to think at him. *It's fine, you can stop.*

Radar kept barking.

Avery sighed and turned back to her father. That was when she noticed the taxicab idling on the street.

"Came straight from the airport," Mr. Miller said, noting her gaze.

"Huh."

The guilt tapped harder on Avery's heart.

"I should head to my hotel," her dad said, chucking her shoulder—a familiar move Avery hadn't felt in over a year, "but I'll call your mom. We'll set up a time for that breakfast."

Then he was running out to the taxi and shutting himself inside, and the taxi was off, nothing more than a dab of yellow fading against the horizon. Avery glared after the car, trying to make sense of her feelings. There was anger there. Sadness. Guilt. But there was something else, too:

A scrap of hope.

Maybe this time her dad was going to make things right.

TWENTY-TWO

DANDELIONS

G low in the Park was one day away, but Lola wasn't thinking of racing. She sat in the backyard, many feet off from Cedar House, where a patch of dandelions grew. They were untouched by the work of the weed control men who visited the Gils' house every month. Mrs. Gil had been complaining recently about the workers' lack of thoroughness, but secretly, Lola was grateful these dandelions had been spared. To her, they were not *weeds*. They were lovely—perfect, spherical clouds of fluff that blew into the wind like tiny umbrellas. Why did that bother people so much? Lola had read once that people in France *ate* dandelions, stirring them into salads and stews. They appreciated their beauty and their flavor.

Lola was certain she would get on very well in France.

Concentrating hard, Lola drew up the burning blue flame inside.

No danger here, she told herself. *There's no one watching, no one you can hurt. No food, no other kids, and no explosions. It's only you and the flowers.*

Lola focused the flame with her mind, directing it toward the biggest and fullest of the dandelions.

Blow, she thought.

There was a faint crackling inside her head, and then—

The patch of dandelions began to sway, blown by an invisible breeze, which pressed hardest against the biggest of the dandelions, bending back its head until its fluffy seeds detached and took flight, drifting upward into the sunlit sky.

Lola let out a soft cry of delight.

Then the wind whipped to a stop, and a hot summer stillness settled on the yard.

Lola plucked the now-bare dandelion stem.

"I can," she said aloud. "I *can* control it."

Lola still had no explanation for the loud popping sound that had filled her ears at Jensen Ranch, or the way the strange sensation had sent her sprawling to her back. It had felt as though somehow, when she'd tethered the Sardines' thoughts, they had joined powers, if only for a moment. And those powers combined had resulted in something *big.*

But it's nothing to be afraid of, Lola told herself. *It's only* different. *It's only* new.

Lola had found that the more she tethered, the more comfortable she became. She was getting to know the flame inside, making friends with it. Her power didn't have to be frightening.

Over the past few days, Lola had been visiting Avery's place to play with Radar or read books, side by side on the back porch. And every so often, Lola and Avery would form memories to share with each other. As days had passed, the images had grown clearer, filled with more vibrant hues. This, Lola decided, was her favorite form of investigation: giving memories of birthdays, Halloweens, and long, lazy Sundays to Avery. She liked to think that Bastian was right about his memory plan, even if he hadn't been right about Glow Expo. She wanted to believe that memories were how they'd convince the aliens what a wonderful place the world could be. But even if memories weren't the solution, Lola loved getting a glimpse inside Avery's head.

She only wished Nando were here to see how she was changing. It didn't seem fair to Lola that her brother was so close—right here, in Callaway!—and yet so distant.

Sighing, she sank into the grass and looked up at a cloudless blue sky. Droplets of sweat had gathered on her face, and she drew an arm across her forehead. As Lola lay steeped in thought, she heard a distant rustling. She sat up, hoping to catch sight of a rabbit or squirrel.

Instead, she saw a flash of silver.

Alarmed, Lola looked harder. There was something moving in the juniper bushes.

"Hello?" she called. "Who's there?"

There was no reply.

The bushes rustled more violently, and then a figure emerged, the height of a full-grown man, dressed in a silver suit. Lola could not see the figure's face; it was shielded by a sharp-edged helmet. Grasped tight in the figure's gloved hand was a metal rod—held aloft, like a weapon.

"H-hey!" cried Lola, her words faltering in fear.

The figure turned its dark-visored helmet toward her. Lola tried and failed to breathe properly. She couldn't see its eyes— didn't know if it was looking straight at her. Still, it held its weapon aloft.

Lola stumbled to her feet and ran.

She flung herself forward, across the yard, toward the house, and swung open the back door with so much force that it sent a hard *slam* through the kitchen. Shutting the door, she pressed her back against its steady frame, breathing in quick gasps.

After many moments had passed, she summoned her courage and looked out the window. The figure in the silver suit was gone.

But Lola knew it wasn't all in her head.

They were watching her.

They were following her.

Lola just wished she knew who *they* were.

TWENTY-THREE
SECRETS

Bastian was trying not to focus on how his plan at Glow Expo had failed. He was trying to believe that memories were still the key to convincing the light beings not to eradicate Earth. He was trying not to worry about the fact that he was still the only Sardine the aliens hadn't contacted.

At night, he drew new glowboard designs, taking breaks to push the limits of his telekinesis, juggling paint tubes one day and writing out his signature the next—all with his mind. During the day, he worked himself weary at practice, fine-tuning his telepathy through Lola's tether. After practice, Bastian liked to take a break and skate down Callaway's streets, a spray of silver glow shooting out behind him. That was how Bastian skated today, down Third Street, on his way to meet Nando for ice cream.

Nando had met with Bastian and Lola several times before

at the Frozen Spoon, but he never spoke about his work, and he never once came by the house or talked to their parents. Bastian was frustrated by Nando's secrets, but then, he was keeping a mountain of his own. He hadn't breathed a word about the alien message, or the truth behind Taft Middle's food fight, or Nando's stolen work memo. One of those secrets was Lola's, and not his to tell. As for the others, Bastian had made his vow to the Sardines.

But then, there were other secrets Bastian kept. Like how Mitchell's taunts and Zander's betrayal made him so *angry*. To tell Nando all the stuff the Grackles had done to him... it'd be too embarrassing.

Still, Bastian had asked Nando if they could meet, just the two of them, and hang out like old times. Maybe Bastian was hiding some truths, but there was one thing he wasn't afraid to share with his brother: his most recent glowboard designs. There were a dozen of them—new daring geometric patterns—tucked in a portfolio inside his backpack.

Glow in the Park was only one day away, and the Sardines had held their very last practice on Hazard Hill. Their method of tethering was almost perfected now, and they'd made 2:12, their best time yet. The Sardines were going to beat the Grackles at Glow in the Park. At last, they were going to prove to Zander that he'd chosen the wrong team. They were going to show Mitchell what a *girl* team could do.

It was in this state of mind that Bastian swished past the big glass windows of Tazza Fresca, Callaway's busiest coffee shop. He skated on for a few more seconds before carving to a stop. Then, slowly, he hovered his board back to the shop-window. He hadn't seen wrong: There was Nando, sitting at a window-side table, his green briefcase by his side.

Nando wasn't alone. Sitting across from him was a broad-shouldered man with a mustache, dressed in a tan suit and a wide-brimmed hat: Carl Jensen, King of Callaway. Bastian stared, uncomprehending, as the two men rose to their feet and Mr. Jensen extended his hand. Nando shook it with a big, friendly smile.

Then Nando's gaze shifted, and he locked eyes with Bastian through the glass.

Panicked, Bastian kicked up his board and fled. Seconds later, he heard the clang of a storefront bell and footsteps thudding behind him.

"Bastian!" Nando yelled. "Hang on! Hold up!"

Bastian kept skating, but only for a few more halfhearted seconds. Then, tense all over, he slowed the board to a stop.

"Hey!" Nando caught up and grabbed Bastian by the shoulder. Bastian waved his arms frantically, but it was too late to correct his balance. He fell from his board, hitting the concrete with a painful *whump*.

"God, Bastian! I'm sorry." Nando reached down a hand, but Bastian, still trembling with pain, swatted it back.

"You can't just— You don't . . . *You don't know anything about glowboarding!*"

Nando drew back. "I . . . You're right. I don't."

Bastian got to his feet. "Why were you talking to Mr. Jensen? What were you doing in there?" He thought of the stolen memo, marked *DGE*. "Were you and him making some kind of deal?"

Nando's eyes flashed. "I've told you before, Bastian, I can't discuss my work."

Nando looked genuinely upset, but that only made Bastian angrier. Words swirled in his mind: *Grackles, freak, skate like a girl.*

"The Jensens are the worst," Bastian spat out. "Just so you know. Mitchell's a bully, and his dad is a jerk. Everyone in Callaway knows that. So if you're with Mr. Jensen, then you're not on the Sardines' side. You're not on *my* side."

Bastian grabbed for his board, but Nando beat him to it, scooping up the still-hovering machine.

"Give it to me!" Bastian shouted.

"Not until you let me explain."

"But you won't explain!" Bastian countered. "It's all work secrets. You say the door is always open, but it's *not*."

"You're right."

Bastian blinked. "Wh-what?"

"You're right," Nando said again. "You're right to feel angry, Bash. But I'd like to explain what I can. And I still owe you an ice cream, don't I?"

Bastian hesitated. He could grab his board from Nando and take off. But that wasn't what he wanted. He wanted things to be like they had been before. Before Nando's fights with their parents. Before he had left for DC. Before Bastian's life had become so confusing.

Bastian just wanted one less secret between them.

"You can buy me a chocolate coconut fudge," he decided aloud. "Two scoops."

"There's something going on in Callaway," Nando told Bastian.

Bastian's shirt was damp with sweat, and melted chocolate ice cream trickled down his fingers. The summer heat kept away eavesdroppers, though, leaving him and Nando alone on the Frozen Spoon's rooftop patio. It was the perfect place to share a secret.

"It's something exciting," Nando continued. "Something brand-new. And I get to be part of it."

"Something...with Gloworks?" Bastian spoke carefully, afraid that any wrong word would make Nando stop talking.

"Maybe." Nando smiled a strange smile. Then he leaned in close, over his praline sundae. "Can I let you in on a secret?"

OF COURSE, Bastian shouted inside. *THAT'S ALL I WANT.*

"Sure" was what he said.

"All right." Nando's brown eyes were twinkling. "It's not a coincidence I'm back in Callaway. My people? They recruited me here, at the university, because they wanted someone who knew the terrain and the residents. Because of what's happening here." Bastian's skin prickled as Nando went on. "We don't know much yet, but we're going to. We have a great team of researchers. And soon...this is going to be big, Bastian. It might change everything."

What's happening? Bastian asked inside, the blue flame waxing. *What kind of researchers? Here to research* what?

"That's cool" was what he said.

"Change *everything*," Nando repeated, his face alight. "Even the war. Think about that: We could even change *the war*."

Bastian blinked. He had that bad feeling again—the one he'd first gotten when he'd read Nando's departmental memo. "So," Bastian said, tossing the sticky napkins onto the table, "what you're working on is important, and whatever's important is happening here in Callaway. I kind of already knew those things. Where's the secret in that?"

Nando rubbed at his bearded cheek. "The *why* is still confidential. It has to be, Bastian. I wish you could understand. All I'm trying to tell you is that I'm working on something *good*. Something worthwhile. And I know how you feel about the Jensens, but please, if you can, believe me? I'm trying to do the right thing."

Bastian stared at the Callaway horizon, brow furrowed. Nando wasn't telling him a secret. He was just telling Bastian to trust him.

"Hey," said Nando, nudging Bastian. "You okay?"

Bastian glanced down, discovering that his right arm was covered in melted ice cream. Nando was already tugging napkins out of a holder, and he handed them over with a cautious smile. Bastian wiped up the chocolaty mess, keeping his eyes downcast.

Did he trust Nando? Did he trust him about this whole business with Gloworks and Mr. Jensen? Maybe not. But he did trust his brother with something else—a secret that Bastian, at least, was willing to tell.

"Mitchell hasn't stopped," he said, then the words came out in a rush. "He's been...*bullying* me even worse. Every single day he sees me in school, in the hallway? He'll say, 'Here comes Mrs. Gil!' Like it's some big joke. In PE, we were playing dodgeball, and he told all his friends to throw their balls at me. And he tripped me at a football game, on the bleachers." Bastian held up his right arm, showing the faint outline of a scar. "I told you things were great, but...they're not. Mitchell and the Grackles, they make me feel like...I'm nothing. And I know I'm supposed to be strong and not let them bother me. I know. But it *does* bother me, all the time. They try to make me feel bad for hanging out with Lola and the others. Like it's something to be ashamed of. But I'm *not* ashamed. It's just hard."

Bastian felt winded, as though he'd run miles. Now the words were out of him, in the open, and he felt...relieved.

Nando was quiet before he said, "Bash, you don't have to feel strong. You don't have to pretend what they say doesn't hurt you." He leaned in closer, smelling of spiced pralines. "You don't play by their rules. You make your own. You do what you're great at, you be *happy*. That's the best revenge you can get on any bully. Their words might hurt, but you're bigger than words. They can't stop you from living your life. From glowboarding like a champ. From making amazing art."

Bastian's heart flipped at that. "I brought some," he said, eagerly, turning to his backpack and zipping it open. "New designs. I wanted you to see, tell me what you think." He threw the portfolio on the table. "If they're crap, just say so."

Nando opened the portfolio. He looked over one glowboard sketch, then turned it over and studied the next. Another sketch, and another. He looked at them in silence as Bastian sat watchful, hands clasped between his knees. The rest of his chocolate coconut fudge was melting in its cup, but Bastian didn't care.

At last, Nando closed the portfolio. His brown eyes were shining—an expression Bastian couldn't read.

"Wh-what?" Bastian asked.

"They're good," Nando said.

Bastian's heart sank. *Good?* That wasn't what he wanted from Nando. He wanted *real* feedback. He wanted—

"You have to stop showing them to me now."

Bastian's stomach twisted. *"What?"*

Was Nando going to tell Bastian that he was too busy these days? That he didn't have time for silly sketches anymore? That he didn't have time for *Bastian?* That—

"I mean," Nando said, "you need to start showing them to other people."

Bastian blinked. "But other people don't—"

"They're glowboard designs," Nando interrupted. "Aren't they?"

"Well, yeah."

"For whose glowboards?"

Bastian studied his sticky, ice-cream-filmed hands. "No one's."

"That isn't right." Nando jabbed his finger against the portfolio. "This is *good*, Bash. I know it's scary, showing your work to people you don't know. People you don't think *get* you. I know Zander let you down before, and that hurt. But this is what I'm talking about: This is *living*. It's something that makes you happy and could make other people happy, too. Don't you think your Sardines would love a Bastian Gil original glowboard design?"

Bastian made a face. "I mean, I don't know."

"They *would*," said Nando. "Stop showing me, Bash, and show the world. That's my advice for this artwork of yours. And that's how you show those bullies how strong you are. You do what you love, and you do it well. Share them, Bash."

Bastian's ice cream was now a chocolate puddle. Very slowly, he nodded. Nando's words weren't easy, and they weren't what Bastian had expected. But they made sense, and more than that, they filled Bastian with new hope.

"Okay," he said, taking back the portfolio. "Thanks for the advice."

TWENTY-FOUR

THE BLUE VAN

Some days, Dani went out to Hazard Hill by herself, with no intention of practicing. But just because she wasn't there to skate didn't mean she wasn't there *for* skating. Glow in the Park was only one day away, and Dani's every waking thought and restless dream had to do with glowboarding. This close to race day, Dani had a tradition: She went to Hazard Hill and sat on its crest, at the very place where the starting line would be activated. There, she envisioned the Sardines' full descent.

With her digiwatch in hand, she whispered each passing second aloud, picturing the draft train and every inch of its formation. She pictured her teammates' faces, drawn in hard lines of concentration, using their newfound advantage of tethering. She pictured the cheering crowd that bordered the track and grew denser and louder the farther down the

Sardines skated. Dani envisioned the finish line, drawn out in glowing red laser light. She pictured Avery crossing that line at precisely the right moment. She could see it all so clearly. One day from now, her vision would turn to reality. One day from now, the Sardines would finally *win*.

There was one thing that Dani didn't let herself envision: the expressions on the Grackles' faces when they were defeated. That, she wanted to save. She wanted to be totally surprised by Mitchell Jensen's reaction the moment the official announced the Sardines' record-breaking time. Then she wanted to look Zander Poxleitner straight in the eye and give him the biggest smile she'd ever smiled in her life.

Lola would be upset if she knew about this part of Dani's plan. She would call it mean. She would call it gloating. But Lola was too nice for her own good, and anyway, *she* wasn't the team captain.

Also, Lola hadn't once had a crush on Zander Poxleitner.

Not that it was a crush *exactly*, but Dani had liked Zander a lot—more than she'd liked any other boy before or since. And Zander, in typical traitor form, had made her think he'd liked her back, before he ruined everything. He'd never given the Sardines an explanation for why he'd moved away from his house at 29 Cedar Lane or joined the Grackles at the start of last summer. He'd simply left.

Yes, Dani would admit, she had refused to speak to Zander in the hallways or after school. His actions had done all the talking, though, hadn't they? She'd had to find out about his defection from Mitchell Jensen himself, in front of his whole horrible crew. So what if she hadn't let Zander explain himself? Nothing he could say would make things right again.

Angrily, Dani got to her feet. She placed her fists on her hips and looked down on the winding track.

Victory, she instructed herself. *Envision victory.*

She closed her eyes and heard the cheer of the crowd, smelled the smoke of a fireworks celebration, saw the gleam of the first-place trophy. Once she had that trophy, Mitchell would have to shut up. Once she had that trophy, her parents would have to hold up their end of the deal; there'd be no more fights at home about swim team, and at last, Dani could get a new board. And once all that was settled, *then* Dani could think a little harder about aliens and the end of the world.

One step at a time—that was Dani Hirsch's philosophy.

Dani skated down Hazard Hill in a lazy putter, careful not to overexert herself or her board. She didn't believe in practicing right before big races. The Sardines had already put in the hard work, and now it was time to store their energy. Now was the great big breath before the plunge.

When she reached the hill's base, she turned east, toward the city, pushing off the ground in long strides. This was desolate, desert land, made of rock and sand, of steep cliffs and crags. Overhead, the cloudless sky stretched out in all directions, and the sun beat down on her face. She was hot and sweaty, sure, but Dani liked the heat. By the time she got home, maybe she'd even want a cold power smoothie.

Cars passed Dani on the road, shimmers of colored metal that winked light into her eyes. She skated at a safe distance, watching cautiously as each zoomed by. Then, glancing back, she noticed a large blue van crawling up behind her. She glided over, past the edge of the road, to let the van pass.

But the van didn't pass. It remained behind her, traveling at a slow, measured pace.

Dani frowned, putting more energy into her push-offs.

She glanced again at the steadily moving van, trying to make out the face of the driver. All she could see was that they were wearing silver, as was the figure in the passenger seat.

Not just silver.

Silver suits.

Dani swallowed hard and looked ahead. Callaway was only minutes away. If she could make it into town, and out of this wide-open space, she could shake the van easily enough.

Dani skated faster.

The thrum of the van engine changed pitch, a slight acceleration. Dani swallowed again. She was too afraid now to look back. She had to focus on getting to town. *She had to get to town.*

Dani skated even faster. As she did, her board began to stutter, hiccuping globs of orange glow behind her. Dani teetered, off-balance, and whispered, "Hang in there. Don't die on me now."

A little green car was approaching from the opposite direction. Frantically, Dani considered if she should try to flag them down.

If they stop for you, she thought, *the van will speed away, and those people in the car will think you're crazy.*

But that's what I want, Dani told her rational thoughts. *I want the silver suits to speed away.*

She raised her hand and waved toward the car, waving and waving ... until they passed.

Maybe they hadn't been looking, or they hadn't understood. Dani was still skating after all. She probably looked like some kid goofing off.

But I can't stop skating, Dani thought miserably. *If I do, the van will catch up, and then—*

Dani didn't know what happened *then.* She only knew she didn't want to find out.

Her board was struggling, shuddering every few seconds, but it hadn't died on her yet. She no longer liked the feel of damp heat on her skin. Everything on her—bangle bracelets, charms on her sneakers, even *sweat*—was weighing her down.

Still, the van didn't speed up, didn't draw nearer. There were no shouts, no blaring horns. The silver suits were simply *following,* in time with every stroke Dani made.

I'm telling Mom and Dad, she thought. *This is why they should let me have my own phone.*

Then, finally, *finally,* a shiny Texaco sign came into view, the first building on the western edge of town. Its red-and-white star had never looked so beautiful. Soon, many other buildings appeared: storefronts and banks and apartment complexes. More cars filled the road, and the traffic became steady. Streets took shape, forming into intersections Dani knew by heart.

Dani took a sharp turn onto Euclid Street and kept on for many more moments, pushing her sneaker off the asphalt in rapid strokes.

Then it happened.

There was an awful groaning sound beneath her feet. A *crash, scrape, swish.*

Dani threw out her arms, desperate for balance as she fell forward onto the sidewalk. When she looked back, she saw the awful reality: Her board had given out and now lay motionless, several feet off, in the bike lane.

"NO!" Dani shouted, lunging for it, just as an oncoming pickup truck honked loudly, swerving to the right. She grabbed hold of the board, tumbling back onto the sidewalk as the truck barreled past.

For several moments, all Dani did was breathe—shallow gasps that ricocheted through her body. Then she sat up, inspecting her scraped palms and bloodied right knee. Blinking, she took in the scene around her. To any other passerby, it would seem like a normal day in Callaway. Light traffic continued to pass on the street. The sun blazed down through leafy green trees. A congregation of grackles, gathered on a telephone line, chattered obnoxiously.

The blue van wasn't around. Dani didn't see it anywhere.

But that didn't mean she felt safe.

Wincing, Dani got to her feet, inspecting her board.

"Come on," she pleaded. "This can't be it. You've got more glow in you, I know it. *Come on*."

Gingerly placing the board on the sidewalk, she flipped the power switch.

Nothing happened.

"Come *on*," Dani demanded.

She reset the board and flipped the switch again, almost violently.

Nothing.

Desperation had brought hot, stinging tears to Dani's eyes. Sitting down beside the board, she placed her left hand atop it, gently stroking the chipped blue paint.

"Please," she coaxed. "I need you to hang on one more day. I need you for this race. We can do it, together."

Then Dani shut her eyes and, one last time, tried the power switch.

There was a low, rickety whirring noise. A garbled cough. Then there was the sweetest sound that Dani had ever heard: the hum of power.

Her eyes flew open.

"YES!" she shouted, fist pumping the air. "We're back in business!"

Dani didn't waste another second. Even though there was no sign of the blue van, that didn't mean it wasn't still out there, searching for her. She had to get out of sight.

Buzzing with determination, Dani stepped on the board and set out onto the street, speeding ahead, tears still blurring her eyes.

Bleeeeeep.

Dani startled at the shriek of a horn, turning in time to see that she had flown through a four-way stop. A man in a giant SUV was raising his hands toward her, shouting. She raised her own in apology, but still, she didn't stop skating.

She didn't stop until she reached Cedar Lane.

The man in the navy suit was having a very bad day.

"It's unacceptable," he said. "What part of *stealth* did those drivers not understand?"

"You did give them orders," replied the woman with the high ponytail. "You said you wanted them monitored more closely, individually."

"I *said* I wanted basic surveillance, not careless incompetence. Now that Hirsch girl is on her guard, and I have a very good reason to suspect the boy is onto us, too."

"The boy," said the woman, looking up from the digipad she'd been typing into. "Sebastian Gil."

The man took a seat, slumping in exhaustion. He placed a hand to his forehead and sighed. "I think he's been placated for now, but there's no real way of knowing. We're *this* close to the twentieth, and now—"

"Do you think," said the woman, "your plan is still viable?"

The man in the navy suit looked up sharply. "Of course it is. I told the DGE they could trust me, and I never betray a trust. The plan will still work." The man pointed to five photographs tacked on the wall. "They're different, each one of them, but what's the common denominator? It all comes back to Component G."

"And glowboarding," said the woman.

"And when do we know the subjects will all be gathered together? At the race, tomorrow. They'll be in one location, and they'll be fatigued after competing."

"They'll practically skate into our hands," murmured the woman, frowning at her digipad. "And after that, they'll be in the department's custody?"

A dark look crossed the man's face. "In theory, yes. That's how the plan works."

At that moment, there was a knock on the door.

"Yes?" called the woman.

A short, owlish man shuffled into the room, looking like he'd rather be anywhere else on earth.

"What is it, Smith?" asked the man in the navy suit.

"That reporter, sir," said Smith. "The, erm, documentarian. He's been quite insistent. It's the third time he's called today. What should I tell him?"

The man in the navy suit glanced at the woman. She answered with an almost imperceptible shrug.

"Tell him I'll speak to him," said the man. "Make a phone appointment for this afternoon."

Smith nodded and left the office.

The woman studied the closed door as she said, "I can't believe we're this close."

"It's staggering," the man agreed. "DC is waiting on tenterhooks. This is going to change everything: our diplomacy, war strategy. With leverage like this, we'll be back in the game. Imagine the threat they'll pose when they're properly trained, when their energy has been harnessed. This war is going to end. *Peace—* what we've all been fighting for—will finally be a reality. And we'll be the ones to make that happen. *Us.*"

The man in the navy suit was having a bad day, but now at least his mind was feeling clearer. He had regained his focus. From here on out, there would be no more mistakes.

Now it was only a matter of waiting for race day.

TWENTY-FIVE

STARS

Tonight, Bastian was working with oranges and blues. Using pastels, he filled in an ink design that he had finished a few days earlier: five stars scattered across a midnight sky. This wasn't a constellation, like the plastic stars above his head. He gave these stars no pattern and no special names. They simply existed, bold and true, on a glowboard stencil.

That's the best revenge you can get on any bully. . . . They can't stop you from living your life.

That's what Nando had told him.

Now, on the eve of race day, before the Sardines faced the Grackles, Bastian meant to take his form of revenge, however small. He was going to live his life. He was going to make art.

The sun was going down, and only Bastian's desk lamp lit the room. Dusk—that was Bastian's time. He felt most alive in the early evening, brimming with ideas, his hands itching to create. Though tonight, his thoughts wandered as he worked. He was thinking about a sheet of paper marked *DGE*, folded into a swan, and about Mr. Jensen shaking Nando's hand in the coffee shop. He was thinking about tethering and a race time of 2:12. He was thinking about the light beings and what they had told Dani about an "elixir." He felt close to a revelation, right on its edge.

Then Bastian looked down at his design.

He had been filling in a star, careful of his work, drawing and coloring in small triangles. At least . . . that's what Bastian *thought* he had been doing. But the paper told a different story.

Bastian's stars had transformed. They had taken on the shape of people—five figures, gathered together in a circle, their hands joined.

"What?" Bastian said, under his breath, afraid to break the spell.

Was this what he thought it was? What he'd been waiting for? Was this *them*?

Hello? Bastian formed the thought and pushed it outward. *Who's there?*

That was when the static filled his ears.

The Grand Canyon, Bastian thought. *Picture it. Show them. Show them.*

He tried to paint the picture in his mind: unthinkably deep ravines, a crystalline blue sky, his grinning face as his family unpacked a birthday picnic. He had to show the light beings. He had to change their minds. This was his chance.

The static grew louder, and Bastian pressed his hands to his ears. The noise was so loud he couldn't concentrate. Then a voice broke through, forceful, flooding his mind.

You must be united when we reach you. All five of you must be joined together. Without unity, we cannot...convey...full message...

The static was back, louder than ever, overpowering the voice.

No, Bastian reached out, frantic. *Wait. What day are you going to meet us? Please, you have to listen. We don't want you to eradicate Earth. We have good memories to show you. Things that make Earth worth saving. Please!*

The static disappeared. The voice did, too. Silence deafened Bastian, and he stared at his art. His stars had resumed their usual shapes, as though nothing unordinary had occurred. They taunted Bastian, shining in a blue paper sky.

Then a new sound filled his mind:

Bastian? You in here?

Light flooded the room, and Bastian cried out, shooting so far back in his rolling chair that he thumped into the bed.

Lola stood in the doorway, looking equally startled. "Dani says—she says..." Lola frowned distractedly at the artwork on Bastian's desk. Quickly, he flipped it over, crossing his arms atop the mysterious stars.

"Dani says what?"

An emergency meeting, Lola told him. *She says we have to talk. Right away.*

Yeah, Bastian answered, his every nerve alight. *Yeah, we do.*

TWENTY-SIX
EMERGENCY MEETING

Dani sat inside Cedar House, cross-legged and stone-faced. Avery arrived first, full of questions, but Dani shook her head in reply to all of them. She wasn't going to speak until every Sardine was present. So Avery finally took a seat, and Radar flopped down beside her, producing a lazy yawn.

"Me too, bud," said Avery, scratching his ears. "This better be good."

At last, Lola and Bastian arrived, taking their beanbag seats. Even then, Dani didn't speak for a few moments more.

"We're being watched," she finally announced. "Someone's after us."

"*What?*" Avery asked, looking around the circle in alarm. Beside her, Radar pricked his ears.

This afternoon, said Lola, breaking into Dani's thoughts. She took a moment to adjust as Lola formed the tether among the Sardines. Then Lola continued with wide, watery eyes. *I was right out there in the yard when I saw someone in the bushes. A silver suit.*

"Lols!" Bastian said aloud. "Why didn't you say so before?"

Lola's eyes grew waterier. "I don't know. I guess... part of me thought I'd made it all up?"

"You didn't," said Dani. "Or if you made it up, then I did, too."

She told them then about the blue van and the nerve-racking chase back to Callaway.

"I don't get it," said Avery when Dani was through. "They didn't try to run you over or send you off the road. They didn't say a thing. They just followed you, and then they disappeared? What does that get them?"

"Maybe they made a mistake," Bastian said. "Or they were waiting for an order that never came."

"Or they're trying to intimidate us," said Dani. "Make us scared."

"They're doing a good job," Lola mumbled.

"There's something else, too," Dani said. "My board—when they were chasing me, it gave out."

"WHAT?" the others cried.

"It's okay now. I got it to work again. But Glow in the Park can't come fast enough, that's all I'm saying." Dani nodded to Bastian and Avery. "Have you two seen anything weird?"

"Not weirder than usual," Avery said. "Not since the aliens showed me their own TV show."

"You, Bastian?" Dani asked.

Bastian looked around at the others. He licked his lips. "Not silver suits. But . . . something else. The aliens. They made contact with me."

"When?" Dani demanded. "What the heck, Bastian? You're just now telling us?"

"Because it just happened," Bastian said, hotly. "Literally *just happened*. They used my artwork."

"Well, what did they say?" Avery cried. "Did they tell you the date? When are we supposed to meet them? *Which* midnight?"

Bastian looked grim. "They didn't give a day. They said something else. Something about how the five of us have to be together. And then . . . the message was breaking up, but they made it sound like, if the five of us *aren't* together, we won't be able to make contact. We've talked about how the aliens keep using our memories, right?"

"Yeah," said Dani. "That's kind of your whole theory for how we're gonna stop them."

"Well," said Bastian, "the art on my paper—it was an image, but I didn't recognize it. There were five people standing in a circle. Not four, *five*. I don't have any memories like that."

The Sardines went quiet.

Then Avery said, "The *five* of us together. Do they mean . . . Radar?"

Bastian shrugged, looking helpless. "I guess? But he usually hangs out with us anyway. I don't see why that was so important for the aliens to tell us."

"You're *sure* they didn't say anything else?" Dani pressed.

"Hey, it's not my fault!" Bastian shouted. "I tried to talk to them. I even tried to share my memories, I *swear.*"

"No one said it's your fault," Lola said, touching her brother's shoulder. "We know you did your best."

"It has to be connected," Dani whispered. "Our powers and the aliens' message and those silver suits. It all has to be connected. I just don't know *how.*"

"Do you think they know?" Lola asked. "The silver suits. Do they know what we can do?"

Dani thought back to her first sight of the suits, in front of Taft Middle. They had been there to investigate what Lola had done in the cafeteria. Now they were showing up in Lola's backyard.

"Yeah," Dani said. "I think they do."

Avery studied the ground. With a pensive expression, she said, "I've been thinking of something else, too. Something about our memory plan."

Bastian flinched. "The plan's going to work. Maybe Glow Expo wasn't the right place, but—"

"No, I know," Avery interrupted. "I still think it's a good hypothesis. But I've been thinking, back at Glow Expo, all our memories—they were nice, but they were kind of random: a glowboard, rainbow sprinkles, the Grand Canyon. Well, Lola and I . . . we've practiced sharing our memories together. And personally, the ones that have stood out? They're not of things, they're of *people*. Memories with my mom and with you all. I wonder if maybe we should focus on memories like that. Memories of people we love." She cast a tentative look at Lola, then the others. "I think those are the most powerful."

Bastian seemed to consider Avery's words before saying, "Yeah. I mean, *yeah*. That makes sense."

"Avery's right," added Lola. "Those *are* the best memories she and I have shared."

"Well," said Dani, "it can't hurt. Memories of people, huh?"

"Memories of people you *love*," Avery clarified. "Connection, you know? That's got to convince the aliens this world's worth keeping around." She scrunched her nose. "Now, what about the DGE? We still don't know what that is. Do you all think it's connected to the silver suits?"

Dani made a face. "The silver suits are creepy, and they're watching us. That's all we need to know. Does it matter who they are, or who sent them?"

"I think it matters a lot," Avery replied. "We don't know who's on our side right now, who we can trust. We all agreed not to tell our parents, but"—Avery pointed at Lola—"you and Bastian showed us that memo from Nando. We never decided we could trust *him*."

Lola's eyes got big. "What's that supposed to mean? You think... Nando is one of the bad guys?"

"No," Avery said. "Not necessarily. But we can't—"

"Hey," Bastian interrupted. "Nando can be trusted. He's our brother."

"Okay," Avery said slowly, "but he *is* with a secret government organization. And you two are his brother and sister." She reached out to touch Lola's arm. "Maybe you're too close to know if—"

"What?" Lola cried, pushing Avery's hand away. She staggered to her feet. "I—I can't believe you'd actually think that. You *know* Nando. He's only been nice to you."

"Yeah, but he—"

Lola shook her head fiercely, her eyes shining in Cedar House's twinkle lights. "How could you say something like that?"

Avery raised her hands. "It was only an idea. I didn't mean—"

"No. *No.* I don't want to hear any more." Lola turned to Dani. "Is the meeting adjourned?"

"Uh..." said Dani, bewildered. When there were fights in Cedar House, Lola was never part of them; that was Dani's territory. Avery looked just as shocked. "Uh..." she repeated. "Yeah, I guess. There's nothing else new to discuss."

And so the Sardines filed out of Cedar House and into the starlit night, Lola stomping ahead past Avery. But just as they were walking away, Radar let out a deep bark.

"Hey, calm down, boy," Avery said.

Radar barked louder, more insistently, pointing his nose back toward Cedar House.

"What is it?" Avery looked around. "A squirrel? *What?*"

"Look." Bastian pointed to a piece of paper tacked above

the clubhouse entrance, fluttering in the wind. Dani stepped ahead of the others and ripped the paper down from the brass tack holding it in place.

The message was in red ink, written in a bold and slanted script:

STAY AWAY FROM HAZARD HILL.
AVOID THE RACE AT ALL COSTS.

SINCERELY,
A FRIEND

TWENTY-SEVEN

PIZZA PALACE

A very sat in a booth alone, a copy of *The Hobbit*, by J. R. R. Tolkien, on the table in front of her. Normally, Avery relished any chance she had to read a chapter or two, uninterrupted, when she had a spare moment. This morning, though, she couldn't concentrate, no matter how much peril the hobbit Bilbo Baggins was in. This morning, her dad was fifteen minutes late (and counting) for their brunch appointment at Pizza Palace. And this morning, Avery was thinking about what awaited her on Hazard Hill. Nothing but danger, if the note tacked to Cedar House was to be believed.

Dani was convinced that the Grackles had written the message.

"Friend? Yeah, right," she'd said. "They're trying to rattle us."

Bastian had agreed with Dani, but Lola had stayed quiet. Avery had asked, "What if it's the silver suits?"

"The silver suits are *after* us," Dani had said. "Why would they warn us?"

Avery had shaken her head at that. "Maybe it's someone who *knows* the silver suits. Who knows something we don't."

In the end, the Sardines had come to no certain conclusion, but Dani had crumpled the note and said, "We won't be scared off. The race is everything. Nothing's changed."

Only, something *had* changed between Lola and Avery.

Wincing, Avery remembered how Lola had pushed away her hand in Cedar House, deep hurt in her eyes. She wished now, more than anything, that she could take back what she'd said about Nando . . . even if she did think it might be true. Avery didn't *want* for Nando to be on the side of the silver suits, but he *had* arrived in Callaway at a very convenient time, and he *was* working for the government, in a top secret job that not even Lola and Bastian knew details about. Wasn't it possible that he could be telling the silver suits secrets of his own? Secrets that Lola and Bastian had shared with him? Only, they'd never suspect him because he was their family.

Still, Avery thought, *you shouldn't have said so.*

She couldn't shake the memory of that terrible look on Lola's face, or the way she'd stormed out of Cedar House. And now, in the morning light, every minute that ticked by felt like an eternity. Where was her dad? Avery was wasting time—time she could be at Lola's house, apologizing.

Pizza Palace was filled with the buzz and bloop of old-fashioned arcade games. Pinball machines lit up in displays of colored lights, beckoning players to plunk down their quarters. In one corner, a couple of kids were taking turns at *Ms. Pac-Man*, shouting whenever one of them lost a round. There were families all around, digging into plates piled high with cinnamon sticks, salads, and Pizza Palace's famous breakfast pizza: crust topped with spinach and home fries and slathered in cheddar cheese.

"Hey, kid."

Dani looked up at the waitress who'd stopped by her table—a grumpy-looking teenager with a chewed-up pen tucked over her ear.

"The place is packed," the waitress said, "and you're taking up a perfectly good booth."

"I know," said Avery. "I'm waiting on—"

"Don't care who you're waiting on," the waitress snapped. "If your party doesn't show in the next five minutes, you're gonna have to get up."

The waitress didn't stick around for Avery to reply. She stalked off to another table to set down ruby-red tumblers of orange juice and soda.

Avery looked at the clock above the salad bar. It was almost nine thirty, which meant her dad was almost a whole half hour late. Avery felt like slumping down in the booth and disappearing from view. The next time the waitress came by, she'd leave before she could get into trouble. She'd just glowboard home with an empty stomach.

Another minute passed, and Avery swallowed, trying to combat the awful dryness in her throat. Had her dad canceled plans *again* and, this time, forgotten to clue her in? She should've known better. She should've—

Mr. Miller burst through the front door, a phone held to his ear, searching the restaurant with frantic eyes. Avery raised a hand to get his attention, and when he spotted her, he hurried her way with an apologetic grin.

"Whew," he said, reaching the table. "You'll never believe the phone call I've been having. Didn't realize a place like Callaway was filled with as many charlatan rental car companies as there are in LA."

Avery, still a little stunned, stammered out, "R-rental car?"

"Well, sure, Veemeister." Her dad laughed. "Didn't think I was going to be chauffeured all around town, did you? Took way more negotiating than I thought, but I finally got something lined up. Anyway, you hungry?"

Avery bit her lip. She'd noted that, for all his excuses, her dad hadn't said he was sorry for showing up late.

"Yeah, I'm starving," she said pointedly.

Still grinning, Mr. Miller waved down the grumpy teen waitress, who didn't get any less grumpy when he ordered two buffets and a coffee with soy milk, *not* regular, and stevia, *not* sugar. Then he and Avery received their plates and filled up at the buffet. Avery picked out two cheese sticks, two cinnamon sticks, and the three biggest pieces of breakfast pizza she could find.

"Healthy appetite," her dad noted when they took their seats.

In reply, Avery shook a hefty helping of pepper flakes on everything—cinnamon sticks included. Then she took a giant bite of her first slice of pizza.

Mr. Miller picked at his house salad. "It's a beautiful day for a race," he observed.

Avery gave an affirmative grunt through her pizza-filled mouth. Then she took a long gulp of her Dr Pepper.

"Do you even know what kind of race it is?" she finally said.

"Sure I do. Your mom told me about it, and you'll be impressed: I did some research online. Draft training, huh? Looks pretty cool."

"So, what?" she asked. "Did your documentary plans get canceled?"

Mr. Miller blinked in surprise. "Why would you say that?"

"Dunno," said Avery. "It's just really weird that you'd want to come here when you've got work to do."

Her dad speared a cucumber slice and chewed it in silence. Then he said, "You know, Vee, I'd really like to talk about *you* this morning. Not work. This is Avery's day."

Avery felt a tap on her heart—a small fracturing. She'd be lying if she said she hadn't wished for her dad to say those exact words. But hearing them now, she didn't feel particularly better. She was still mad.

"So," she said, "what do you want to know about me?"

"Well, what have you been up to? How's school been? Why

did you decide to get a dog? All of that. *Any* of that. Whatever you want to talk about."

Avery studied her dad's hazel eyes. *Her* eyes. Then she decided to be honest. Partly honest, anyway.

"I've been skating, mostly. Practicing for the race. School's been okay, but I'm glad it's out for the summer because there's this kid there named Mitchell that I don't like. And I got a dog because Mom said I could, and he's great. I'm going to train him to jump a four-foot fence."

Mr. Miller's eyebrows shot sky-high. "Impressive."

Avery found herself smiling a little. "Yeah, I know. Radar's the best."

"I imagine," Mr. Miller said after some silent eating, "it's a strange new time for you. I remember being your age. A lot of changes, but a lot of excitement, too. You'll be in high school soon. That's a big deal."

"Yeah," Avery said noncommittally. "I guess."

"So, you've noticed changes? In your life?"

Avery squinted. She suddenly felt less like she was talking to her own dad and more like she was chatting with Taft Middle's guidance counselor.

"What kind of changes?" she asked.

"Oh, I don't know. In your mood, your day-to-day life."

Avery squinted harder. "Are you . . . talking about *puberty*?"

"What?" Her dad looked shocked at first, then burst into laughter. Avery had forgotten the way her father laughed—lightly, like popcorn kernels popping. "Veemeister, you're something. I forgot what a killer sense of humor you have."

The fracture in Avery's heart got bigger. Did her dad really think that? Sure, Lola laughed at Avery's jokes, but did her dad think they were *really* funny?

"I guess things have changed a little," Avery admitted, careful with her words. "Life's definitely harder now than it was when I was, like, nine. I have competitions to worry about, and homework's harder, and we've got the Grackles to beat."

Mr. Miller nodded at everything Avery said, but he didn't look exactly satisfied by her answer. There was a kind of impatience in his eyes as he listened to Avery elaborate on the Sardines' rivalry with the Grackles.

When she was finished, he didn't say anything for a while, just ate his salad.

Then, right as Avery was swallowing a chunk of cheese stick, he asked, "Do you remember what happened at your school in LA? That . . . meeting with the principal?"

Avery almost choked. She coughed a few times, pounding a fist to her chest, and somehow managed to swallow the rest of the cheesy bread lodged there.

Did she remember? What kind of question was that?

"Uh . . . yeah?" she managed. "I remember."

"Were you telling the truth that day? You really didn't vandalize the bathroom, like that girl said?"

"I told you I didn't," Avery said.

And you didn't believe me, a cold voice inside her added.

Her dad nodded, thoughtful, then asked, "Is there anything else you want to tell me about that day?"

Avery could have told him a lot. She could've told him how

that was the day everything changed. It was the day she'd lost Katelyn as a friend and found out she had tele-whatevers. It was the day she'd learned that he, her own father, didn't have her back.

Avery only crossed her arms and said, "That was a long time ago. I've got nothing left to tell."

Her dad studied her then, with those same almost impatient eyes. He seemed ready to say something else, *ask* something else. But then he smiled, very broadly, and said, "I'm so glad this trip worked out. And the food's fantastic, Veemeister. Excellent recommendation."

Avery didn't see how some iceberg lettuce, cucumbers, and carrot shreds could be *fantastic*, so she offered her dad one of her breakfast pizza slices. He was reluctant at first, but once he tried it, he wouldn't stop raving. Then he and Avery talked about normal things, like the documentary he had been working on and the books Avery had been reading, including the one on the table. Mr. Miller told her that he'd first read *The Hobbit* when he was thirteen, too, and he'd been such a fan he'd made drawings of Gandalf every day in study hall for months—so often that once some kids caught wind, they'd called him Gandalf the Goof for the rest of junior high.

Avery made a face. "I guess you had to deal with your own Grackles."

Smiling, Mr. Miller said, "Something like that."

Talking became easier, and both Avery and her dad went back to the buffet for seconds. They didn't leave Pizza Palace until it was almost noon. Avery patted her stomach as they walked out into the sun.

"Dude," she said. "That was good."

"Dude," her dad said back. "It was."

Then he offered to take Avery back to Cedar Lane in a cab, and since Avery really was afraid she'd work up a cramp skating in her stomach-bursting condition, she agreed.

They pulled out of the parking lot, and Avery watched the Pizza Palace sign in the taxi's rearview mirror: a giant neon pizza. Slice by slice, it flickered from a whole pie to a darkened one, like some invisible mouth was munching it up.

Then, in a matter of minutes, the taxi was pulling up to 25 Cedar Lane.

When Avery opened the door to leave, her dad nudged her arm.

"See you in a few hours," he said. "At the race. I'll be the super-loud dude, cheering you on."

Avery gave a cautious smile. "Sounds good."

With that, she got out of the car and began to run toward her house.

"Wait!" her dad shouted from the open door. "What team do I cheer for?"

Avery's fractured heart suddenly shattered. She stopped on the lawn and turned to face her dad.

He didn't know.

He didn't even know her team name.

"Sardines," she mumbled.

"What's that?"

"Sardines!" she shouted toward the cab.

Mr. Miller threw out two thumbs-up and shut himself into the car. Then the taxi was gone, and Avery was left with a bellyful of food and a head full of confusion. She wiped a tear from one eye, unsure of how it'd gotten there. Then, as she was about to head inside, she heard, *Avery, wait!*

One yard over, Lola Gil was running her way.

TWENTY-EIGHT

SUMMER SUN

"I came as fast as I could," Lola panted, reaching Avery's front porch. "Was that . . . your dad?"

Lola couldn't explain how she'd known that Avery needed her. The feeling had simply been there, in the place where the blue flame burned—a sudden and sure conviction that she should go to Avery's house. Then she'd seen her saying goodbye to an unknown man, watching a taxicab turn the corner off Cedar Lane.

"I—" Avery began, before more tears appeared in her eyes, and she threw her arms around Lola. The two girls stood there for a long time, hugging each other in the summer light.

At last, Avery loosened her arms and whispered, "I'm really confused."

Want to talk about it? Gently, Lola pushed the thought her way.

Avery nodded, and together the girls sat on the porch's top step. The afternoon sun had warmed the concrete. Birds were calling from the trees. Somewhere close by, a lawn sprinkler was on, whirring along with a *chuh-chuh-chatter-chatter-chuh*. It was a perfect summer day. Perfect, except for the tears drying on Avery Miller's cheeks. Lola wanted to blot them away, to tell her that everything would be all right.

"He just *showed up*," Avery said. "Out of nowhere. He said he wasn't going to make it to Glow in the Park, but he changed his mind last minute. I've been so mad at him, I told my mom I never wanted to see him again."

Lola listened, nodding occasionally.

"But now? I don't know. He seems like he might actually be sorry. Part of me wants to forgive him, but the other part . . . it can't."

The lawn sprinkler carried on: *chuh-chuh-chatter-chatter-chuh*.

Avery released a shaky sigh. "I never told you this, Lols. I never told any of you guys. But back in California, things weren't so great. I got in trouble because of my powers. I didn't know what they were then. I lost my friend, and my dad? He wasn't there for me."

Avery shut her eyes, and Lola felt a familiar kind of nudge. Images appeared in her mind, but they weren't of her own making. Avery was sharing a memory with her. Lola watched as yellow bathroom tiles shattered, giving way to a violent spray of water. Then she saw a principal's severe countenance, along with the face of a man she now knew to be Avery's father. Hurt and disappointment—both Avery's—welled within her.

Then the memories faded, and Lola said, "Vee, I'm so, *so* sorry."

"I guess I never told you all because…I don't know, you might think I was a freak. If you knew my friend had left me, maybe you'd leave, too."

Lola squeezed Avery's freckled hand. "You think I'd do that? Avery, you're my best friend."

Avery looked up, dumbstruck. "What about Bastian?"

Lola crinkled her nose. "Well, he's my *twin*. That's different. But best friends are the people you choose. And I'm not un-choosing you."

Avery shook her head. "I thought you were still mad at me. About last night. What I said about Nando."

"I was mad," Lola admitted. "I was scared, too. I still am. I don't like all this stuff about the silver suits, and then the note on Cedar House…Something doesn't feel right."

"I *don't* think Nando's a bad person," Avery said, with feeling.

"I know," Lola replied.

"I'm just scared, like you. It's hard to not be suspicious."

Lola studied her knees. "It hurt, though. What you said about him. I'm *not* blinded because he's my brother. I know who Nando is. I know he'd never do anything that would hurt me or Bastian."

Avery nodded. "I'm sorry. It wasn't right for me to say that. And maybe I'm suspicious, but I do trust you."

"I forgive you," Lola said, feeling an instant rush of relief. "Who knows how I'd feel about Nando if he wasn't family. Top secret government stuff is always suspicious."

Avery sighed again, but this time the heavy murk had cleared from her eyes. "Good," she whispered, resting her head on Lola's shoulder.

The girls sat in yellow light, the sun winking out rays onto rooftops and tall cedar trees.

"Anyway," Avery said after a while, "it'll all be over tonight."

"Thank goodness."

Avery smiled against Lola's arm. "You sound relieved."

"I'm nervous," Lola said, in a small voice.

"About tethering?"

Lola frowned, thinking. "Not about that, actually. I was at first, but...it kind of feels nice to have a job all to myself. One that I'm good at."

"*Really* good at," Avery said. "You're the reason we're going to win, Lols."

Lola blushed, her heart quickening. "It's teamwork. We're *all* the reason why."

"But you most of all," Avery insisted, and before Lola could argue further she added, "I get it, though. Wanting it all to be over with. I mean, I like racing a lot, but...it can be stressful. Especially when Dani gets into one of her moods."

"She just wants us to win," said Lola. "I like that about her: Dani goes after what she wants. She doesn't take no for an answer."

"Especially from Mitchell Jensen."

"Especially him." Lola laughed. "But…" She paused, turning thoughtful. "I do want us to win. Not to show the Grackles who's boss, or to get the money, though. I want to win because it'd make all of you happy. That's all I want: for us to be happy."

A memory prickled in Lola's mind of Nando at the dinner table, his voice raised, and of angry looks on her parents' faces. She closed her eyes, shutting the images out. Why couldn't everyone around her be happy for one moment? No war zones and gunfire on TV, no fights in her family, no silver suits lurking close by, no confrontations with Mitchell and his Grackles.

Maybe that was impossible, but Lola was still going to hope.

"My dad's coming to the race tonight," Avery said. "I don't even know if I want him there."

"Well," said Lola, "we'll be there, too. If you want us to chase him away, then that's what we'll do."

Avery laughed, sitting up straight but leaving behind the scent of her coconut sunscreen on Lola's shoulder.

"Like you could ever chase someone away, Lola Gil," she said, getting to her feet.

Lola stood, too, the sudden movement sending her rose crown askance. She righted it, then shrugged. "I could try." Squeezing Avery's hand, she asked, "Feeling any better?"

"A little. But still confused."

Me too, Lola replied. *About aliens, and our powers, and everything.*

Avery started for the door but then stopped.

"Did you know," she said, "your thoughts—they're different

from the others'. It's hard to describe, but they feel...like a color."

Lola grinned, her stomach fluttering happily. "They *feel* like a color?"

Avery's cheeks pinked. "Guess that sounds stupid."

"No. It doesn't sound stupid at all."

From inside the house, Radar barked in agreement.

Today was *the day*, and the man in the navy suit started it off with a strong cup of coffee. By this time the next morning, the terms of the contract would be fulfilled, and he would go down in history as a *discoverer*. A *peacemaker*. The man who brought an end to the worst war the world had ever seen. He would make his family line proud.

The man's digipad chimed, and the screen informed him of an incoming video call from the department.

When the man pressed the accept button, the woman with the high ponytail appeared on the screen.

"Ira," the man said, brightening into a smile. "Good morning."

Ira nodded at the greeting, then said, "How is everything on your end? I know you don't need the reminder, but it's policy to inform you that our contract expires at—"

"Yes, I know," the man interrupted. "Don't worry. Everything's going according to plan."

"Then you still intend to apprehend the glowhosts tonight?"

"We do," said the man. "We're using every resource available to us. We've even brought on that reporter—someone to chronicle the process. Everything will be done in the proper way."

"Very well. I look forward to your next call."

The digipad screen went dark, and the man in the navy suit drained the last of his coffee. He set down the mug with a forceful *clank*. Then he looked out his window, at the dawn-kissed horizon of Callaway, Texas. This great town had sprung out of nothing, a wasteland turned to a bustling center of commerce. Over the decades, it had changed and expanded, and now it stood on the edge of yet another transformation—one in which he would play a part.

Tonight, at the race called Glow in the Park, everything would change.

The man rose from his chair and picked up his green briefcase. Then he set out to do the day's work.

TWENTY-NINE

RACE DAY

On the first day of summer, meteorologists predicted clear skies for Callaway, with temperatures taking an unusual dip, down to the low seventies. It was the perfect weather for Glow in the Park. For the Sardines' sweet victory.

Dani thought about victory while choking down her morning power smoothie. She thought about it while reading the same sentence of an article in *Glowboard Monthly* over and over again. She thought about it as she fixed her own dinner, alone in the kitchen, opening a can of tomato soup and pouring it into a pot on the stove, all without using her hands. While the soup was simmering, she noticed the note her parents had left on the digipad:

Work party, be home late. Bedtime at ten o'clock.

Typical. Her parents had left for a party and completely forgotten about the race. The race they'd made a deal about. Not that Dani *wanted* her parents to come. If the Sardines didn't win first place—which *wouldn't* happen—she couldn't stomach seeing her mom and dad's triumph.

After eating, Dani went through her pregame exercises. She ran in place for three minutes and did twenty-five jumping jacks. She breathed in and out, facing herself in the mirror.

"You've got this, Danielle Hirsch," she told her reflection. "It's race day, and nothing's going to bring you down."

Then she grabbed her glowboard and headed outside.

It was still daylight, just after dinnertime. Registration at Glow in the Park began at seven thirty, which gave the Sardines a half hour to skate out to Hazard Hill. Bastian and Lola were sitting on their front lawn, Lola adding to a clover chain that she'd draped around Bastian's neck. Avery was at her front door, arguing with someone: Radar.

"I can't take you!" she was saying, shooing his nose back inside. "There's no one to watch out for you, bud."

Radar barked loudly, then whined, and Dani wondered, not for the first time, if that dog really could be one of them. Dani thought of the message Bastian had relayed last night, direct from the aliens: *The five of us have to be together.*

"Hey," Dani said, jogging up to Avery. She held out a hand for Radar to happily lick. He barked some more, as though entreating Dani to reason with Avery. He really *did* seem to know what was going on.

"Mr. and Mrs. Gil are coming," Dani said. "I bet they could bring Radar along."

"Huh," said Avery. "Should I ask?"

Dani wondered if Avery was thinking the same thing, about Radar being one of them. A tele-whatever. A true Sardine.

"Wouldn't hurt," she said.

"Ask what?" Lola was skipping up to them, Bastian trailing behind, attempting to rid himself of the cumbersome clover chain.

"Would your parents bring Radar to the race, you think?" asked Dani.

"Sure!" Lola's eyes brightened at the suggestion. "They love Radar. Don't they, boy? They love you!"

Lola knelt and patted down Radar, who was bursting with energy, jumping and wiggling his tail in anticipation. Together, the team walked him over to the Gils' house.

Nando's car was gone from the driveway, as it had been for nearly three weeks now. All the twins had shared with Dani was that he was still in town but no longer staying with their family. She had noticed, though, that the usually chipper Mr. Gil had developed a perpetually creased brow. He greeted the Sardines at the garage door, where Lola explained the situation and her father said that of course, he and Mrs. Gil would be happy to bring Radar to the race.

The Gils always offered to drive the team to Hazard Hill, but that would take the fun out of the pre-race. It was tradition for the Sardines to skate to races together, swishing in with style, glowstreams trailing behind them. That was how winning teams behaved, Dani insisted, and the others never argued with her. She was pretty sure they all liked the grand entrance, too.

So the Sardines left a barking Radar with Mr. Gil and set out for the street. There, they kicked on their boards and mounted.

"Give me one more good race," Dani whispered to her board, flipping the switch.

This time, it turned on without a hitch, as though it knew what tonight meant to her.

The road stretched out before the four friends.

Forget Mitchell Jensen and his note.

Forget the silver suits and their unknown mission.

Forget columns of blue light that spoke of an unknown alien world.

Tonight was about the race.

"All right, Sardines," said Dani, clicking her helmet into place. "Let's win this thing."

THIRTY

SARDINES VS. GRACKLES

Hazard Hill was bustling with people: fans, family, officials, and racers all gathered for the big event. At the base of the hill, past the finish line, vendors had set up tents, selling hot dogs, hamburgers, and fresh lemonade. Farther up, fans had gathered along the official racing track, edging as close as they could to the neon spectator lines. But the main attraction for the Sardines, once they'd arrived, was the registration table set up beneath the hill's abandoned gate. There, the organizers of the Junior Glowboard League were signing in teams and handing out glow sticks to all participants. Lola had taken several small sticks and connectors and was threading them through her crown braid. Bastian cracked the stick in his own hand, revealing a bright magenta, and shoved it into his back pocket. He couldn't believe pointless glow sticks like this were the extent of the fun before *real* glow had been discovered.

But why do you like Component G so much? Bastian thought, strapping on his slider gloves. *Because it's weird and unexplainable . . . like you?*

Quick as he could, Bastian shook the question from his head. Now wasn't the time to be thinking about his powers or the light beings. It wasn't the time to consider that, last night, when he'd tried to send the aliens his memory, they hadn't heard. That maybe his memory plan to save the world was all wrong.

No, now was the time to focus. Now was the time to *win*.

Draft train was the first event of the night, beginning before sunset, at eight fifteen. Dani retrieved a schedule from the sign-in desk, which she held up for all the Sardines to see. Once again, their team had been assigned the very last racing spot, so they stayed at the base of the hill awhile longer, wedged into the crowd that had gathered behind the spectator lines.

Even as the first of the racers flew past, Bastian's eyes strayed from the track. Nando had said he couldn't attend the race, but Bastian still found himself searching the faces of the crowd. Instead, he caught sight of his parents, newly arrived, walking past the food vendors. A leashed Radar trotted by Mrs. Gil's side, tail wagging. When the Gils saw Bastian, they shot excited waves and then raised a sign above their heads. *SARDINES!* was written in giant pink bubble letters on poster board.

Bastian's cheeks burned in embarrassment.

Lola was grinning. She blew her parents a kiss.

"So much for competition," snorted Dani, still focused on the track. "Two twenty-five? And they're ninth-graders! Skate more like kindergarteners."

That caught Bastian's attention again. A racing time of 2:25? From a high school team all the way from Dallas? That was a very good sign.

The Sardines continued to watch draft trains swish by. Every five minutes, a new team raced, but none were even close to competition. The Sardines' newest race time still had the best beat by a full five seconds. Bastian noticed, as they watched, that Avery kept looking around.

"Vee," he said eventually, "who're you looking for?"

"Huh?" Avery turned to him, startled. "Uh, no one."

But he watched as, silently, Lola reached out and squeezed Avery's hand—a single, silent pulse.

Then the Grackles were up. Bastian was surprised that Mitchell hadn't found them beforehand, to throw some more taunts their way. Not that Bastian wanted him to. He could do without Mitchell Jensen for a whole race day. For his whole life, actually.

You don't play by their rules. You make your own. Nando's advice echoed in Bastian's head. That's what Bastian would do: He would do what he was great at and skate his heart out. That's how he would prove Mitchell wrong.

"They're off!" shouted the finish line official, listening to the race report through his earpiece.

The crowd at the base of Hazard Hill waited. All they

could hear was the distant cheering from those who had stationed themselves farther up the track, at the starting line. Two minutes passed like this, with the occasional update from the game official—"They're skating strong!" or "The players continue in formation!"

Then there was a burst of sound and sight. The Grackles rounded the corner, Zander leading the pack, elbows tucked in, helmet forward, in perfect form. Beside Bastian, Dani stared at her digiwatch, speaking under her breath. In a flash, the Grackles crossed the line, and the crowd around them erupted into cheers.

This is it, thought Bastian. *The time we have to beat. It can't be more than—*

"Race time!" the game official shouted through his bullhorn, and in that moment, the world seemed to lose its sound. Bastian waited, hands clenched at his side.

"Looks like we've got a new all-time record, folks!" the official bellowed. "Grackles take the lead with *two eleven!*"

The crowd went wild.

Bastian felt all his breath wither and die in the back of his throat.

2:11. No. That wasn't possible.

Someone rammed into his shoulder, hard. It was Dani. She was pushing against bodies, slipping away into the crowd.

"Hey!" Bastian called after her. He looked to Lola and Avery, who were wide-eyed and openmouthed.

Without another word, the three of them followed after Dani, pushing past sharp elbows and sweaty bodies, making their way up Hazard Hill's walking path. The crowd thinned out the farther up they went—the farther away they got from the finish line—until there was no crowd left at all. No one ever watched races from this part of the track. For spectators, the beginning and ending were the interesting parts of a race, not the middle.

With no crowd in the way, Bastian caught sight of Dani running uphill.

"Dani!" he shouted after her. "Hey, slow down, would you?"

Dani groaned loudly but whipped around, waiting for the others to catch up.

"I don't get it," she spat, once the others reached her. "Two eleven can't be right. *We* were going to set an all-time record. Nobody's come close to two twelve before. *No one.* How could the Grackles have gotten that fast, that quick?"

"Well." Avery looked nervously at the others. "*We* got fast quick."

"Yeah, because we're telepaths," Dani said, raising her voice. "Because we're *freaks!*"

"Say it ain't so."

Bastian froze. He knew that voice. He couldn't stand that voice.

Mitchell Jensen had followed them up the hill, out of the crowd. He stood a few yards off, sweaty from fresh victory, his Grackles flocked around him. A smirk stretched across his hateful face.

"So you finally admit to being freaks, huh?" he asked. "I knew you'd have to admit the truth eventually."

Beside him, Kyle Bridges and Ross Mondt snickered. Zander stood at a distance, his mouth set in a thin line.

All eyes turned to Dani. She was the one who always said not to pay attention to Mitchell. Bastian wondered if this time she'd follow her own advice.

Dani said nothing, only turned and resumed her walk up Hazard Hill.

The Sardines followed her.

But the Grackles did, too.

"You could save some face and drop out now!" Mitchell shouted after them. "You *freaks* shouldn't even qualify for the races!"

Dani kept stomping up the path.

"Well, that's what you are!" Mitchell yelled. "I know about the creepy stuff you can do. I saw you here on Hazard Hill. And guess what? I told my dad, and he said he could have you disqualified if he wanted. How would you like that, Sardines? How'd you like it if you could never race again? If I— AAAAAH!"

Mitchell's taunts turned into a bloodcurdling screech, and when Bastian looked back, he saw why: Mitchell was hanging upside down in midair. His hair fanned out beneath him, and his face was bright red, blood rushing to his forehead. Mitchell kept screaming, thrashing in the air. It looked as though some invisible hand was holding him up by his right sneaker.

Then his glowboard came to life. It hovered, spraying a bright red glowstream, and, in a blinding flash, shot out, past the rocky terrain that bordered the walking path, and right off the hillside. It stopped for one moment, out in the open air, wobbled unsteadily, and then fell, plummeting out of view. Seconds later, Bastian heard the *crash*—shattering plastic, total destruction. Mitchell's glowboard was gone.

"Let's get out of here!" shrieked Kyle Bridges.

He took off running down the hill, Ross Mondt following suit, each of them shouting and casting back terrified looks.

Only, there was one boy who hadn't fled. Zander Poxleitner remained where he was, looking up at a dangling Mitchell.

"That's right!" Dani shouted, pushing past Bastian and the other Sardines. She walked down to the place where Mitchell hung. "You say stuff like that one more time, Jensen, and I'll *really* give you something to cry about. Tonight, us *girls* are going to beat your sorry ass."

Bastian was horrified. Bastian was grinning. Bastian didn't know what to think. It was the first time he'd heard Dani cuss.

Then Mitchell dropped to the ground with a *thud*. He scrambled to his feet, not meeting anyone's eye, and ran after his Grackles, stumbling the whole way down the hill.

Dani folded her arms and shifted her glare to Zander. He shook his head at her—slowly at first, and then more quickly. There was an urgent look in his eyes: fear, or maybe sheer panic. He, too, set off, running down the path.

"Welp," Avery muttered. "So much for keeping a low profile."

THIRTY-ONE

THE FIERY FINISH

t wasn't me.

Dani wanted to shout it: *I wasn't the one who held Mitchell upside down!*

But the Sardines were next at the starting line, the last team to race in the Glow in the Park draft train competition, and now they had a new time to beat: 2:11. They'd never made 2:10. How would they do that tonight, when everyone's nerves were alight, and Mitchell had just *dangled in midair*?

And the Sardines all thought Dani was the one who'd done it.

"What was *that*?" Bastian asked her as they reached the top of the hill.

"Do you think he'll tell anyone?" whispered Lola.

Avery clapped Dani on the back and said, "It was awesome. Kind of stupid, but awesome."

It wasn't me.

Dani thought the words again, but she still couldn't say them, even *think* them from her mind to the others. She was too confused. Because if the others thought she had done it, and if she most definitely hadn't—then who had?

Maybe I did *do it, and it was an accident,* Dani thought as they took their places at the starting line. *Maybe I was too angry, like Lola in the cafeteria. . . . But she* knew *the food fight was her fault. She felt it, inside. Not like me. Not like this.*

Dani, hey. Bastian's words bit into her brain. *Don't let it bother you, okay? We'll figure it out later. After the race.*

He was right. She had to focus.

A crowd of spectators was gathered around them—though not nearly as big as the crowd awaiting them at the finish line. There was a man taking photographs, his flashbulb zapping every few seconds. A racing official stood at the line, stalwart, flag in hand. Dani caught bits of conversation, like "unprecedented" and "impossible to beat."

She stopped listening. She focused. She shut her eyes, drowning out sound and taking in the smell of dry Texan dirt and the desert shrubs that grew between the boulders lining the path. She focused on her breath and the quick patter of her heart. Then she opened her eyes and kissed each of her elbow pads, her good-luck ritual. She looked down to her hoverboard, which hummed discordantly beneath her feet, a foot from the starting line.

"One more race," she whispered to it. "I know you've got one more race in you."

273

2:10. They could make 2:10. If they skated the best they had ever skated. If they all remained unshakably synchronized.

They could do it with Lola's tethering.

They could beat the Grackles, once and for all.

Mitchell's shrieks rang in Lola's ears, no matter how hard she tried to shake them.

He had been *upside down.*

His glowboard had *shot off the hill.*

And Dani had done it.

Was that right? Was that who the Sardines were? Were they... dangerous?

Lola, focus, Bastian spoke in her head. The others might not have been able to hear her private thoughts, but Bastian could sense her distraction, same as she could always sense his. Twin telepathy.

Lola focused as best she could. She kicked on her board and lined up with the others behind the starting line.

At every race before this one, Lola hadn't had a reason to be nervous. She'd been a mid-player, the one team member with no job but to stay in formation. But now she was in charge of the most important task. Now she had to fight down the fear of silver suits, aliens, and even the power inside herself.

Don't be afraid, she told herself. *You can tether. We can win this race.*

The game official approached the green laser starting line, raising a checkered flag above his head.

You control it, Lola. Don't be afraid.

Lola still felt afraid.

Even so, she was going to skate.

Bastian caught Lola's tether, hooking it firmly in his mind. Then, in an instant, he felt the connection prong outward to Avery and Dani.

No way we can lose after that, you guys, Avery's voice said in his mind. *Let's skate like the wind.*

Bastian's heart thudded hard in his chest. The rules were theirs to make now, and they would show the Grackles. They would race their best time ever.

The flag dropped.

They were off.

And the race timer began.

Tethered like this, Avery could almost hear the creak of Bastian's ankles as he crouched. She knew exactly when to grab his hand, forming the final link, completing their train.

This time, there would be no confusion, no mix-ups. She and Bastian had practiced this moment so many times before, from the perfect amount of force to put into the whip to the perfect positioning of their hands to the perfect form of her body as she crossed the line. She readied herself as they sped down the hill, gaining speed, coasting through air, their glowboards following the curve and incline of the track.

2:11.

They'd never gotten 2:11.

Tonight, they would have to beat it.

Avery could feel her teammates' concentration burning along all tethers—that familiar, blue-hot flame, swelling within the four of them, radiating out from their minds. Sweat trickled down her cheek. She ignored it. The heat washed around her, blue and white sparks sizzling under her ribs. Avery focused only on the track, her team, and this one important task.

At last, they rounded the final bend, and the glowing red finish line came into view. Avery breathed in deeply, as she'd practiced. Heat burned through her, drawing out more sweat, sizzling against her skin. She kept ignoring it, tuning her thoughts only to Bastian's tether.

I'm ready, she told him.

This is it, he thought back.

She felt every muscle and nerve in Bastian's hand. She felt his intention, knew just when to move. He swung her out, and Avery went flying forward, the night wind stinging her sweat-streaked face. It was still so hot, and she was going so fast, *so fast*. Faster than ever before.

In that moment, a thought flashed in Avery's mind: She hoped her dad was there, watching her, like he'd promised. She hoped this moment would change everything.

Then Avery flew across the finish line, past the officials and a blur of faces. She crouched low to carve into a stop, pushing her sliders into the ground. Sparks flew up from the asphalt, and Avery felt a painful sear of heat on her palms. Her already-threadbare sliders were disintegrating from the friction. She was still going too fast.

Snap.

The tether released from Avery's mind, three cords cut loose at once. She ducked, flying from her board into a somersault, tumbling against the hard ground. Pain shot through her elbows and knees, but finally she came to a stop.

Slowly, Avery pushed herself up from the ground. She knew it, without a doubt: The Sardines had skated their best race. Lola's tether had connected them, and their blue flames had merged together just like they had at Glow Expo. Only this time, there had been no *POP!* This time, the merge had given the Sardines more speed.

They had never gone this fast.

And Avery had never felt so sure.

They had won.

"Our time?" Dani shouted, not bothering to dismount. She carved around the finish line, skating straight up to the game official, her face aflame.

"Our time," she panted. "What's our time?"

But the official wasn't paying attention. The stopwatch lay idle in his open hand, and he was staring at something in the distance, mouth agape.

"Hey," Dani said, snapping her fingers in front of him. *"Hey."*

It seemed as though the official was in a trance.

"Dude, seriously?" Dani demanded. "You have *one job.*"

What was wrong with the guy? Didn't he know how important this race was? What was so distracting—a two-for-one special at the hot dog stand? Or maybe the Grackles had paid the guy off to have him fix the race.

Well, not if Dani could help it. If he wouldn't do his job, then she would.

Dani grabbed the stopwatch from the official. She expected him to snap out of it, but he went right on gaping. She looked at the watch.

2:04.

No. 2:05.

2:06.

No. The timer was still counting. The official hadn't stopped it. Dani did so quickly, heaving out breaths, sweat dripping down her face. She felt so hot inside, like a fire nearing the end of its fuse. She stared at the now-stationary numbers.

2:07.

Less than 2:07. It had been ten seconds at least since Avery had crossed the line—which meant a race time of *less than two minutes.* But that couldn't be right. No one could race this hill in so little time. 2:10 was near impossible enough.

It couldn't be under two minutes.

It couldn't—

"We did it!" Dani shouted. "We did it! We beat them. WE WON."

She turned to find her teammates, to throw her arms around them, scream, and celebrate.

But the Sardines weren't there.

She'd been so preoccupied before, but now Dani noticed that the crowd was pressing in around her, rippling with gasps and cries of alarm. Fingers pointed to the sky, others to the track itself. At last, Dani saw for herself what had frozen the game official in shock.

The fire was everywhere. It was eating up sagebrush and cedar trees alike, grasping for any kindling it could find along the rocky hill. The flames that shot into the sky were bluish-white, too large, too strange to be real. But they *were* real, and they had begun to send the crowd running. In the distance, fire truck sirens wailed.

Dani didn't move. She stood, staring up, the stopwatch clutched to her chest.

When the Sardines had been racing, she'd felt pure fire burning along their tethers, the blue flames within them raging, joining together as one. That's why they'd gone so fast. And that's why...

Dani gulped.

Mitchell hadn't been her fault.

But these flames—they might be.

THIRTY-TWO

FLAMES

Lola's eyes watered from the heat. Sweaty bodies pressed in on all sides, and she gasped for air. She held her glow-board close to her chest, ducking under elbows as she pushed her way through the crowd.

"Avery!" she called. "Bastian! Dani!"

Her shouts were swallowed up in the commotion. Someone bumped into her, hard, throwing Lola onto her knees.

Please. Blindly, she pushed out the plea to her friends. *Please, someone find me. I'm here, I'm* here.

She managed to stand again, struggling with her glow-board, avoiding more arms that threatened to knock her down.

Bastian. Avery. Dani. Find me here, please.

A hand clamped around Lola's arm. It was bloodied and wet, and Lola cried out. Then she saw who it was.

"Avery!" she shouted, throwing her arms around her best friend.

"Ow," squeaked Avery, putting space between them. "Hey, I just . . . ow."

Lola got a better look at Avery. Her hands were badly scraped, smeared with blood.

Came in too fast for my sliders, Avery said, and when Lola widened her eyes, she added, *Doesn't matter, I'm fine. Let's get out of here.*

Hand in hand, the girls followed the crowd away from the roaring flames on Hazard Hill. The fire truck sirens drew closer. People ran for their cars, and others shot off into the night on their glowboards. Car doors slammed and horns honked, and men in uniform appeared in the crowd, shouting for everyone to remain calm and *move over there.*

No one was remaining calm, though, and Lola didn't want to go anywhere without finding the others first.

Listen for Radar, said Avery. *I bet he's barking up a storm.*

So Lola listened for barks while searching all around for the faces of her parents. She heard the click and static of a nearby walkie-talkie. A man's garbled voice came through, shouting things like "seal off" and "contain."

Then Lola heard something else entirely.

"Avery! *Avery!*"

She turned abruptly, gripping Avery's wrist. *Someone's calling for you.*

A man appeared in the crowd, making his way straight for

them, red lights flashing across his face. He was tall, a foot above the rest of the crowd, with swishy blond hair and hazel eyes that Lola recognized. They were Avery's eyes.

"Mr. Miller?" Lola gasped.

"Don't worry," he said. "You two are safe with me."

THIRTY-THREE

TRAPPED

"**R**ADAR!" Avery shouted, even as her father dragged her across the road.

Her dog was here, somewhere. What if, frightened by the commotion, he'd broken off from the Gils? He could be alone, terrified, waiting for Avery to rescue him. She couldn't let him down.

Radar, Avery thought desperately, because even if he couldn't speak back, maybe he could hear.

Deep inside, Avery was sure of the truth: They had done this, somehow. The Sardines' thoughts had been so intertwined, so concentrated, and the speed of the boards and the fierceness of the race had been so great—somehow, all of it combined had created this mess. Which meant Radar might be in danger because of *her.*

"RADAR!" Avery shouted again, but there was no reply. No barks, no flash of his blue merle coat.

"Come on," said Mr. Miller, pulling Avery and Lola, his grip unyielding.

When her dad had first found Avery in the crowd, she'd been filled with relief. He'd come to the race, like he'd promised, and maybe she had been wrong to be mean to him before—giving up on him, refusing to let him visit ever again. But now Avery just wanted to find her dog.

They arrived at the side of the road, in a cooler, quieter place. A cargo van was parked there, windowless save for the windshield. Avery frowned as her father slid open the side door. What kind of rental car was this?

She stayed where she was, feet planted beside Lola.

"Radar," she said. "We have to find him. And my friends."

"Ray . . . what?"

Avery glared at her dad. "MY DOG."

"Oh! Right. We'll get him, Veemeister. But we can find everyone better from the van."

Avery continued to stare at the vehicle. "It looks creepy."

Mr. Miller laughed at that, in his popcorn-kernel way. "It was best for carrying my equipment," he said.

"Equipment?"

"Well, yeah." Her dad leaned against the driver's door. "I thought your mom told you: I'm working on a new project here. Got a great lead. You and your friends can even help out."

Avery's mom had certainly *not* told Avery that. What's more, her *dad* hadn't told her, not during a whole Pizza Palace brunch. In an instant, Avery put the pieces together: Her dad was here for work, which meant he hadn't just come to see Avery at Glow in the Park. He'd lied.

Avery's heart sank.

Come on, Lola, she thought, taking a step back. *Let's go.*

Before Avery could think another word, silver suits flashed around her. The faceless attackers grabbed hold of her arms.

"Dad!" she screamed. "Help!"

But the silver suits weren't dragging her and Lola away. Instead, they were moving *toward* the van, throwing Avery roughly inside and shutting the door with a vicious *slam.* Avery blinked rapidly, trying to adjust her vision.

"Lola?" she called out. "Dad? Dad!"

She was surrounded by spooled cables, lights, and packing trunks, and she could hear soft, quick breaths close by.

"Avery?" whispered Lola. "What's going on?"

"I don't know," said Avery. "But we're getting out."

She crawled toward the door, hissing against the pain from the cuts in her hands. When she reached out, she felt nothing but cold, smooth metal. There was no handle here. They had been locked inside.

Avery heard movement at her back, but it wasn't Lola.

"No!" she shouted. "Dad! Dad, help! There's someone here! There's—"

A sharp sting pressed into her neck.

Then Avery Miller's world went dark.

THIRTY-FOUR

FALL

Bastian was inside Dani's head. Somehow, in the chaos, he'd managed to find her.

I'm by the boulders, he said. *Have you seen Lola?*

Dani darted out of the way of two running firefighters. Her clothes and hair were soaked in sweat.

I haven't seen anyone, she thought back. *And in case you hadn't noticed, there are A LOT OF BOULDERS AROUND HERE.*

Stop screaming, would you? My head's about to explode.

Sorry, Dani thought, in as small a way as possible. Because if the Sardines could create raging fires, maybe they could make heads explode, too. At this point, who knew?

I'm at the boulders near the stop sign at Sunset Street, Bastian elaborated.

I can work with that, Dani told him. *Just stay where you are.*

Resolute, she ran down the road. Sunset Street was far off

from Hazard Hill, and the farther away Dani got from the fire, the cooler the air became. The night was dark, but emergency vehicles illuminated her path in blue and red bursts. Dani cut off the main road to a dusty path, running hard, but careful to stay away from the edge of the steep desert cliffside. She could see Bastian now, standing by a towering cluster of boulders, his head craned toward the sky.

"Bastian!" she shouted.

He looked her way.

In that very moment, a van pulled up on the road beside Bastian. A blue van. Its back doors opened, and hands reached out, grabbing hold of Bastian's shoulders and hauling him inside.

It happened in an instant, as Dani watched in horror.

"BASTIAN!" she screamed. "NO!"

The doors slammed shut.

Then the van sped off, screeching onto the main road. Before it disappeared into the night, Dani caught sight of the writing scrawled on its side: *Gloworks, Inc.*

There was a sharp *snap* inside Dani's head as her connection to Bastian broke.

Where were the people in the van taking him? What did Gloworks have to do with it? If someone had found out the Sardines' secret...what was going to happen to them? Horrible possibilities flew into Dani's head—images of wires and machines, of tests and interviews.

Avery! Lola! Dani's mind called out. But like before, there was no response. Wherever the others were, they were too far away, out of reach. Tears and sweat mixed on Dani's face, and she turned a full circle, thinking wildly.

Mr. and Mrs. Gil. They had to be somewhere close by. They wouldn't leave without their kids. The Gils could help her.

Dani ran up the dusty path she'd come down, rejoining the crowd on the street. A policeman shoved into her, distracted by a conversation with his walkie-talkie. She winced, rubbing her shoulder, and then she saw them: the silver suits. They were everywhere, swarming the base of the hill with their rod-shaped glow detectors in hand.

Dani quickly turned the other way.

"Oof."

She'd run into someone. Someone with an opaque visor where a face should have been.

"Hey," said a staticky voice from inside the silver suit's helmet. "*Hey.* Stop right there."

Dani didn't hesitate. She ran.

"STOP RIGHT THERE, KID! STOP THAT GIRL!" the voice shouted after her.

Dani heard rapid footsteps behind her, but she kept running. She leapt forward, each step propelling her in a desperate sprint, until she broke from the crowd. When she reached an open space, she pulled her glowboard from her backpack and threw it down. With one swift jump and a kick of the power switch, she was skating off, down the darkening street.

The suited men were still following, but the distance between them and Dani was growing.

"Ha!" she shouted back at them. "Take that, losers!"

At that moment, the board beneath her shook, throwing her off-balance. Dani cried out, frantically righting herself. Then she saw the problem: While she'd been gloating over the suits, she'd run the board right off the road and over a steep-sloping cliff, into sheer air.

No, she just had time to think. *Help.*

The board, strained beyond its limits, gave one last stuttering cough of orange glow. Then Dani was plummeting down, down, down.

She shut her eyes. The fall was too far, the ground below jagged.

All for nothing, she thought. She had worked so hard, she'd beaten the Grackles, and it was ending *now.* What would the aliens up above have to say about that?

Dani readied herself for pain, for darkness, for some sudden end.

They didn't come.

The wind no longer whipped at her hair. Her arms stopped flailing about. Dani opened her eyes to find that she hung suspended, only yards above the rocky ground. Slowly, her body tilted until she was standing upright in the air. Then she lowered, steadily, until her sneakers hit a soft patch of dirt. Her glowboard hovered beside her, caught by the same invisible force that had stopped her fall. It sputtered out a few coughs of glow and shut down, hitting the ground with a *thump.*

"What the—" Dani began. Then, "AAAH!"

Someone else was falling from the sky. Though not falling, exactly—more like *floating down*. A moment later, he landed beside her on a smooth stretch of rock.

"Whew!" He looked over at Dani with a nervous grin. "That was close."

It was Zander Poxleitner.

Dani stared. "What," she whispered. "Was. That."

"Well," said Zander conversationally, "you skated your glowboard off a cliff, and then I rescued you. Now we're hiding from the bad guys, and we're *not* shouting, because if we did that, they would track us down here."

Dani continued to stare as Zander jumped from rock to rock, until his back was pressed against the cliffside. He motioned for Dani to join him, but only when she heard the crackle of walkie-talkies overhead did she understand: They needed to hide. She hurried toward Zander just as a shadowy figure looked over the cliff's edge. The two of them stood still together, holding their breath, inches apart. A flood of light suddenly burst before them, sweeping across the rocks.

"Well?" called a voice from above.

"No sign of 'em. Send a team down to investigate, you know protocol. But if we're going off Smith's report, these suckers might be long gone. Levitation, teleportation, even. Tell your people to watch their backs."

The light shone down for several more breath-stopping seconds. Then, abruptly, it cut out. Engines revved overhead, and as they did, Zander grabbed Dani's hand.

"What do you—" she began, but stopped short at the voice in her mind that said, *Just run.*

It was Zander's voice.

Zander was in her head.

Dani, too stunned to react, did as Zander asked. Carefully, they dodged around rocks until the ground smoothed out, and streetlights appeared in the distance. But Zander didn't head toward the lights. He pulled Dani off to the side, into an opening in the cliff. She found herself in a small cave, hidden from the light of the moon. Dani couldn't even see her own two feet.

Then there was a *crunch*, and Zander's face was illuminated by a freshly cracked glow stick. He looked different in the green light.

Very different.

"Before," Dani whispered, realization crashing on her. "Mitchell hanging upside down . . . that was *you*."

Zander blinked at her. Then he said, "Yeah."

"Why?" demanded Dani. "Why'd you act like I was the one who did it?"

"I dunno. Guess I figured it was your big moment, not mine."

"But you—you—" Dani sputtered, trying hard to think.

A car engine rumbled nearby. Zander held a finger to his lips, and once again, he spoke into Dani's mind.

I shouldn't have left you all. I was supposed to be with the Sardines all along.

Dani stared at Zander's green-lit face, uncomprehending. Then, slowly, she began to understand. Once, Zander had lived on Cedar Lane. Once, he'd been a Sardine. But he wasn't just talking about the team. He wasn't just talking about glowboarding.

The fifth person. Cautiously, Dani pushed her thought toward him. *The fifth person the aliens were talking about—it's you.*

"There's something I have to tell you," Zander said aloud. "Something happened the night of the food fight. I...can't really describe it."

"Let me guess," said Dani. "You sleepwalked your way outside, and a giant blue light told you life-changing stuff. And *then* it got in your head, showed you memories, and told you *more* life-changing stuff."

"Uh..." Zander stared at Dani. "Well, yeah. Only I don't know exactly what the message was. It was all crackly. They just kept repeating the same two words, over and over."

"Wait," Dani said. "Did they tell you what day they're coming here? When we're supposed to meet?"

"I don't—"

Dani wasn't sure how she'd ended up grabbing Zander by the shoulders, but she squeezed them tight now and shook with all her might. "ZANDER POXLEITNER, WHAT TWO WORDS. WHAT DID THE MESSAGE SAY."

"Whoa, *whoa*!" Zander wrenched away, looking at Dani like she'd gone crazy. Maybe she *was* crazy, Dani reflected. She had started to believe in aliens after all.

Another engine roared by on the road. Dani and Zander

breathed in together, and after some silence, together, they breathed out.

"Okay," whispered Zander, rubbing at his arm. "What I was going to tell you, before you resorted to *violence*, was that the message kept saying 'summer solstice.' Just that: *summer solstice.* But I don't know what—"

"Holy crap," said Dani, putting her hands to her face. "The solstice. The first day of summer. *That's today.* At midnight. At Hazard Hill. All five of us. Holy, holy *crap!*"

"What?"

"Don't you *get it*?" shouted Dani. Then she checked herself. "No, of course you don't. None of us did. You didn't hear the first part of the message, and we didn't hear the last. Because we were all supposed to be together, like you said. The message was jumbled because you were missing. But now we have all the pieces, and we have to *do* something about it. The others are in trouble, Zander. I don't—"

"DANIELLE HIRSCH, WHAT DID THE MESSAGE SAY."

Dani gaped. It appeared Zander could yell as well as she could. Also, he'd called her *Danielle*.

She gathered her composure and said slowly, "We're special, right? We can move stuff and talk with our minds. And these aliens from a galaxy far, far away figured that out. Actually, they're probably the ones who *gave* us our powers— something about an elixir, maybe it was *the incident*, we don't know for sure. But what we do know is that they don't like the way we've been treated on Earth. They're coming to 'rescue' us, whatever that means. And the rest of the world?" Dani brought her hands together, then pushed them away, fingers dancing. *"Kapow."*

Now Zander was the one gaping. "That...can't be right."

"Yeah, well, there've been a whole lot of things going on that *aren't right.* Like you talking in my head, and cafeterias exploding with food, and, I dunno, the fact that *Hazard Hill is on fire.*"

Zander scratched his nose. "Good point."

Dani gave him a look. Had Zander agreed with her? And before that, had he stood up to her bully? Had he even saved her life, back on that cliffside?

Gross, Dani thought.

"What?" Zander asked.

"Huh?"

"What's gross?"

Dani crossed her arms. She hadn't meant for that thought to leak out. She was going to have to be careful from now on.

"You are, obviously," she said.

Zander scowled. "Yeah, you're welcome. Go ahead and forget that I saved you from certain death."

"Okay, I will," said Dani. But she was growing distracted with other thoughts.

Gloworks. The blue van that had chased her the other day, the one that had pulled Bastian off the street minutes before, was a *Gloworks* van. For all Dani knew, those same people had grabbed Avery and Lola, too.

The memo that Bastian had stolen from Nando—what exactly had it said? Something about Gloworks. Something about *negotiations* and *delivery of new resource.*

Dani got an awful, twisted-up feeling inside. The blue flame sputtered as she met Zander's eyes.

"The memo," she said.

"The what?"

"Come on," said Dani. "We're going to find my friends."

THIRTY-FIVE

COASTING

"**N**O. WHY? WHYYY?"

Zander was watching Dani from a safe distance. She really could be scary, especially at a moment like this, when her glowboard wouldn't budge. Though the board turned on easily enough, and though Dani could hover like the star skater she was, there was no power left in the machine. It hung motionless in the air while Dani yelled, "MOVE, WOULD YOU. *MOVE.*"

"Uh..." Zander said, but not until he'd put several more steps between himself and Dani. "I don't think it's going to work anymore. Not after the cliff. All that strain zapped the glow. You'll need a new cartridge. Or, um, with that old of a model...maybe a new board."

"YES, I UNDERSTAND THE PROBLEM," Dani screeched. "I'M JUST VERY, VERY MAD."

Zander glanced around, nerves tingling. He and Dani may have escaped the silver suits for now, but that hardly meant they were safe on this dark, deserted road. Still, he stood by and let Dani be angry. He would be angry, too, he figured, if it were his board. Plus, he knew how much that glowboard meant to Dani. He'd been there when she'd bought it, using two years' worth of allowance and birthday money. She hadn't even ridden it on the way home, but squeezed it to her chest like it was a check for a million dollars.

Zander looked at his own board, a top-of-the-line turbo model direct from Gloworks, Inc. He hadn't paid a penny for it; Mitchell's dad donated all the team's gear. But he also didn't care about it anywhere near as much as the starter model he'd first got in fifth grade.

Dani had once called Zander a sellout. Moments like this, he wondered if she was right. He wondered what she'd say if she knew about the brand-new boosters Mr. Jensen had installed on the Grackles' boards, and how those boosters were most definitely against racing regulations. How *that* was how they'd made their record-breaking 2:11 time. If Dani knew all that, she'd probably yell even louder than she was yelling now.

Eventually, Dani grew quiet. She hopped off the board and turned to Zander, a strange look on her face. Like she was . . . unsure.

When was Dani Hirsch unsure of *anything*?

"Okay, genius," she said. "What are we supposed to do? There's no way we can walk back to my neighborhood. That would take hours. We don't have hours."

Zander didn't have a plan. He wasn't like Dani, didn't see the point in preparation when stuff like *this* could happen, blowing your careful plans to smithereens. What Zander did have was a fancy glowboard and a last-minute idea that just might work. He switched on his board, and it came to life with a powerful hum. In the moonlight, its gold-painted body seemed to shine.

"Maybe you're out of power," he told Dani. "But you can still hitch a ride."

He knelt, opening a compartment at the back of the board, right above the glowstream cartridge. From it, he pulled a retractable cord with a thin plastic handle on its end. He tossed the handle to Dani, who caught hold.

"Gloworks really thinks of everything, don't they," she muttered.

"Done this before?" Zander asked as they mounted their boards.

"What, coasting? Not... exactly."

"Well, we could always switch places, if you want."

Dani glowered at him. "What, you think I can't do this?"

"Nope. Just an offer."

"Offer denied."

Zander didn't know why, but suddenly he was smiling. Dani was the worst, but she was also kind of... the best. Not that he'd ever tell her so. She already hated his guts, and there was no need to make her hate him more.

"So, where are we headed?" he asked her.

Sudden energy sparked in his mind. Dani was there.

I'll tell you on the way, she said.

Which, weirdly, made Zander smile some more.

They set off. Zander started at a slow, careful pace, glancing back every few seconds to check that Dani was okay. Her board hovered behind his, skating smoothly through the air, hitched to his power. Dani's grip on the handle was tense at first, but as they went on, he felt the tension loosen. Then Dani was in his head, saying, *Is that as fast as you can go?*

Zander smirked. He'd show Dani Hirsch *fast.* He kicked the board to full power, and they picked up speed in an instant, zooming along the desert road. Cars began to appear, and the desolate path eventually led to buildings, sidewalks, and streets. The whole time, Dani thought out directions: *Left,* and *right here,* and *stay straight awhile.* The houses became more familiar, until Zander recognized their route.

Got it from here, he told Dani, and sped the rest of the way to Cedar Lane.

Hey, slow down, Dani thought minutes later as they rounded a corner. Zander glanced back, knees slightly bent, a warning to Dani that he meant to carve. She nodded once and bent her own knees, turning her body with his in precise synchronization.

This mind-meld thing really helps, he thought to himself. *Just* himself. And as he eased to a stop, one slider glove extended, he found his face heating up.

"You okay?" he asked Dani, getting to his feet.

But Dani was already standing, board in hand—more than okay.

"Come on," she said, tossing Zander the connector cord. "We keep to the backyards, stay in the dark. The silver suits are probably watching our street, so we gotta go the back way."

Zander had forgotten how bossy Dani could be. But he was kind of grateful, too; he wouldn't have thought to keep off the street. He followed Dani as she cut across yards, moving with ease, avoiding ditches, ducking under branches, and opening gates, until they reached a familiar yard. Zander spotted Cedar House, and his stomach knotted in ten different places. He hadn't realized until this moment how much he missed the place. The late-night chats, the Sunday-night games of sardines . . .

Hey. Dani shook him out of his memories, motioning for him to follow her to the Gils' back porch.

But your place is one more over, he said, confused.

Yeah, I'm aware. We're not going to my place.

Dani reached the trellis that ran up the porch's far left column. Without hesitation, she grabbed hold, finding footholds in the wood-hewn diamonds and working her way up.

"What the heck are you doing?" Zander whispered.

In a matter of moments, Dani had reached the porch roof. She stood atop it and waved for Zander to climb.

It's easy, she told him. *I do it all the time at my house.*

"Like that helps me," Zander muttered, but what choice did he have? He climbed the trellis, taking much longer than

Dani had and ending up with several scratches from the splintery wood.

"The price of stealth," Dani told him, holding up her own scarred, callused hands. Then she opened the nearest window and climbed inside.

Zander dropped in after her and found himself in a room that smelled of lavender. A collection of paper creatures lay on a white wicker dresser. This was Lola's room. Zander had only been here once before, when a storm had caved in the roof of Cedar House, forcing the Sardines to meet indoors. Now he watched as Dani opened and shut drawers, then stepped inside the walk-in closet and rummaged around.

"What're you looking for?" he asked, scratching a brand-new mosquito bite on his cheek.

"The memo," Dani said. "Or something more. Come on, let's check Bastian's room."

She opened the bedroom door onto a dark hallway, looked both ways, and crept out. Once again, Zander had no choice but to follow.

Bastian's room was opposite Lola's, and way different in style. A host of stars twinkled above their heads, casting eerie light on dark plaid wallpaper. Artwork was tacked to every wall, most of it colorful glowboard designs done in pastels, pencils, and chalk. Zander felt weird about being here, seeing artwork that Bastian had once shared with him in private—artwork Zander had told Mitchell and his Grackles about. Standing here now, without Bastian's knowledge, made Zander feel like a traitor twice over.

Dani picked up notebooks and papers from Bastian's desk, turning some over, flipping through others.

"It's got to be here," she said. "Check the floor. Maybe under the bed. It might still be shaped like a swan."

"I don't get what we're looking for," Zander said, but he still got on his hands and knees to check under the bed. It was spotless there—no dirty clothes, no boxes, not even dust bunnies. He hadn't known that Bastian was such a neat freak.

"You met Nando," Dani said, pawing through desk drawers. "Their older brother?"

"Yeah," Zander said, now tugging the pillows off Bastian's bed, checking under the sheets. Nothing suspicious-looking there, either.

"Well, he works for the government, and he came to town on secret government business. Now think, what secret government business is there in *Callaway*?"

"Uh..." said Zander. "Drug bust?"

Dani groaned, slamming the last of the drawers shut. She slumped into the desk chair, looking defeated. "Bastian and Lola stole one of his papers. It was about a deal with Gloworks. And that van I saw picking up Bastian—it was a Gloworks van. Connection?"

"Uh..."

"*Connection,*" Dani said with conviction.

"*The* Gloworks?" Zander asked. "Mr. Jensen's Gloworks?"

"Yes. And that memo was on a special letterhead. I'm almost sure there was an address. A clue to where the others could be."

"Well," Zander said slowly, trying to sort it all out, "what if they're at . . . Gloworks?"

Dani frowned. "That's too obvious. Anyway, why would anyone take them to a glow factory?"

"It's not just a factory," Zander said. "There are meeting rooms, and some special lab . . . but they didn't let us go back there on the tour."

Dani was looking at Zander as though he'd transformed into a flying cockroach. "You went on a *tour* there?"

Zander shrugged. "With the Grackles. Mr. Jensen was pretty nice."

"Whatever," Dani sighed. "So if they *are* at Gloworks, what do we do? It's all the way across town, and my glowboard doesn't work." Dani pointed to the clock on the bedside table. It was 10:13. "Today's the summer solstice. That's what your message said, right? *Summer solstice.*"

Zander nodded, feeling a lot less smug than he had a minute ago.

"That was the final clue we needed," Dani said. "The aliens— they're meeting us on Hazard Hill at midnight, *tonight.* And if we're not there . . ." Dani shook her head. "We *have* to be there, that's all."

Now Zander felt like he might puke. "Maybe," he said weakly, "the others aren't really in trouble. Maybe it's one big misunderstanding."

Dani gave Zander a look that said, *Don't be stupid.*

"Just saying," Zander mumbled. "It's possible. And it's not like we've got a lot to go on."

Suddenly, the desk lamp flickered on. Zander blinked against the light, looking to Dani.

Did you do that? he asked.

It was dark, Dani thought back. In the new light, he saw a blush spread over her cheeks.

Zander smiled a little. "It's nice to know I'm not the only one who can do weird stuff."

"Yeah." Dani looked pensive. "We thought the fifth person was Radar."

"Wait. You thought I was a *dog*?"

Dani's entire face was red now. "Well, what else were we supposed to think? The aliens said 'five.' Radar hangs out with us a lot. It made sense."

"A dog," Zander muttered, hardly comforted by Dani's explanation.

"When did you know?" she asked after a moment's silence. "About the powers."

"A year ago, I guess? Around when I turned twelve. That's when I first started to feel..." Zander frowned, searching for words. Finding none, he tapped his chest.

"The blue fire," Dani said.

He looked at her, surprised. "Yeah. That. We were at a restaurant, and the waiter brought out a tray with desserts. You know, the special ones they use for display. I wanted the brownie sundae. I was *thinking* that I wanted it. And all of a sudden it fell off the tray, right onto the table, in front of me. Everyone thought it was a funny accident. The waiter apologized, and the manager even came out to say our meal was free. But it wasn't an accident. I knew it was me. I'd felt it on the inside."

"Yeah," Dani said. "That's how it felt on the hill tonight. When we were skating, our thoughts were combined—tethering, that's what we call it—and suddenly it was like our flames combined, too. We were connected, all over. I felt the heat inside, and I told myself it was just adrenaline. But now..." Dani's face crumpled. "The fire. I know it was us."

"Because you were connected?" Zander guessed. "Like, you were stronger with your powers combined?"

Dani gave him a look. "It sounds super corny when you put it like *that*."

"Hey, I saw that fire. I don't think it's corny."

If anything, Zander was jealous. The others had connected their thoughts, and maybe it had resulted in disaster, but they had shared a bond, like a real team. A team where they belonged. Zander had never felt that way with the Grackles.

"Am I really the reason you left?"

Zander started at Dani's question. "Wait, what?"

"You left because of me," Dani said in a whisper. "Because I sucked out all the fun. Right?"

"Uh..." Zander cleared his throat. "What do you want me to say?"

"The truth."

Crap, Zander thought.

Now he wished that Dani hadn't turned on the lamp, because he couldn't hide the weird feelings he was sure were on his face. "It wasn't the *only* reason. When Mitchell asked me to join the Grackles, he seemed pretty cool back then. His dad gave us all brand-new equipment so we didn't have to buy it for ourselves."

"What," said Dani. "You couldn't buy it for yourself?"

"Not everything." Zander looked down, picking at his knit wristbands. "You had to have noticed, all my stuff was in rough shape. Secondhand gear."

"But I . . ." Dani scowled against the light. "You knew how bad *my* board was. You weren't the only one who didn't have great equipment."

"Yeah," said Zander, "your board was bad, but the reason you couldn't buy a new one wasn't because your parents were *broke*. My dad got laid off and didn't have a job for a long time. I never told you all that."

"No," said Dani. "You didn't."

"And the reason we moved? It wasn't because we wanted to live in a cooler part of town. My new house? It's half the size. We couldn't afford our place on Cedar Lane. That's the truth."

Dani blinked. "I . . . didn't know that."

"You didn't ask," Zander said—not an accusation, just a fact. "Even after we moved, it got so bad, Dad said he might have to send me away, to live with my mom's family in Vancouver."

"Vancouver?"

"It wouldn't have been *so* bad," Zander said. "The Kwons are really nice, and I didn't get to know my mom before she died. It would've been a good experience. That's what my dad said. But I didn't want to leave here. I liked school, and I liked glowboarding, and I liked . . . you."

Dani's eyes got big. "Me?"

"I mean, all of you," Zander said quickly, feeling flushed. "You know, the Sardines. But then my board broke, for good, and I couldn't tell you all. It seemed like the only way I could keep skating was to do something you all would hate me for. And I did it. I joined Mitchell's team. And...you hated me."

The room was quiet. Zander felt the way he had once when he'd gotten a stomach bug and barfed up chili cheese fries into a restaurant toilet.

Finally, Dani spoke. "I didn't hate you. None of us *hate* you. We didn't understand why you left, that's all. Why didn't you tell us what was going on?"

Zander lowered his eyes. "I guess I was too embarrassed. Mitchell made everything easy, and you guys made it so hard. And then suddenly we weren't friends anymore. But I never wanted that to happen. And I never meant for them to use the things I told them to hurt you all, especially Bastian. I know that part was wrong: I shouldn't have stood there and let the Grackles be awful to you. When I left the Sardines, I wasn't trying to be a traitor. But taking Mitchell's side—I guess that made me one."

The room got quiet again, and Zander listened to the *tick tick tick* of the bedside clock.

Dani said, "Maybe I hated you a *little*."

Then she laughed, a sort of muffled sound, and Zander laughed, too, and found he could look at her again.

"I never told you congratulations," he said. "For winning the race."

Dani snorted. "They didn't announce an official time, so technically we didn't win anything. And if we didn't win, we won't get the cash prize, and now my board is toast." Dani motioned limply toward her backpack. "That's the end of the line for me."

"But you *won*," Zander insisted. "And you deserved it. All of you."

"Two eleven, though," said Dani, pointing at him. "That's pretty great. You must've practiced hard."

"Yeah. Um...About that..."

Dani's face changed, her brow scrunching up.

She knows, thought Zander. *She probably suspected the whole time.*

Still, he had to say it.

"We cheated," he blurted. "Well, Mitchell did. He made us all—"

Dani's brow stayed scrunched. She waved for Zander to stop talking.

"No," he said. "I've got to tell you. I know it was wrong. I—"

"*Shut up*," Dani growled, lunging forward to clamp a hand over Zander's mouth.

That's when he heard the footsteps outside, in the hallway.

They weren't alone.

The footsteps came closer, closer, and then Bastian's door creaked opened.

Everything happened at once.

Dani screamed, and rough hands caught Zander, pulling him off his feet.

A man's deep voice boomed out, "What's going on here?"

Then Zander heard a name flash in his mind, Dani's thoughts sharp with fear:

Nando.

THIRTY-SIX

SLEEP

Lola woke choking. There was a strange object in her mouth, cold and metal, tasting of blood. A pinching sensation shot through her arms, and she blinked against harsh white light. Strangers stood over her, speaking in low voices.

Avery! she called out.

Beside her, a machine began to beep.

Avery, where are you?

The beeps grew louder, more rapid. There was movement around Lola, and powdery gloved hands touched her arms and legs.

Avery, she called. *Dani! Bastian, where are you?*

The foreign hands were rotating her arms. She felt a cold, sticky substance drop on her skin, and though she strained upward, restraints kept her pinned flat against a hard surface.

She couldn't see their faces; she could only hear their staticky voices.

"Let's go with a sedative, it's not time."

"At least we've got the twins."

"They'll bring in the rest, Smith. Focus on your job."

Lola's eyelids drooped shut against the too-bright light. She felt tired all over, like she could sleep for days.

She drifted away, while the strange machine beeped on.

THIRTY-SEVEN

RESTRAINTS

Avery fought against her bonds, but struggling did no good; they were too tight. She tried to speak, but no words came out of her mouth. All the while, a man in a silver suit sat across from her, the visor of his helmet opaque. His tenor voice crackled out from the helmet speaker, a terrible thing.

"Not to worry, Ms. Miller. You're in good hands."

Avery glared. Good hands? Good hands didn't lock kids into vans. Good hands didn't kidnap girls and take them to strange, windowless white rooms.

Secrets. Bad things. Pain. That was all that could possibly await her here.

Lola? she called out. *Bastian, Dani?*

She listened, but there was no answer.

Avery shut her eyes. She took hold of the fear inside, stoked by a blue-white flame. She tried to form it, to reach out, the way she had on Sardines Night, when she'd saved Dani from her fall.

Out, she ordered it. *Move. Set me free.*

The flame stayed inside her, dancing and sparking, but not expanding. It remained stubbornly small.

A chill passed over Avery. These people had done something to her, somehow taken away her power. Which meant they knew all about her tele-whatevers. They had been watching, waiting. Now she was their prisoner.

Avery was too angry to cry, and far too scared. She could only watch as a sleek white door swished open, and yet another silver suit walked into the room.

"How's this one?" The man's voice raised gooseflesh on Avery's skin.

"Well enough, Smith," replied the other silver suit.

"Wh-why don't you ask *me*?" Avery wheezed. "I'm not okay. I—I'm not okay at all."

The man named Smith turned to her, folding his arms.

"Sorry to hear that, Ms. Miller," he said. "From what your father told us, we thought you might have come to us willingly."

"What—" Avery swallowed, trying to rid her throat of its scratchiness. "Wh-what did my dad tell you?"

"He's an employee of ours, you understand." Smith leaned against the table where Avery lay bound. He spoke breezily, as though Avery were not, in fact, tied up. "We hired him to do some important video work. Once all this is said and done, no longer a government secret, the public will want to know what happened here. It's the documentarian's dream, really. The chance of a lifetime."

With difficulty, Avery shook her head. "He wouldn't do that. He's my dad."

"My dear." The man patted Avery's ankle sympathetically. "He's the one who turned you in."

In response to Avery's silent stare, Smith went on. "People do odd things at times like these. I'm sure he was only doing what he thought best."

"B-but you can't just tie up kids," Avery sputtered. "It's illegal!"

"That's... a gray area," the man said in his sympathetic tone. "I wish you'd see—I hope you will—that we're doing this for your own good. For your good, and the good of our country."

He gave Avery's leg a final pat, then turned and walked to the door. "Continue monitoring," he instructed the seated silver suit. "We're interrogating the boy first."

Bastian, Avery thought, panicked. *They have Bastian.*

"Where's Lola?" she cried out.

The man did not answer her.

"An hour," he told the silver suit. "Maybe more."

"Very good, sir," the silver suit replied.

Then the door swished shut behind the man, and Avery shut her eyes in despair.

He's lying, Avery told herself. *Dad would never do that. He wouldn't turn me in. Not me. Not his own daughter.*

But you're not his daughter, a sullen side of her countered. *You're a freak. He never believed you. That's why he didn't take your side last year. It's why Katelyn Sumner stopped being your friend. They both saw you for what you are. They saw you didn't belong.*

"No," Avery whispered, anger pooling inside her. *"No."*

Still, the raging blue flame inside refused to grow.

THIRTY-EIGHT

GOING ROGUE

"*Watch out!*" Dani screamed as the man—*Nando*—took hold of Zander.

The next moment, bright blue light filled the room. A magnificent *pop* resounded in Dani's ears, and she staggered back, shielding her eyes until, as instantly as it had appeared, the light vanished. When Dani lowered her hands, she saw Zander on his feet, flushed and breathing hard. Nando was lying on the ground, knees to his chest, groaning. That's when his eyes met hers.

"D-Dani?" he said.

Nando looked as stunned to see Dani as she was to see him.

"I'm s-sorry," Zander stammered, backing away. "But you grabbed me, man, and—"

"I get it," Nando grunted, getting to his feet. "No sweat."

He felt around his chest, then surveyed his arms and legs. From what Dani could tell, Nando seemed unharmed. With that fear dispelled, she instantly turned suspicious.

"What are you doing here?" she asked, edging toward Bastian's window. If things got bad, she decided, she could make a jump for it.

"I'm looking for my family." Each of Nando's words was slow and deliberate. Because he was lying? Dani couldn't tell.

Don't trust him. Dani pushed the thought toward Zander.

Then she made a grab for something—*anything*—off Bastian's desk and ended up with a box of watercolor paints. She held it in front of her, like a shield. "Don't come near us!"

"Dani," said Nando, still deliberate. "It's me."

"Yeah," said Dani, "and we know all about you. You're working with *them*—the silver suits. You're on their side."

"If you let me—"

"WE DON'T NEED YOUR EXPLANATIONS!" Dani tossed the box of paints at Nando. It missed him completely and hit the wall, bursting open, little circles of color flying out.

"Uh, Dani?" Zander glanced her way. "We kind of *do* need an explanation."

In the frazzled silence that followed, Dani considered. Even though Nando might be the enemy, he might also have the answers they needed. If Dani was smart about it, maybe she could get those out of him.

Stiffly, Dani pointed at Nando. "Okay. Talk. But keep your distance! You've seen what Zander can do."

And what I *can do,* Dani thought, in sudden realization. Instead of throwing a box of watercolors, what could she have done with the blue light inside her?

She could think about that later. Now she had to focus on Nando.

"Where are they?" Dani demanded when Nando didn't speak. "What are you people doing to my friends?"

"I'm not doing anything," Nando said slowly. "And I understand why you don't trust me, but I swear, I didn't take them. I had nothing to do with that."

"You're working with the government, though," Dani said. "That's what your secret project is, right? It's *us.*"

Nando released a fatigued sigh. He sank to sit on Bastian's bed, resting his head in his hands.

"We've been monitoring GARs—glow activity readings—in Callaway," he said. "The Department of Glowhost Engagement, that's our job. The enemy's already found others like you in their territory, and they're weaponizing them for the war. Our government wants to do the same thing."

"Weapon...what?" Dani asked.

"It's tied to the glow," said Nando. "When the Jensens found the first deposits here, Component G seemed like an anomaly. But then the glow started showing up in different places across the globe. And wherever the glow appeared, strange things began to happen. Reports of electrical disturbances, an inexplicable blue light. Glow was unusual, the government knew that early on. At first they thought they could harness it for big technology."

"But they couldn't," said Dani.

"They couldn't," Nando confirmed. "Decades of testing, and all the best glow was good for was..." He motioned to the glowboard jutting out of Dani's backpack, and she grimaced at the reminder that it was broken for good. "During all that time, the government was working with private businesses."

"Like Gloworks," said Zander. He was standing at a distance, holding his hands behind his back, as though to stop himself from doing more damage.

"Gloworks has never been just about the toys you kids use," Nando replied. "They used that sales money for the labs, the experiments we outsourced there. So when the disturbances here in Callaway got worse, and when we got more reports of unusual GARs, we—the DGE—came to investigate. We concluded that the glow was a deposit, an alien substance. And these deposits, spread across the world, affected certain humans born nearby. The DGE calls these humans glowhosts."

Dani looked to Zander, feeling suddenly uncertain. He looked back, his eyes wide, hands still hidden away. Dani's idea that *the incident* somehow connected the Sardines, Bastian's guess that "elixir" might be glow—it was all true. They'd guessed right.

"Nando," Dani said. "How long have you known it was us?"

"I *just* found out, I swear. Jensen and his people have been keeping all the details under wraps. They claimed they had a master plan, and we agreed to give them jurisdiction for a while. Then we got news of the fire on Hazard Hill. The GARs went off the charts; there's been *nothing* like that before.

That's when Ira told me everything she'd learned, and what she suspected."

"Who's Ira?" Zander asked.

"My coworker." Nando looked embarrassed. "And...also my girlfriend."

Dani raised her eyebrows.

"See," Nando went on, "she'd been working closely with Mr. Jensen, as our departmental liaison. She had concerns when she found out glowhosts were just kids; we both did. But she didn't know at first that I was Bash and Lola's brother. The photos of them weren't great, and she's never met them, not even on video chat. She didn't recognize their names, either, because they were listed by their full names: Dolores and Sebastian. Around her, I call them Lola and Bash. And I use the last name Jones at the DGE for security measures."

"So," said Dani, crossing her arms. "You only decided to help us when you figured out Bastian and Lola were involved. Shouldn't you have cared that we were *kids*, period?"

Nando sighed loudly, rubbing a hand down his face. "I know what it looks like, and I'm not proud of myself. But you have to understand: It's a high-pressure job. Ira and I have been training for this work for years. I always felt conflicted about it, but tonight, when Ira shared your names, we knew what we had to do. She stayed there, to monitor things. And I left the lab and came here first, on my way out to Hazard Hill. I hoped maybe Bash and Lola had gotten away. That if they had, they'd be hiding here."

"But they didn't get away," Dani said, narrowing her eyes. "I saw the silver suits take Bastian. They kidnapped him, right off the street."

Nando's features slackened.

"And that's *your fault*," Dani went on. She turned to Zander. "Come on, we've heard enough. They've taken them to Gloworks."

"Wait," Nando said—not a shout, but a plea. He looked between Dani and Zander, entreating. "We're on the same side. I promise, we both want to save my brother and sister."

"And Avery?" asked Dani. "What about her? What about me and Zander? Or do you only care that Bastian and Lola ended up being the glow kids you're trying to hunt down?"

"You don't get it," Nando said. "I'm not trying to capture *anyone*. I started working for the DGE because I wanted to make a difference in this war. I thought, when we found glow-hosts, they'd be . . . I don't know, but not *kids*. Not *you*. I don't want to use you as weapons. And Ira doesn't, either."

"Oh yeah?" Dani's voice dripped with disdain. "The one who's been working with Mr. Jensen? Your departmental lasagna, or whatever?"

"She's on your side, too," Nando said heatedly. "We'd been talking about it, even before we found out who you were. How the DGE is handling this all wrong, and how we don't like Jensen. Ira told me she got so upset about it yesterday, she tracked you all down to your clubhouse and left a note."

Dani started. The note. The note from *a friend*. How could Nando have known about that? *Was* he telling the truth?

She shook her head angrily. "A little too late for notes now, huh?"

"It doesn't have to be," Nando said. "Ira's still stationed at Gloworks. She has inside access. You have to trust me."

Zander looked to Dani. *I think he's telling the truth,* he told her mind.

"No," Dani said, for Nando to hear, loud and clear. "No way."

Nando looked exhausted. "Look, don't trust me. Fine. You two could leave now, skate out to the factory, and try to save your friends on your own. But I'm telling you, if they've been taken, they'll be in the lab under heavy surveillance. You don't know Gloworks. You don't have someone on the inside. I do. And I'm telling you, I want to get my brother and sister out of there as much as you do. Get *everyone* out," he added loudly as Dani began to protest. "You don't have to trust me, but you'd be better off working with me."

Dani stayed silent, thinking. Whether she liked it or not, what Nando was saying made sense. Maybe she and Zander needed him right now. She just wished she didn't. What if this was a trap? If Nando took her and Zander, and if the silver suits had captured all the others, as Dani feared they had—who would be left to save them?

And midnight was less than two hours away.

If the Sardines didn't make it to Hazard Hill...

"We have to get them out," she said. "And when we do, all five of us have to go to Hazard Hill, no questions asked. We have to be there by midnight."

"What—"

"No questions asked!"

Nando licked his lips. Then he nodded. "All right. Deal."

"But we're keeping our eyes on you," Dani told Nando, glowering.

He looked at her quizzically. "You know you're the ones who have the upper hand, right? You set a whole hill on fire. This kid"—he waved at Zander—"threw me to the ground with his mind. If anyone should be scared here, it's me."

Once again, Dani wondered why she hadn't thought of her powers. Maybe it was because she'd never considered that they could be used to protect herself, even to *hurt* other people. The memory of Mitchell dangling upside down flashed in her head. Dani shook it out.

"Yeah," she said to Nando. "Well, you stay scared."

Nando turned to Zander and said, "Sorry I grabbed you, kid."

Zander shrugged. "It's fine. We kind of broke into your house."

"So," said Dani, "are we going to save the Sardines, or what?"

THIRTY-NINE

PINK LEMONADE

A paper bowl sat before Bastian, and in it was a single scoop of ice cream. Chocolate coconut fudge. His favorite.

"No doubt you need nourishment after such a big night." That's what the silver suit had told him before leaving Bastian alone in this room.

Bastian knew better.

He sat in a swivel chair, eyeing the ice cream but not touching the spoon that rested beside the bowl. The cameras were obvious, mounted in every corner of the room. A boardroom—that's what this place was. It was nothing like the bare white room he'd been kept in before. This place had color. There was a wooden table, surrounded by a dozen orange swivel chairs—all of them empty except for Bastian's. A chipper piano melody piped in from an overhead speaker. Posters lined the wall featuring photographs of soaring eagles and mountainous terrains, with words like *Perseverance* and *Teamwork* printed beneath them in big black letters. At one end of the room hung a whiteboard. At the other, letters were painted on the wall in bright yellow:

GLOWORKS, INC.

Bastian didn't trust any of it. He vividly recalled the moment that rough hands had pulled him into that van and slammed the door. He reached inside, to where the blue flame burned, but he couldn't coax it to grow. *They* had done something to him when they'd jabbed him in the neck. These were bad people, and he was their prisoner, and *somehow* this all had to do with Gloworks, Inc.

"Bastian." A man's voice came through the overhead speaker, interrupting the music. "We know you must be hungry."

Bastian folded his arms.

He could guess what the people were doing on the other side of that speaker. They were watching him through those cameras, marking down observations, talking about him like he was an animal caged in the zoo. Maybe Mr. Jensen was one of them. Maybe even Mitchell was there, too, watching and laughing.

For the second time that night, Bastian remembered his brother's words: *You don't play by their rules. You make your own.*

Bastian smirked as the idea came to him. They may have found a way to stifle his powers, but he still had his own two hands.

He had his art.

And he was great at that.

Bastian stood up, ignoring the bowl of ice cream, and walked across the room to the dry-erase board. There were several markers sitting there. He picked up the red one, uncapped it, and began to draw. Then the green marker. Then the black. Minutes passed, and Bastian's strokes grew bolder. When he was finished, he stepped away, surveying his work.

He had drawn a cartoon UFO—a flying saucer—with a ray of light beaming down. Bathed in the light stood four figures and a barking dog. Satisfied with the final image, Bastian uncapped the black marker and wrote the caption: *Take us to your leader.*

The music cut out once more. "Very funny, Bastian," said the man on the speaker. "But this would go better for everyone if you would eat your meal."

Bastian looked up, straight into the lens of the nearest camera. He said, "No way."

"As you wish," the man's voice replied.

The music came on again, twinkling piano arpeggios.

Bastian returned to his chair, sat, and swiveled slightly, pushing back and forth off the floor. He had stopped trying to use his mind to call for the others. Without control of the flame inside, he couldn't reach out to find them. All he knew for certain was that he was trapped in this prison. Alone.

There was a sudden commotion at the boardroom door. Locks slid from their places, the door opened, and a woman walked inside.

She wasn't a silver suit. She looked like a perfectly normal businesswoman, wearing a finely tailored gray pantsuit, her curly black hair tied up in a high ponytail. She was young—Nando's age, maybe—and she looked at Bastian kindly.

He didn't trust her.

The woman drew out the chair directly across from Bastian and set down both a thin folder and a plastic cup on the table between them.

She studied Bastian first, silent. Then she said, "You really should eat."

Bastian said nothing. He glared fiercely ahead, past the woman, pretending he could bore a hole through the wall using his eyes alone. Maybe he *could* have, if they hadn't injected him with whatever poison was suppressing his flame.

"We know you like this flavor, Bastian," said the woman. "Would it be more appetizing with a lemonade, perhaps?" She nudged the plastic cup toward Bastian, and pink liquid sloshed out, splashing onto the table.

He didn't move.

"No," said the woman after some time. "I can't say I blame you, Bastian. You've been through a lot today."

"Stop saying that," Bastian mumbled, eyes fixed to the table.

"Excuse me?"

"Stop saying my name."

The woman raised her eyebrows. "Yes, I understand. That's very rude of me, considering I haven't introduced myself. My name is Ira Mehta."

Bastian frowned. Why did that name sound familiar?

"So what," he said. "You work for Gloworks?"

"No, I'm with the DGE. That's the Department of Glowhost Engagement."

"Who's been talking to me on that speaker?"

"That..." The woman named Ira hemmed, scratching at her neck. "That would be Carl Jensen. You see, my people are working in tandem with his organization to—"

That's when Bastian realized: "You work with Nando."

"Yes, that's correct."

"You're *dating* Nando."

"I...that isn't..." Ira touched her hair. "I think it's best we focus on the task at hand."

"Nando knows I'm here?" The flame burned hot inside Bastian. He kept his shaking hands hidden beneath the table. "He knows what you guys are doing to me? To *us*? Where's my sister? Do you have her, too?"

"I'm very sorry, Bastian, but I can't answer those questions."

"Then I don't have anything to say to you."

The woman named Ira didn't seem deterred. She opened the folder before her, turning one page and then another.

"Why aren't you wearing a silver suit, like the rest of them?" Bastian asked. "Aren't you afraid you'll get freak germs?"

Ira looked up. "I'm not afraid of you, Bastian."

"That's why they sent you in, huh? They thought I'd talk to someone who seems nice."

"We're trying to help you," Ira said. "I wish you'd understand. We want to help both you and your friends. Now,

Danielle Hirsch and Zander Poxleitner—do they have favorite places in town? Places they like to hang out?"

"I'm not friends with Zander," Bastian said, on instinct.

Then he realized what Ira's words meant. The silver suits hadn't caught Dani yet. And Zander...

"Please, Bastian. We only want to help."

"If you really wanted to help us, you'd let us go. You wouldn't kidnap us and keep us locked up here."

"This is for your safety."

Bastian met Ira's eyes. "You all want me to talk? Then send in Nando."

"Bastian." Ira sounded sad. "It'd be best if you drank your lemonade."

She nodded to the beverage between them. Then she stood, folder in hand, and made her way to the door. She tapped the touchscreen there, then seemed to consider.

Slowly, she turned to face Bastian and said, "Remember: The door is always open."

Ira nodded once at him. Then she was gone, and Bastian was alone again.

Anger burned where the blue flame lived, begging to be set free. The heat of it seemed to be drying up every particle of moisture inside Bastian. He *was* thirsty. Terribly thirsty. He eyed the cup of pink lemonade with resentment.

A taunt, that's what it was. A trick.

The door is always open.

His mind replayed Ira's parting words, and Bastian looked to the lemonade once more.

The door is always open.

Nando. Nando had told Bastian that at the Frozen Spoon. Nando had been telling him that for years. It was *his* saying, not Ira's.

What did that mean? Was it only coincidence?

Or was it... a message?

It'd be best if you drank your lemonade.

Bastian looked at the cheery pink liquid.

Maybe it was a trick, but what more could these people do to him? He was already captured and powerless.

Bastian grabbed the cup and, in one go, gulped down the lemonade.

Cool relief swept through his throat, and he wiped his mouth, satisfied.

He waited—for what, he couldn't say. He was waiting... for something to change.

And something did change.

The blue flame flared, and then it began to grow. At last, it was expanding, straining hard. Then it was breaking free of its restraints. Bastian gasped, rising from his chair, placing his hands on his chest.

The door is always open.

He pushed his chair aside, fixing his eyes on the door.

Come on, he told the flame as it grew larger still, eating up his insides, pushing out toward his skin.

In a burst of light, the door flew from its hinges, opening Bastian's boardroom prison cell.

He ran free.

FORTY
REUNION

Find me.

The voice woke Lola from sleep.

She blinked open her eyes against blinding light, wondering if the words had only been a dream.

Then the voice reached her again, louder, clearer:

Find me, Lola. Break free.

It was Bastian.

Straps pressed against her arms and legs, and the awful machine beeped on. Lola strained her neck to see a silver suit sitting in the corner of the room. One silver suit, that was all. And Bastian was in her mind.

The blue flame brightened inside of Lola, shooting out eager sparks. She felt her tether to Bastian strengthen, felt energy cross from his mind to hers. Then her power began to return, warming her body through. As it did, the machine beeped faster, turning frantic. The silver suit jumped up and flung open the door, running out, calling for help.

Lola inhaled one grounding breath. Then she pushed the fire out to fill her bones, her veins, her every muscle. The restraints tightened against her skin until, in a burst, they broke free. Lola sat up, prying out the tube jammed up her nose, pulling at the wires hooked to her body with cold, sticky suction cups. She freed herself entirely and dropped from the table to the ground. The blue fire was giving her weak legs the strength she needed to run.

And Lola ran.

I'm here, she called to Bastian, padding barefoot down a sterile white hallway. There was a commotion of shouts and footsteps behind her. She didn't look back, but turned a corner into another corridor that looked the same as the first.

I'm in a stairwell, said Bastian's voice. *Near some kind of garage. See if you can follow my voice.*

Lola paused, forming a firm connection that would lead her to him, as it had so many Sunday nights, during all those games of sardines.

"Stop her! Up there! Stop!"

The silver suits had reached her. Lola turned to see them barreling down the hallway.

And in that moment, Lola was not afraid. The blue flame raged within her, too great to be contained. She knew the flame well. She had used it, day after day, to tether her best friends together. She'd used it to fold paper flowers, to blow

332

dandelions skyward. She wasn't the Lola who had stood petrified in a cafeteria food fight. Not anymore. She could control her power. She *could.*

You *stop,* she thought, and the flame swept through her, shooting out to form a solid wall of blue-white fire. The silver suits skidded to a halt at the fiery barrier, yelling out orders to each other.

And once more, Lola ran.

Her heart beat fast as she followed her connection to Bastian, sliding her mind along it like hands on a guiding rope.

It's easy, Lola told herself. *Treat it like another game of sardines.*

She turned through white hallways, on and on, until she reached a large metal door. When she pushed the door open and stumbled through, she found herself standing in a dark stairwell.

Down, Bastian told her. *Farther down.*

Lola raced down the stairs.

Behind her, the door swung open, and new footsteps echoed in the stairwell.

They had caught up to her.

Lola couldn't think right, could barely breathe. She ventured a glance back and saw—

"Avery!"

The freckled, hazel-eyed girl threw herself forward, and she and Lola fell into a tight embrace.

"I—I couldn't hear you," Lola gasped out. "I was so scared."

Avery nodded against her. *Me too. Then Bastian reached out. He found me. My powers came back.*

They held each other a moment longer as relief flooded Lola's heart. Then, hand in hand, the girls ran down the remaining stairs, until there were no more stairs to follow. There, hidden in the dark corner of the landing, sat Bastian. He raised his head at their approach, and when he did, Lola gasped.

"Bastian," she said. "Your eyes . . . they're glowing."

The blue shine on his face revealed a smile as Bastian replied, "Yours are, too."

FORTY-ONE

ESCAPE

Zander looked at the passing city as Nando sped his car down its dark streets. Houses flashed by, and storefronts, but none of them were familiar. Nando explained that he was keeping to the less-traveled roads of Callaway. The silver suits could be watching, waiting around any bend.

"The DGE knows now," he said. "I haven't reported back. They know I've gone rogue."

Beside Zander, in the backseat, Dani grunted a skeptical "Huh."

Zander had noticed her rubbing at her eyes, now red with irritation.

Itchy contacts? he asked, attempting to break the silence.

Dani looked up sharply. *Get out of my head, would you?*

Zander felt a zap of force in his mind, Dani's thoughts

pushing his out. Maybe, he considered, he and Dani were still too closely connected from coasting. His face got hot.

Sure, whatever. Zander crossed his arms and went back to staring out the window.

Whatever? Dani demanded. *Like you've got a right to be mad at me, after your big confession.*

Oh.

That.

Zander's face got hotter—*lava*-level hot. Dani had heard his confession in Bastian's room after all.

The boosters were Mitchell's idea, he told her, feeling small and miserable. *His and Mr. Jensen's.*

Doesn't matter, Dani shot back. *You went along with it. So that makes you not just a traitor, but also a cheater. I should've known. You Grackles always play dirty.*

Zander ran his knuckles along the seat upholstery. He didn't argue with Dani or give another explanation. It was obvious that she was back to hating him all over again, and if Zander knew one thing for sure, it was that there was no winning with Dani Hirsch when she decided to hate you.

The car stayed quiet, the only sound the engine and the quick, hard shifts as Nando changed gears. In the silence, Zander revisited the memory of throwing Nando to the ground in Bastian's room. Back on Hazard Hill, he'd meant to teach Mitchell a lesson by lifting him off his feet. But at the Gils' house, the force that had come out of him had been instantaneous, like a reflex. The burning blue light in his chest felt stronger than ever.

Soon, there were no more storefronts out his window. They'd crossed through Callaway and were now on a desolate country road, in a sprawl of flat dust and shrubs leading past city limits to their destination: Gloworks, Inc.

Many minutes later, Nando called out, "Here we are."

The glow factory rose before them, concrete and chrome. The building had few windows and fewer doors, and just ahead stood a gate and two guard boxes. Over the gate arched a sign that read, *THE FUEL OF THE FUTURE.*

"How are we going to get past *that?*" whispered Dani, who sounded less angry now and more afraid.

"We're not going that way," said Nando, and in that instant, he made a sharp turn.

Zander's heartbeat quickened as they sped alongside a fence—tall and ugly, made of metal, and lined at the top with spiraling barbed wire. Zander got the feeling that this fence wasn't the only precaution Mr. Jensen had taken to protect his factory.

"What's your plan?" he asked Nando, leaning toward the front seat.

"Ira's inside," Nando replied. "She's working on it."

Dani grunted another one of her skeptical "huhs." Zander didn't feel too sure about Nando's plan, either. This place felt dangerous. And plans could so easily go wrong.

Nando slowed the car to a stop and turned off the engine and lights, then looked back, studying the road behind them.

"Trouble is," he said, "she hasn't called me yet."

"So, what," said Dani, "we wait here? Those guards at the

gate had to have seen us. They're gonna follow us here and ask questions."

"She'll call any second," said Nando. "I know she will. Stay calm."

Nando didn't exactly sound calm himself. Zander's heartbeat was ramping up to top speed.

That's when words filled Zander's head in a sudden, light-filled rush:

We can break down the wall. Together.

It wasn't Dani talking, though. Another voice had reached him. And it sounded a lot like—

"Lola." Dani turned to Zander, eyes big. "It's Lola. I can hear her."

Zander nodded. "Me too."

Nando looked back at them. "What are you talking about?"

"She's somewhere close by," said Dani. "She has to be."

"She's talking about a wall," said Zander. "I think the others are trying to use their powers."

"Of course," said Dani. Even in the dark, Zander could see the light growing in her eyes. "Why didn't we think of that?"

She threw open her car door, despite Nando's shouts, and ran onto the dirt road, right up to the towering factory fence.

"What's she doing?" Nando cried.

"She's going to tear it down," said Zander, somehow knowing without a doubt that what he said was true. "And I'm going to help her."

"What? No, you'll—"

But Zander was out of the car, running up to Dani's side.

Hey, he said, planting his feet in the dirt beside her. *I know you're mad at me, but I can help. We can do this together.*

When Dani looked at Zander, he stumbled back in shock. The light he'd seen in her eyes had grown brighter, and now it was washing all over her face. Her eyes were *glowing.*

Dani said nothing, only nodded. Together, they turned toward the fence, and Zander focused the energy that burned inside his chest. The energy he'd used to secretly open envelopes and shut doors, the energy he'd used to dangle Mitchell Jensen by his feet, the energy he'd used to protect himself from the intruder in Bastian's room. This energy was powerful. And now it was everywhere at once.

The metal fence began to rattle, then *move.* The chain link broke, tearing away, and a sliver of fence folded down, as though Zander and Dani were peeling open a tin of sardines. It was strange, working with Dani, using their powers together. But somehow, this feeling, these powers combined, also felt like the most natural thing in the world.

Nando was shouting behind them. Zander couldn't make out the words, but he didn't care. He was too focused on his work, dragging the fence down with Dani until an open path lay before them.

Then the way was clear, and the two of them ran forward, hurtling over the crumpled metal, heading for the factory.

At the same time, a rumbling sound filled the air, and ahead, light exploded from the factory. Concrete fell away, revealing an opening in the side of the building. The others had done it: They had torn down their own wall.

They came running out, faces aglow, and in seconds the five of them converged. Lola threw her arms around Dani, then Avery did, too, forming a laughing hug. Bastian stood at a distance, watching Zander with his glowing eyes.

Zander wanted to explain, to say something like *I'm the fifth person, not the dog!* But he found that he didn't have a voice; it was like the blue flame had dried it out of his throat.

Then the alarms went off—earsplitting, spiraling wails.

"Come on!" shouted Dani, pointing ahead to the opening in the fence and, beyond it, Nando's car.

They ran as white lights flashed nearby, drawing closer, breaking across the night in eerie strobes. Nando was standing beside his car, looking stunned and holding on to the open door as though his legs might not support him. But before the Sardines could reach the car, the bright lights flashed into Zander's eyes, sending him stumbling. He heard the roar of engines and the hurried slams of van doors.

A loud voice broke through the night, amplified by a megaphone. "STOP WHERE YOU ARE. WE HAVE YOU SURROUNDED."

A heavy weight threw Zander to the ground. He looked back and saw a silver suit grappling with his wrists, closing them into cold metal. He heard the others' shouts and violent scuffling.

They hadn't gotten away after all.

No.

The silver suit hauled Zander to his feet and dragged him forward, calling to the driver of a nearby van, "Prep an injection!"

Panic burned inside Zander.

No, raged the blue flame. *NO.*

The fire burst out of him, throwing off the silver suit that held him and knocking several nearby suits to the ground. The handcuffs fell away from his wrists, and Zander looked to Dani, nearby, struggling with her captors. His fire raged on, pushing at the suits that were holding her down. They flew back into the air before hitting the ground. Then Dani stumbled to her feet.

Thanks, she said, and for one second, Zander was stupid enough to grin.

Then the two of them turned, together, toward their struggling friends.

The fire rushed through both of them now—that still unfamiliar but *right* feeling—and Zander and Dani reached out, dragging the silver suits off Bastian first, then Lola and Avery. As each of the Sardines stood, their thoughts joined Zander's.

Let's run, Avery was thinking.

The car, Bastian added.

This is our chance, said Dani.

Each thought felt as though it had been cast out like a string with a hooked end, and each of these hooks caught in Zander's head. Tethers.

Zander, said a soft voice in his mind. *You too?*

He met the gaze of Lola, whose hook was strongest of all, and he realized that she was the one bringing them together. The connection was strong, and so dizzying that Zander felt a little like puking. Inside, the flame burned hotter. All their eyes were alight, glowing blue where pupils should have been. It was a terrifying sight, but Zander wasn't afraid. He was one of them—a Sardine.

Get to the car! Dani shouted into their heads.

The five of them ran toward Nando's sedan, past fallen silver suits. Then, abruptly, they stopped.

One man remained standing, facing Nando. His suit wasn't silver; it was navy. And in his hand was a small black object.

In the flickering lights, Zander recognized the face of the man in the navy suit. He'd seen it tons of times on television commercials, and he'd seen it in person way more often ever since he'd joined the Grackles.

It was Carl Jensen, the King of Callaway.

"Unfortunate," Mr. Jensen said loudly, aiming the gun at Nando's chest. "A contract simply doesn't mean what it used to."

Zander watched, stock-still and openmouthed, as Nando raised his hands. "Your deal isn't with us, Jensen," he said in a low voice. "Ira and I—we're not with the DGE anymore. If you understood what you're dealing with here . . . they're kids, Jensen. *Kids.* You've got one of your own, you told me over coffee. Think about it. Help us out. The DGE doesn't need to know you were involved with their escape."

In reply, Mr. Jensen cocked his gun. "They're an asset," he

said. "I've been investing in them a long time. I went all the way to DC, struck a deal."

"You're plenty rich, Jensen," Nando replied, keeping his hands aloft, but—Zander noted—edging toward the car. "You don't have to do this."

"This isn't just about the money," said the man in the navy suit. "It's about this country's national security. With their powers, those kids are going to win us the war. As a DGE agent, you should know that. You should see why this is necessary. Sometimes, country comes before self."

What happened next was a terrible commotion of sight and sound.

A loud *pow*,

Lola's scream,

and a blinding blue flash of light.

It took moments for Zander's vision to clear. When it did, he saw Mr. Jensen thrown to the ground, unconscious. Lola was bent over him, shaking badly, hands at her side. And then there was Nando—slumped against the car.

"NANDO!" Bastian shouted, running to his brother's side. He skidded to his knees, eyes searching Nando's body, as Zander, Avery, and Dani gathered close.

"Nando," he pleaded. "Nando, be okay."

The world around Zander fell dead silent.

Then Nando coughed, pushing himself up. He breathed in deeply.

"I'm...fine," he said hoarsely, looking at the gathered Sardines. "It's all right. He missed. I'm okay."

"Lola," Avery said, and the others looked to where Lola was still slumped over a fallen Mr. Jensen—in shock, it seemed. "She used the flame to knock him out."

As Zander put the pieces together, he heard more engines rumbling closer, more car doors slamming. He tensed, but before he could move, a woman's voice called out, "Jones! Nando, it's us!"

Nando struggled to stand as a woman rushed toward them. She was dressed in a gray pantsuit, and her dark curly hair whipped around in the night wind. She reached Nando, helping him to his feet and speaking too low for the others to hear. Then both of them turned toward the Sardines.

"Come on," Nando said, waving to the car. "We're getting you out."

But Bastian was already in the car.

He had taken the driver's seat.

None of the Sardines spoke; they didn't have to. Somehow even Zander knew, on instinct, what to do. He scrambled into the back of the car, alongside Lola, whom Avery had helped up from her shocked state. Dani slammed herself into the passenger seat, pressing the power lock and sealing them in.

"Hey!" came Nando's muffled voice. He pulled on the driver's side handle, then banged on the window, looking in, bewildered.

"Hazard Hill!" Dani shouted.

"Midnight!" Zander added, pointing to the clock on the car's dash, which read *11:54*. "C'mon! We have to *go*."

Then a remarkable thing happened.

The vehicle began to rumble and shake, even though there were no keys in the ignition. Nando's car lurched—not forward, but *up.*

The blue flame heaved among the Sardines, shooting out tendrils, blue strands that curled beneath their seats, drawing them up into the sky, tugging the tires off the ground.

Then they were airborne, climbing upward. Nando's beating fists fell away from the window, and Zander looked out to see the earth expanding fast beneath them. The silver suits looked as small as action figures on the ground. They passed the shining sign that read, *THE FUEL OF THE FUTURE.*

The Sardines pushed the car forward, and they were no longer rising but *flying,* high above Callaway.

Beneath them, roads wound out and crisscrossed in long black ribbons. The car soared over rooftops into the light of a full moon. Zander knew exactly where they were headed. The blue column's message was clear, made complete in their shared thoughts. The five of them had an appointment tonight, at midnight, on Hazard Hill. The car flew on, and Bastian guided the wheel, but really, all five of them did the steering, charting a course to their destination.

At last, Zander let out a sigh of relief.

That's when the car shuddered, dropping a few feet. Zander and Avery let out startled screams. Something was wrong. The connection the Sardines had formed outside Gloworks had frayed somewhere, and there was a plucking sensation behind Zander's eyes.

"Lola?" Avery said, touching Lola's shoulder. Then louder, *"Lola?"*

Again, the car shuddered, and Zander looked across the backseat.

Lola was huddled against the window, her eyes glazed and distant. Slowly, she held out her hands.

They were covered in blood.

FORTY-TWO

FLIGHT

A very watched in horror as more blood emerged from Lola's side. The bullet must have gone deep for there to be so much of it, and though Avery was pressing her hand against the wound as hard as she could, it wasn't enough to stop the bleeding.

"It didn't miss Nando," Avery whispered. "You jumped in front of him."

Lola smiled weakly, her eyelids drooping. "I wasn't afraid."

"We have to do something!" Avery shouted to the others. "We have to get her to a hospital!"

But Bastian was shaking his head. "There isn't time!" he shouted back. "The light beings—they can help us. They can *fix* her. Don't you feel that?"

Avery did feel it; the blue flame was urging her toward Hazard Hill. The light had faded from the Sardines' eyes, but

Avery still saw the determination in their faces. Somehow, they all understood what had to happen next, where they needed to go. And it wasn't to a hospital. It was to Hazard Hill.

They just had to make it there in time.

Lola was trying to say something, but Avery couldn't make it out. The car shuddered and dropped several more feet.

Then Lola closed her eyes.

"No." Avery pressed more firmly against the wound. "No, Lola. Stay awake!"

In her head, Avery felt a telltale *snip*. As Lola was growing weaker, so was her tether. The little threads connecting her to Avery were pulling loose, one by one. The familiar hue of Lola's thoughts was fading from lavender to lifeless gray.

Just hang on. Avery pushed the words over the damaged connection. She dragged Lola into her lap, trying to prop her up. She'd heard once that when someone was injured, you had to keep their heart raised over the wound. Or was it that you had to keep the wound raised over the heart? And what did you do when the wound and the heart were so close together?

The car jolted violently, losing more altitude. Avery felt weak, deep inside. She was too weak to think straight, let alone keep a car aloft. She couldn't even form a thought to send to the other Sardines, and though they remained tethered, none of them reached out to her. Avery wondered if they felt the way she did: that their tele-whatevers were ebbing away.

"We're close to the hill!" Bastian shouted. "We're almost there!"

Zander leaned over the console, pointing out the

windshield. "Steer it toward the road," he said. "Watch out for those boulders!"

"Yeah, great advice, man, thanks," Bastian growled.

"Stop fighting!" Avery screamed.

Snip, snip. More threads cut her loose from Lola. But that couldn't happen. Not now, after everything—their victory at Glow in the Park, their escape from the silver suits. And Hazard Hill was close. They couldn't lose Lola now.

"We're gonna make it!" Bastian yelled.

But, thought Avery, *what if Lola can't?*

"Please," she whispered, wondering if Lola was beyond hearing now. "Please, Lols. We need you. We love you."

She looked out the window to the moon-drenched terrain below. They had reached the base of Hazard Hill, but the car was descending rapidly, now only yards off the ground. As they juddered over the dusty, boulder-lined road, Avery saw the red-and-white police barriers ahead.

The car swerved as Bastian and Dani shouted over one another: "Stop, stop!" and "I'm going for it!" The next moment, they were crashing through the barriers, knocking them over in a great *wham.*

"Brace yourselves!" Bastian shouted as the car slammed into solid ground, sending Avery sprawling.

The car clunked and skidded to a stop. Then all was silent.

"She's fading," Avery whispered, watching the rattling rise and fall of Lola's chest.

Bastian shook his head fiercely. "She won't. We'll take her to them. If anyone can help us, it's them."

Everyone knew who Bastian meant by "them," just as everyone knew that they had to reach the top of the hill. It was time.

It was midnight.

On the summer solstice.

And they were on Hazard Hill—all five of them.

The others got out of the car, circling to where Avery sat with Lola in her lap.

"We shouldn't move her!" Avery cried, but Dani and Zander were already lifting Lola into their arms. She floated up between them, their blue flame keeping her aloft.

"H-how are you doing that?" Avery asked, feeling so weak.

Dani and Zander shared a look. Then, softly, Zander said, "Avery, you have to break the link with her."

"She's letting go," Dani said. "If you don't break your connection, she's going to keep draining your powers. I know you can feel it, Vee. We all can. It's why we crashed."

"I'm not doing that!" Avery shouted, even as more *snip*, *snip*s echoed in her ears. "Maybe I'm *how* she's hanging on. Maybe she needs our powers to live, and that's why she's draining them!"

"I'm not breaking mine, either," Bastian said, his eyes wide. "We can't shut her out. She needs us. I *won't* shut her out."

"Okay," Dani said as she and Zander stepped away, drawing out Lola between them. "But we have to get her up there. We have to reach *them* in time."

FORTY-THREE
SUMMIT

A storm was brewing overhead. Dark clouds crowded across the big Texan sky, eating away the light of the moon. Hard rain began to pelt Bastian's face, but it didn't matter. What mattered was reaching the top of the hill. What mattered was his sister's hand in his.

Bastian walked alongside Zander and Dani, who were moving Lola on the invisible stretcher they'd formed with their linked minds. Avery held Lola's left hand, and Bastian held her right. Lola's skin was far too cool, her fingers limp.

Bastian's flame was diminishing. He knew that was Lola's doing, but he couldn't cut his tether any more than Avery could hers. This was his sister, his twin. Lola would always be his closest connection of all.

The light beings can save her, he thought. *We just have to walk faster.*

He reached his thoughts outward, trying to find Lola, but she was hidden somewhere in a swirling white mist that muddled his mind. He stumbled once, then righted himself, still gripping Lola's hand.

Then the mist was no longer in Bastian's mind, but all around him. Along the path were the blackened, smoking remains of trees and shrubs. The fire—*their* fire—had made its mark on Hazard Hill.

Bastian knew, was sure, that someone was waiting for them at the summit.

The wind picked up, causing Bastian's shirt to billow and ripple.

He kept walking.

He kept holding Lola's hand.

Minutes passed. The incline began to flatten, little by little, then more and more. The wind blew into Bastian, rougher than before. Then he saw it through the mist, glowing the faintest green: the starting line.

They had reached the top of Hazard Hill.

Bastian knew, by instinct, what to do. He knelt as Dani and Zander lowered Lola to the earth. All of them gathered, kneeling, forming a circle around her. Bastian began to form a memory—so familiar, so vibrant in his head. A memory of beauty, of the good there could be in life. He was ready to speak to the aliens. He only hoped they were ready to listen to him.

The world was quiet for one moment. There was no sound but the wind.

Then the light appeared, and the darkness around them scattered.

FORTY-FOUR

CONTACT

L ola was bathed in a haze of blue. She couldn't speak, couldn't move. But she knew she was where she was supposed to be.

A bright blue column appeared above her head, gently pulsing, and from it a form emerged. It stepped down from the light to Lola's side and embraced her in its many arms. It spoke tenderly in her mind, with a voice that was several but one.

Rest, child of ours. Rest.

Lola no longer felt scared or pained. The vision of Avery's worried face drifted away, replaced by a cooling sensation. The air around smelled of mint and newly budded flowers, and the coolness drifted from Lola's eyes to her wound. It settled there, intensifying, working through muscle. Lola felt a stitching sensation, as though she had been torn before and was now being woven whole.

The voice returned to her mind.

Rise, it said.

Energy shot through Lola's legs and, no longer tired, she found she *could* rise. She beamed at the sight of the other Sardines. They were all there—Bastian, Dani, and Avery. Even Zander stood in their circle, and somehow Lola knew he belonged there, too. All their heads were tilted upward, toward the column shooting down the very center of the hill's crest. There were stars shining in their eyes.

More figures emerged from the column. Their hair floated down in thick, long strands. Their many arms stretched out in a gesture of welcome. And inside each of the figures, blue light burned beneath their transparent skin.

Greetings, children of Earth, their voices spoke in unison. *We have come to rescue you from this place.*

The blue column began to transform. Colors appeared on its surface—greens and oranges and reds, projected there by an unseen source. The column rotated clockwise, faster and faster, like a spinning top. The colors on its surface blurred, disorganized and dizzying. Eventually the spinning slowed, and the blurs distinguished themselves, forming shapes—*images.* Then the spinning stopped utterly, and the images sharpened, so clear that they now looked like a broadcast on a TV screen. There was news footage of the war, shattered buildings, crying children, bloodied soldiers. Then there was Dani, taking a bad fall off her glowboard, Bastian in bed with a fever, and Zander placing flowers at a tombstone marked *Celeste Kwon Poxleitner.*

Lola felt more memories being siphoned from her mind:

the unfeeling look in Mitchell Jensen's eyes, the day she'd fallen down the stairs and fractured a bone in her left arm, the overheard shouts between Nando and her parents.

Such pain, said the beautiful figures. *Senseless suffering. It extends over all this planet and has affected each one of you.*

The figure who had touched Lola stepped forward, reaching out its arms, turning a deliberate circle, facing each one of them. When it spoke, there was no static obscuring its words.

We are the source of what your kind call Component G. We deposited it in many planets less developed than our own, intending that your civilizations would, over time, evolve to the level of existence we have long enjoyed. We had hoped that our gift of elixir would raise this Earth's civilization to new heights. Instead, your world continues to war, and to bring you—a new generation— into that war's crosshairs. Humans have chosen to capture others of your kind and use them for evil, violent purposes. We were wrong to believe this planet would prove a hospitable environment for gifted creatures like you. And so we have come to remove you from this planet, and to destroy what remains of its unenlightened inhabitants.

Come now. Come with us.

Lola felt the cooling sensation again—like a splash of water, drenching her mind. The light beings' words had awakened her. She saw now the sense of their message. In so many ways, Earth *was* a terrible place, filled with people who wanted to hurt Lola: silver suits, who would tie her down to a table and take away her power. Bullies like Mitchell Jensen and his

Grackles. Unknown faces on the other side of the war, who would hurt Nando if given the chance.

Maybe, Lola thought, the light beings had been right all along.

Maybe it would be best to leave.

NO!

Bastian's shout broke into Lola's head.

REMEMBER, Bastian cried. Her brother was staring wildly at her, gripping her hand. *REMEMBER WHAT WE CAME HERE TO DO.*

And with difficulty, as though dredging out a heavy box from under water, Lola began to remember: *Remembering.* That's what they were here to do. They had practiced, they had prepared. They had made mistakes, but now it was time for the Sardines to share their message.

Bastian looked afraid, though.

Lola, he said, his thoughts quieter. *I've been trying to share my memories, but it's like they're bouncing back. They're not going through. I don't think I'm strong enough to do it on my own.*

Lola! cried another voice. Dani. She stood opposite Lola, her face cast in a bright, blue glow. *Lola, I can't get through to them. We have to try something else.* You *have to try.*

Lola didn't need Bastian or Dani to explain. She knew. Here, on Hazard Hill, she had tethered them together. *Together,* the Sardines were more powerful. Together, they'd set this place ablaze. Now it was up to Lola to bind the Sardines again, and *together,* they would try to reach the light beings.

She began the tether as she always did, hooking a steady link in Bastian's mind. Then she turned to Avery, who was clasping her other hand.

You can do it, Lols, Avery told her, eyes shining. *I know you can.*

Avery's tether caught hold in an instant.

Then Lola turned to Dani and cast another link. Dani grabbed hold with so much force, Lola stumbled a step, tightening her grip on Bastian's and Avery's hands.

And then there was Zander.

Lola frowned, suddenly uncertain. The first time she had reached Zander had been outside Gloworks. Until that moment, she hadn't known she *could.* This connection was new, uncertain. But she would try.

Lola shut her eyes. She concentrated on the flame inside— so familiar, so volatile.

I can do this, she told herself, and herself alone. *I'm in control.*

She unraveled her newest tether and, opening her eyes, she threw it out to Zander, hoping that he would sense it and take hold, as he'd known to do before. She saw the moment it happened: Zander's eyes widened, his lips parting in slight shock. And then the link found its place in his mind.

Bastian's memories were the first to shoot down the tether, vivid and fierce: the day he'd shown Avery how to skate, gripping her hand for balance as she wobbled down Cedar Lane; family car rides with Lola, the twins laughing at knock-knock jokes they passed between their minds; talks with Dani atop Hazard Hill, the setting sun in their eyes.

Memories of people, of friends—the best kind of memories. They trembled along the threads that bound the Sardines together, and Lola saw, with gasping delight, that the images were not merely in her mind, but outside of it, projected onto the column of light.

Lola's heart warmed as new scenes filled her mind: Avery's memories. She saw herself and Avery on Sardines Night, sitting on the branch of the big oak tree, so close that their knees were touching. She saw Avery eating strawberry ice cream with the team at the Frozen Spoon, after a racing victory, giggling at something Dani had said. Then the images shifted again, and memories flooded in from another source: Dani. She saw the Sardines gathered at the May Day Draft Train Bonanza, piling their hands and cheering. She saw the sunny day when Avery and Dani had first met, talking over the fence between their backyards. She watched in surprise as Zander and Dani looked over glowboards in a shop, and Dani picked up one, joy flooding her face.

It was as though this memory of Zander had sparked his own, because even he seemed to know what to do. His memory was fainter, fuzzy at the edges, but it was strong enough for Lola to make out Dani, Bastian, and herself skating with Zander down Cedar Lane. Lola recognized the memory: It was the team's very first practice, the day they'd decided to call themselves Sardines.

The glow enveloping the light beings gave a shaking pulse. Whispered words, spoken in a language Lola couldn't understand, spun around her like wind.

Then the figure who had spoken to Lola stepped forward. It reached out, placing one of its three-fingered hands on Lola's forehead.

Lola knew then that it was her time to share. Concentrating, she formed her practiced memories—the ones she cherished most.

See them, Lola pleaded. *Please. Understand.*

Then she allowed the images to take over: A rainy morning when she and Bastian had gathered in her bedroom to make paper boats, with Lola folding and Bastian painting the sails. The day on Hazard Hill when Dani had agreed to a free skate. The morning on Avery's front porch when Avery had told Lola her thoughts felt like a color. Then Lola retrieved an old, untried memory of Zander, of the gift he'd given her two birthdays ago, when they'd been friends: sheets of floral-patterned folding paper.

The memories rushed from her like a shimmering wave.

The figure took a step back. *Why would you wish to remain here, children? Should you stay, further pain is inevitable.*

Another memory shook along the tether, exploding in vibrant color: an ordinary day on Hazard Hill, the Sardines laughing and sweeping along the dusty track with their boards. A free skate. Lola didn't know if the memory was hers, or another Sardine's. In the end, she realized, it didn't matter. What mattered was the message: *We want to stay here, no matter how hard it is. We want to stay here, with the people we love.*

More whispers swept around Lola. Then the joined voices said, *They've grown attached.*

It was only an observation, yet Lola felt instinctively that something was wrong. Attachment was not a thing to be desired.

There is such evil, such ugliness, the voices continued. *And yet, there is also beauty. Great capacity for love and happiness. These two extremes exist together, in a perplexing tension. It is incomprehensible to us...and to you, too, dear children.*

Still, said the speaking figure. *One thing is clear.*

Light swept around their circle, touching the face of each Sardine—Avery, then Dani, Zander, then Bastian, and, last of all, Lola. She felt a tingling sensation in her head, as though she was being fed spoonfuls of electricity. The light beings were inside her mind.

The memories returned to Lola of Gil family dinners, complete with their fights, her shared birthday parties with Bastian, the long afternoons spent practicing right here, on Hazard Hill.

Yes, Lola told the light. *I want to stay. I do.*

The electric buzz subsided, and the light curled back into the blue column. Then the many figures began to slip away, stepping into the column, absorbed by its glow. One by one, they disappeared until only the first figure, the speaker, remained.

It is futile, the light being said, *to work against such deep desires as these. And we would never eradicate a world where life-forms like you still exist. We will visit again, perhaps at a time when we can all better comprehend.*

The figure stretched out its many arms, as though it were

reaching for each of them, trying to show that it cared. *Until then, we will protect you as best we can from afar.*

A magnificent light burst from the column. Then the last figure was gone, vanished, and the column pulsed radiantly until, in a great *whoosh*, it shot into the sky.

FORTY-FIVE

SHATTERED

Avery blinked, wondering if the world around her really was so dark, or if her eyes had been permanently changed. The column was gone, sucked into the storm clouds from which it had emerged. A roll of thunder swept overhead, and then, the very next second, rain sheeted down on the Sardines.

Beside Avery, Lola coughed, wiping at her eyes and pushing back soaked strands of hair from her loose braid. Avery didn't hesitate. She threw herself on Lola, wrapping her arms around her shoulders.

"Y-you're okay," she sputtered through wet, chattering lips. "You're okay, Lols. You're *okay*." Then a sudden fear seized Avery, and she pulled back. "You *are* okay, aren't you?"

Lola smiled and wordlessly tugged up her T-shirt to show

the place where Mr. Jensen's bullet hole had once been. There, in its stead, was a faint blue circular scar.

The others gathered close, wrapping Lola into a group hug. Then they looked toward the sky. Avery wondered if, like her, the others were trying to figure out everything that had happened. Feather-soft words still circled her memory: *We will protect you as best we can from afar.*

Avery couldn't say how long they had spent with the light beings. One moment, she was sure they'd only touched down for a minute. The next, she was convinced they'd been on the hill for hours. Maybe, she reflected, the important thing wasn't the time, but the message.

"Lola," she said. "You tethered us. You did it."

Lola smiled. "No, *we* did it. Together."

"Do you hear that?" said Dani, peering at the others through the rainfall.

Avery listened. Thunder crashed above, and the rain continued to patter. But she knew that Dani wasn't talking about the storm. She listened harder, finally making out the sounds of . . . a crowd.

The Sardines were not alone.

In unison, the five of them turned toward the slope of Hazard Hill. People—adults and children alike—had gathered below. They were gaping and pointing. At *them.*

Avery took Lola's hand in hers. The rain had drenched Avery's clothes, but somehow she didn't feel cold. She was on fire.

Well, she said to the others. *We have to go down there eventually. Let's do it together. Let's show them we're not afraid.*

She felt a lavender thread unspool in her mind. *Lola.* She was tethering them together once more.

The Sardines joined hands. Then they walked downhill into the waiting crowd. Dozens of people had gathered, but none of them approached the Sardines. They only stared, whispered, and pointed.

The Sardines kept walking, following the path they had skated so many times before. Still, no one called out, and no one stood in their way. It was only as the Sardines rounded the final bend in the track that the lights flashed and the shouting started up. The crowd was much denser here, gathered so close together that they blocked the Sardines' path. And right there, forming the front of the blockade, stood a dozen silver suits.

Avery's breath caught, but not for long. It was startled out of her by a too-familiar voice shouting her name.

"Veemeister! Vee! Hey, honey, look here!"

A man was racing toward her, a video camera hoisted on his shoulder. Even through all the layers of plastic that covered his camera and clothes, Avery knew in an instant who it was.

"Look here!" Eric Miller called. "Come on, Vee! What did you experience?"

Avery faced her father.

He had turned his back on her in the principal's office. He had canceled plans on her, again and again. He had lied. He had given her away. He had allowed bad people to take her and hook her up to machines. Now he stood before her with his camera and all the nerve in the world.

The blue light burned inside Avery, but she wasn't angry anymore. Now she knew the truth.

With calm concentration, she focused her gaze on the lens of her father's camera. There was a moment of silence. Then the lens shattered, little pieces of glass crumbling onto the muddied earth.

Avery didn't wait to see Eric Miller's reaction. Instead, she turned to her friends. The Sardines nodded to each other, the last of the starlight fading from their eyes.

Things will never be the same, Avery thought.

And the others thought back, in unison, *No, they won't.*

Avery didn't know what they were walking into. She only knew that they were walking on.

FORTY-SIX

THE FINAL SHOWDOWN

"Stop right there!"

The words pelted off Dani like the rain. She didn't care that Mr. Carl Jensen himself was standing at the base of the hill, lit by a floodlight and flanked on both sides by his silver suits. His threats meant nothing now. Who did he think he was yelling at? *Kids?*

They weren't kids.

They were the Sardines.

The silver suits barred their path, and Mr. Jensen shouted on. His navy suit was soaked through, beads of water stuck on his mustache and gathering on his wide-brimmed hat.

"Step away, they're dangerous! They *attacked* me earlier!" he yelled at the crowd. Then, to the silver suits, "Stand your ground!"

With one mind, the Sardines stopped walking and faced

their enemy. This was the man who had tracked and hunted them down, the father of their biggest bully—just a bigger bully himself. He had tried to kill Nando, nearly killed Lola, and he was a cheater, too; Dani hadn't forgotten Zander's confession. What made the richest man in Callaway want to cheat?

Together, the five of them pooled their fire, forming a single force. The force pushed gently into the crowd, sending bystanders shuffling back. Then it reached Mr. Jensen and held him firmly in place. It stilled the bodies of the silver suits, froze the entire crowd, as the Sardines passed them by.

"Look what they're doing!" Mr. Jensen shouted, straining against his invisible bonds. "Do you see their power? Do you see the danger? Someone stop them before they get away!"

No one stopped the Sardines. They walked on to the finish line.

There, at the base of the hill, was a gold car. A man emerged from the driver's side.

It was Nando.

A question rippled through the Sardines, filled with uncertainty:

Can we trust him?

Dani glanced at Zander, and together they shared with the others what Nando had told them about the DGE, and how he and Ira had gone rogue.

But, thought Dani, *those could be more lies. Another trick.*

No. Lola's thought reached out to the others, firm with

conviction. *It's not a trick. He's my brother. I took a bullet for him, didn't I?*

With that, Lola released Avery's hand and stepped ahead of the others.

"Lola," Nando said, throwing his arms around her.

"Nando," she said into her brother's shirt. "Take us away from here."

With that, the Sardines piled into the car.

Thunder rumbled all around, and the rain fell harder.

But there was something different about this rain. Through the still-open car door came the scent of roses and lemons, heavy and sweet.

We will protect you as best we can from afar.

Dani knew this new rain was *their* doing. She watched from inside the car as the crowd regained movement and wiped at their eyes, looking around in confusion, as though utterly unsure of how they had ended up there.

"What's happening?" asked Nando as he slowly backed the car away, toward the desert road, headlights on.

"Their memories," Dani said, knowing it to be true. Bastian had been right all along: *Memory* was what the light beings knew best. "The aliens are taking their memories away."

FORTY-SEVEN

THE DECISION

The Sardines sat in Nando's apartment, in a small living room with plaster walls and two worn leather couches. Minutes after they'd arrived, the woman in the gray pantsuit had shown up—Ira Mehta, Nando's coworker and girlfriend. But, Nando explained, what the Sardines most needed to know was this: Ira, like Nando, was on their side.

"I just want to be safe," Avery said. "*Really* safe."

"I want to see Mom and Dad," said Lola. "They must be so worried."

Dani muttered, "Bet my parents don't even know I'm gone."

Zander said nothing at all. He could still feel tingling, electric waves running down his skin, the same sensation he'd felt as he'd watched the strange, memory-cleansing rain.

The true nature of the rain became clear when Ira showed

up, soaked. She couldn't recall any of the past day's events, even though Bastian swore she'd been the one to give him a lemonade filled with the antidote to the DGE's anti-power injection.

"Once I was cured," Bastian explained, "it was like I could pass it on to Lola and Avery, because they were close by. The three of us were connected again. That's how we escaped and found the others. That was because of you, Ira, remember? You told me Nando's secret phrase: *The door is always open.*"

Ira frowned intently at Bastian, wringing out her hair. "I remember the *plan*," she said. "The antidote and the code. I remember going to a clubhouse, leaving a note to warn you away from Hazard Hill. But your names, your faces, this *day*—" Ira touched her head. "There's nothing."

Now, though, Ira knew the Sardines' secret for good.

And, of course, so did Nando.

"You'd better be the good guys," Dani said. "If not—"

"They are!" cried Lola, turning to Nando, who sat by her side. "They have to be."

Nando hugged Lola close and said, "We're trying to be, anyway."

"So what do you want from us now?"

All eyes turned to Zander. He'd surprised even himself by asking the question. A part of him felt he didn't have the right to speak. He had stood on Hazard Hill with the Sardines, seen the light beings, and shared their memories with them. But none of that stuff made him a true Sardine. He could still remember the looks on the team's faces when they'd first seen him hanging with Mitchell's crowd. He could remember Dani's expression when he'd told her the Grackles had cheated at Glow in the Park, and the look on Bastian's face when Mitchell had spat on him at Glow Expo, and Zander had done nothing—just stood by and watched.

Maybe the Sardines were all outsiders; maybe they shared that bond. But Zander wondered if he would ever be one of them again.

"What do you want?" Zander asked Nando and Ira again. "Now that you know our secret, what'll you do with it? Same as what Jensen's people did? Connect us to wires? Perform experiments?"

That got an answer out of Nando. "No, nothing like that. We don't want to use you. We want you to live normal, peaceful lives. We want to protect you. We want to be your friends."

Beside Zander, Dani squinted. "Friends, huh?" She looked at Bastian and Lola. "Do you two want to be *friends* with your brother?"

Lola said nothing, only laid her head on Nando's shoulder.

Bastian looked hesitant, but there was a glimmer of hope in his dark brown eyes. Zander guessed that's how he felt, too: He wanted to believe that Nando was good. After the running, the sirens, the fights—Zander wanted to feel safe.

"So," he said, "what do we do now?"

Nando looked to the television. The sound was muted, but on-screen, the local early morning news was airing. The weatherman was cheerily reporting on rain showers that would likely last all day. A news anchor began a story about a lost neighborhood cat.

There was no talk of Hazard Hill. There was nothing about strange columns of light or rain that smelled of flowers, not even about the fire that had raged there the night before. It was enough to make Zander wonder if the last twenty-four hours had only been in his head.

But when he looked at the Sardines, at Nando and Ira, he knew he hadn't imagined a single second. All of it was real, and the seven of them in this room—maybe they were the only ones left who knew the full truth.

"I guess," said Nando, gesturing to the very normal news, "life can go back to the way it was. If this rain does what we think it does, the DGE and Jensen might not even know who you are, or that Ira and I went rogue. If that's the case, we can get them off your trail and out of Callaway. Make up false readings that will lead them away from you."

"Then what?" asked Bastian. "We're supposed to go back to life like none of this ever happened?"

"Well," said Nando, "there are worse options, right?"

Yes, thought Zander. There were worse options. Options involving Gloworks, Inc. and a government organization intent on turning five kids into weapons for the war.

There were *way* worse options.

"I don't think we'll ever really be the same." Lola spoke softly, looking around at the others. "But it's what they wanted, don't you think?"

Zander, like the other Sardines, knew who Lola meant by

"they." He remembered the light and the cooling breath that had filled his lungs on Hazard Hill, the many arms held out like a hundred embraces.

"Yeah," he said. "It's what they wanted."

Dani turned to the others, a cautious smile on her lips. "You all get that we did it, right? We convinced aliens not to blow up the whole world."

"Not that the whole world will ever thank us," said Avery. "*Sooo* ungrateful."

"I just didn't think our plan would actually work," said Dani.

"Uh-*huh*." Bastian crossed his arms. "You mean, you're shocked that *my* plan worked."

Dani thought about this, then shrugged. "Yeah, I guess so. Consider me impressed, Gil."

Avery nudged Lola's shoulder and said, "Let's not forget who really saved the day. That was expert tethering, Lols."

"It was nothing," Lola replied, grinning.

All four of them exchanged glances, a happy triumph in their eyes. Zander sank into the couch, feeling suddenly alone. Maybe he'd shared a connection with the Sardines atop Hazard Hill, but he hadn't shared the past *year* with them—all the meetings in Cedar House and nighttime games of sardines, the glowboard practices and the inside jokes.

Then he felt slight pressure on his wrist.

It was Dani.

"Zee," she said. "We couldn't have done it without you,

either. The aliens said it had to be all five of us, or it wouldn't work."

"Yeah," said Avery. "Face it: You're stuck with the smelly Sardines, whether you like it or not."

Zander turned to Lola, who, though she remained quiet, gave him a kind smile. The only Sardine he didn't dare look at was Bastian. Zander wasn't sure Bastian was ready to approve of him just yet, and to be honest, he understood. First, Zander would have to make up for all he had done—or, more importantly, all he *hadn't* done—while he'd been with Mitchell and his Grackles. That would take time.

A chiming sound filled the room, and Nando started, looking down at his digiwatch. He read the message there, then frowned. "Uh," he said, "Mom and Dad say they've got some dog named Radar?"

THREE MONTHS LATER

The man in the navy suit looked out his window at the town of Callaway. His mind was wandering, as it often did these days. He was trying to remember something.

He was always trying to *remember*.

There were still papers tacked on his wall, each of them blank. There were empty files on his computer. And there was a note on his desk that read, simply,

WATCH YOUR BACK.
SINCERELY,
AN ENEMY

The man had made plenty of enemies over the course of his career. He had fought for wealth, position, and power. "An enemy" could be one of hundreds. His memory was hazy, but he had the distinct impression of a blazing blue light. A powerful presence. Somehow, he knew that this particular enemy was not to be crossed.

A September sun was setting over town,

spilling out an umber hue. The sight of it made the man unspeakably sad.

He shouldn't have felt sad. He was, after all, the King of Callaway.

But as Carl Jensen turned from the sun, he came to a grim conclusion: Maybe, just maybe, being king wasn't all it was cracked up to be.

FORTY-EIGHT
FREE SKATE

Tonight was Sardines Night, but today was all about skating.

Not practice, just *skating*—nothing but glowboards and Hazard Hill and all the time in the world.

"INCOMING!" Dani shouted, curving hard down the track, orange glowstream trailing behind her. A breeze blew against her face, knocking Dani breathless. It was the best feeling in the world. Around her bloomed shrubs and green-leafed trees, and more plants than had ever grown on the hill before the twenty-first of June. Only the Sardines remembered the fire that had happened here, just as only the Sardines remembered their draft train victory.

To the rest of the world, it was as though Glow in the Park had never happened. The official story was that the event had been canceled at the last minute, but if you asked a participant to their face what the reason for the cancellation had been, their eyes would glass over, their gaze turn distant, and they would say, "Well, I don't remember now."

Dani knew the truth. She knew their race time. She knew the Sardines had beat the Grackles, as they'd set out to do.

That was what mattered.

Mitchell Jensen could call them freaks all he wanted. He was the cheater, and to have a dad like Mr. Jensen? These days, Dani spent less time hating Mitchell and more time feeling sorry for the guy.

The next big race wouldn't be until October—the Haunted Halloween Bash—but Dani wasn't worried about that yet. For now, she was forgetting race times. For now, on this warm fall day, she wanted to have fun.

As she crossed the finish line, she whirled into a sharp carve, throwing out a hand to slide to a stop.

"Woo!" shouted Avery, clapping from where she sat, perched on the iron gate. "Moves like that, you should enter single speeds!"

Dani grinned and waved Avery off. Single speeds... *maybe*. She'd be old enough to qualify soon. And maybe she needed to try something different from draft train. The school year might have only begun, but Dani could already feel it: This was going to be a year of changes. A year when she knew who she was and what she could do.

She looked down and, not for the first time that day,

admired her new glowboard. A new *old* glowboard, really, bought secondhand—but it was hers.

When the rain had washed away all memory of the Sardines' victory, it had also washed away their chance at the first-place cash prize. Dani had thought that was the end of everything. After all, she couldn't skate without a board, and the Sardines couldn't compete without their captain. And so, she resigned herself to her fate.

Then, to Dani's surprise, her parents had offered to replace her broken board. Even though they hadn't seemed to have cared all this time, and even though Glow in the Park had been canceled for reasons unknown, Dr. and Mr. Hirsch had apparently taken note of Dani's daily departures to Hazard Hill, recognizing the long hours she'd spent practicing.

"If you care about it that much," Dr. Hirsch had said, "it seems unjust to stop you. It may not be a legitimate sport, Danielle, but you're certainly a legitimate glowboarder."

Dani had been too thrilled to tell her mom that the correct term was "skater."

The next day, her parents had given Dani the money to buy a brand-new board, and it was far more than what her new secondhand was worth. What Dani had done with the rest of that money was something her parents didn't need to know about.

Dr. and Mr. Hirsch still brought up swim team. They still made Dani drink power smoothies, and they banned both pets and candy. They hadn't promised to attend any races yet, but they *had* bought Dani a board, and that wasn't nothing.

Dani wondered if her parents might actually come around to glowboarding one day.

She could always hope.

This Sunday was perfection. There was no pressure to skate, and she was surrounded by friends; Lola Gil couldn't think of anything better.

She sat beside Avery, on the gate by the finish line. They'd skated for hours, and when Avery had announced that she was taking a break, Lola had joined her. They sat together now, shoulders occasionally bumping, cheering on the other three Sardines as they swished up and down the hill. Every so often, Avery turned her attention to a paperback book in her lap—a worn copy of *Tuck Everlasting*, from which she read a few pages at a time, stopping to share the lines she liked best with Lola.

The September air was crisp, and Lola breathed it down deep. As she did, she felt the slightest pang in her side. The faint blue scar was there, a reminder of the wound that had been healed by the hands of the light beings. A reminder that Lola was lucky to be breathing.

I know, she thought, wondering if her words could reach past the stratosphere. *I'm making the most of it, and I'm learning what I can.*

Her scar was also a reminder of the girl Lola had become. A girl who was brave, in spite of fear. A girl who could control her powers, saving them for when she was alone, or with the people she loved most.

Like now, as she plucked a bright red wildflower from off

the track with her mind, lifted it through the air, and tucked it neatly into Avery's ponytail.

Avery grinned at the surprise, wrapping an arm around Lola. And Lola had never felt so safe and known.

Zander was officially a Sardine, and this time for keeps. The *apart*ness he'd felt in June was finally fading, eased away by weeks of practice and Sunday Sardines Nights. In some ways, it was like no time had passed since he'd left the team for the Grackles. So many things were familiar to him, from Lola's flower crowns to Bastian's dry jokes to Dani's impatient commands. Other things had changed, though. Now he was getting to know Avery and hanging out with Radar. Now games of sardines were even better, with another member to hide away. Now the Sardines knew who they were and were learning all they could do with the fires inside them.

It wasn't like everything was perfect, though. Bastian, especially, hadn't been wild about letting Zander back on the team. Zander had apologized for what he'd done the year before—especially the secrets he'd told Mitchell. But Zander knew that words weren't enough for all the times he'd gone along with Mitchell's mean jokes, or his cheating. Still, he was working on it. He really was. And Bastian *might* have smiled just a little when Dani had told the group that Zander had been the one to dangle Mitchell upside down at Glow in the Park.

Then there were the Grackles themselves. They weren't too happy about Zander turning *double* traitor. Mitchell had thrown him to the ground the first day of school and punched him in the face. But that was the worst thing someone like Mitchell could do. Zander gave back his brand-new glowboard and all the fancy gear. It felt good to be out from under the looming shadow of Gloworks, Inc.

The day after he'd gotten his black eye, Zander had opened his front door to find an envelope wedged there. Inside the envelope were folded bills. There were some fives, some tens, and even a twenty. He'd studied the writing on the envelope. It was his name, and nothing else. The writing was disguised— big box print done in black marker—but Zander suspected who the money was from, and what it was for. He'd paid for his old, junior glowboard to be repaired.

"HEY." Dani's voice broke Zander out of his reverie. She was approaching him on the left, shooting a stream of orange glow behind. "Slowpoke!" she shouted, swishing past.

Yes, thought Zander. Just maybe he'd be forgiven.

Nando wasn't in Callaway anymore. In the weeks after Glow in the Park, he and Ira had been hard at work, leading the DGE down another path, to a remote town up in Montana. Only after many more weeks had he resumed his weekly video calls. Nando made up with Mr. and Mrs. Gil, and there was no more talk of war between them, but Bastian had a feeling that he might never again sleep a few doors down from his brother.

The war raged on, and bombs dropped, and angry men yelled on TV. But Nando, at least, was on the Sardines' side, and maybe one day things really could be all right again. In the meantime, as Nando often reminded Bastian, the door was always open.

Bastian jumped off his glowboard, waving to Lola and Avery, who shot back lazy salutes.

"I see you, man," Dani shouted at Bastian, passing him by with a flourishing swish. "Eyeing my board. You know it's the best one on the team now!"

Bastian smirked. He *hadn't* been eyeing Dani's board, but he'd spent plenty of time looking it over before, hand-painting it with his own design. "Flashy but classy" was what Dani had requested when Bastian had offered, for the very first time, to show her his glowboard designs, and to make one especially for her. He'd sketched and then painted her design with care—thick white stripes over tangerine orange.

When Dani had first suggested that Bastian make board-designing a job, he'd laughed at the idea. Lately, though, he'd been wondering if other people might want to see his designs. Nando had said they were good. He'd said they were meant to be shared.

So maybe, just maybe, Bastian would try.

If he could steer a flying car . . . well, anything was possible, wasn't it?

The sun was setting over Hazard Hill, shooting out its golden rays. Avery was the good kind of tired, sore all over from skating the day away. She heaved out a yawn and then, lifting her head off Lola's and putting away her copy of *Tuck Everlasting*, slid from the gate to the ground.

"Gonna head back," she announced. "Mom will be home for supper in an hour."

"But Sardines Night tonight, right?" Lola asked eagerly.

"Of course," said Avery, grinning.

She called out her plans to the others on the track, then waved one last time to Lola before skating away.

Callaway's streets seemed different to Avery now on her rides home. Maybe it was because she'd once been kidnapped and driven across them, all thanks to her father's plotting. After that day on Hazard Hill, he'd sent one last email:

Dear Vee,

I can't remember why I came to Callaway, but if you really don't want to see me, I'll head home.

This time, Avery had responded. She'd written,

I don't want to see you. Have fun with your more important projects.

She hadn't heard another word from Eric Miller since.

It wasn't as easy as sending an email, though. Avery could still remember the slam of a van door and the tone of her father's voice as he had shouted at her from behind a camera lens. He had known her secret, but even before he'd known it, he'd stopped treating her like a daughter. Avery wasn't sure she would ever really understand that.

She couldn't explain everything to her mom without revealing the truth, and the Sardines had all agreed to keep their vow of secrecy. But it had been enough for Avery to simply tell her mother what she'd decided.

In reply, Ms. Sills had said, "It's my full custody, Vee, and your full decision."

Since then, Avery had noticed that Ms. Sills came home earlier from work. As she'd promised, the rest of their summer was full of less overtime and more family dinners. Gone were the days of burnt pizza bagels. These days, they ate at the table together.

Tonight, Ms. Sills had promised a lasagna, and Avery's stomach was already grumbling as she swept her board onto Cedar Lane.

Strange Street—that's what people called this place.

Now Avery knew the truth: It wasn't the street that was strange, but Avery herself, and her very best friends.

And maybe *strange* was a good thing.

When Avery walked inside the house, the television was blaring—coverage of war news, which Avery hardly wanted to hear. Instead, she knelt to greet Radar, who was wiggling with excitement, tail wagging hard.

"Hey, buddy," she said. "Up for lasagna leftovers?"

Radar barked once, and then, very clearly, he said, *Don't mind if I do.*

ACKNOWLEDGMENTS

We did it! We crossed the finish line, and I'd like to express my "glowing" gratitude to everyone who helped bring this story to life. Thank you to my agent, Beth Phelan, for cheering on the Sardines from the beginning. As always, my story is stronger and better for all your insight. And thank you to the entire kick-butt team at Gallt & Zacker for your support.

Hannah Allaman, editor extraordinaire—your enthusiasm and brilliant editorial eye made this book shine ten times brighter. Thank you for believing in this weird story of mine and for treating its characters with such care and attention. Thank you to Violet Tobacco for the stunning cover art and to Tyler Nevins for the *stellar* book design. My thanks to Melissa Lee and to all the other members of the Disney Hyperion team who contributed to *Midnight* with invaluable behind-the-scenes work.

Thank you to powerhouse book ladies Destiny Soria, Mai Shaffner, Ashley Herring Blake, Leila Sales, Seoling Dee, and Kristen Comeaux for supporting, encouraging, blurbing, interviewing—*all* the things. A big thank you to Gail Nall and Kristin Tubb for your kind blurbs. Thank you, dear Jen at *Pop! Goes the Reader*, for rooting for my books these five years and tirelessly contributing to the book community with grace and style. A special thanks to St. Stephen's Episcopal and to Cynthia Bartek. My thanks to BookPeople superstars Meghan Goel, Shannon Brewer, and Eugenia Vela for taking me under your bookselling wings in Austin. And thank you to the brilliant booksellers at Parnassus Books and Joseph-Beth Booksellers for your ongoing support. Endless gratitude to the booksellers, librarians, and educators who have shared my stories with young readers; I will forever be grateful for the work you do.

Shout-out to Nicole Williams for constant love and makeup, to Shelly Reed for the week-brightening polos, to Kayla Powell for peaceful trips spent sunbathing, and to Hilary Rochow for our existential musing sessions. Shannon Burnette, fellow writer and witchy lady supreme—rock on. Sasha Esquivel, style icon and musical kindred spirit—you're fabulous. Thank you to the ladies of Phoebe's Book Club—Alex, Caitlin, Lauren, Libby, and Phoebe—for the infectious enthusiasm and riveting conversations. And thank you to Vicki and Bob Rymill for taking me in as your own and for the cheese plates, merlot, and unconditional love.

Love and thanks to the Ormsbees and Bullocks, aka Best

Family Ever, for cheering me through this publication journey. Thank you to the Ashby and Moore families for supporting me all the way from Kentucky and Tennessee. Thank you, Annie and Matt, for continuing to be the coolest and best siblings; I love you like whoa. Mom and Dad, thank you for seeing me through Book Eight with just as much excitement as you had for Book One.

Last but opposite of least, thank you to the woman first in my heart, Alli Rymill. You're my rock, my person, my soup-snake. I'm the luckiest, and I love you to the moon and back.